LORD KINVER'S CATEGORIES

The Viscount Kinver wanted his wife to be one sort of woman—a ladylike creature who would bear his children to perpetuate his family name, command his staff of servants to smooth his domestic life, and not disturb his dedicated pursuit of pleasure.

The viscount wanted his mistress to be another sort—with beauty to stir his amorous appetites, and the skill to satisfy them.

What then would he want with someone like Emma, who was far too bright to live in his shadow as a wife and had far too much self-esteem to hide in the shadows as his mistress?

The answer was all too discouragingly evident—which left Emma with a far more difficult question.

If Kinver did not want her as she was, what sort of woman should she be . . . ?

The Secret Bluestocking

More Delightful Regency Romances from SIGNET

The Secret Bluestocking

by Eileen Jackson

A SIGNET BOOK

NEW AMERICAN LIBRARY

NAL BOOKS ARE AVAILABLE AT QUANTITY DISCOUNTS WHEN USED
TO PROMOTE PRODUCTS OR SERVICES. FOR INFORMATION PLEASE
WRITE TO PREMIUM MARKETING DIVISION, NEW AMERICAN LIBRARY,
1633 BROADWAY, NEW YORK, NEW YORK 10019.

SIGNET TRADEMARK REG. U.S. PAT. OFF. AND FOREIGN COUNTRIES
REGISTERED TRADEMARK—MARCA REGISTRADA
HECHO EN CHICAGO, U.S.A.

SIGNET, SIGNET CLASSIC, MENTOR, PLUME, MERIDIAN AND NAL BOOKS
are published by New American Library,
1633 Broadway, New York, New York 10019

First Printing, November, 1985

1 2 3 4 5 6 7 8 9

PRINTED IN THE UNITED STATES OF AMERICA

To my mother, with love

1

"Every young lady of quality must marry to oblige her family. There can be no exceptions."

The lady who made the pronouncement did so in the certain knowledge that she would not be contradicted. It was not only the unassailable veracity of her words that assured this, reflected Emma; her impregnability to disagreement lay also in her personality and appearance. In all her years, the number of which varied according to her audience, it seemed doubtful if anyone—man, woman, or child—had dared to raise a dissenting voice to her ladyship. Probably even her nursemaids had deferred to her superiority. Emma's lively mind pictured Lady Augusta in her crib, her baby nose already beginning to take on the form of its present autocratic beak, her sharp, heavy-lidded eyes a match for anyone reckless enough to attempt to thwart her wishes.

When Lady Augusta Brancaster had announced that she and her granddaughter, Miss Lucy Venables, were about to pay a morning call at the rectory, Emma's mama, Mrs. Maria Waring, had been thrown into confusion. Although they were related through the Reverend Mr. Waring, she had not seen her ladyship for years and never met Miss Venables. The lives of Lady Augusta and Miss Lucy were far removed from those of a country rector and his family.

Not, thought Mrs. Waring, lifting her chin, that they were better born. No, indeed, for Lady Augusta's deceased sister had been Lady Lavinia, Mr. Waring's grandmama. She glanced at her two elder daughters, the only members of her family present in the pleasant drawing room, Mr. Waring having been called to attend the last hours of a parishioner. Emma was in full beauty, her creamy skin flawless as always, her figure shown to advantage in a Grecian-style white gown, which her sister Sophia had embroidered with sprigs of spring-green leaves and ornamented with tiny ribbon bows. It was a pity that nature had endowed Emma with red-gold hair, which, though thick and richly lovely, was not at present fashionable. She was gazing at Lady Augusta, her blue-gray eyes fixed in rapt attention. Mrs. Waring sent an involuntary prayer winging heavenward that Emma did not betray to this sharp-tongued old lady the fact that she was clever. What, wondered Mrs. Waring, had she ever done to deserve a bluestocking for a daughter?

She was jerked back from her thoughts by the realization that everyone in the room was staring at her, and became distressingly aware that she was guilty of the discourtesy of inattention. Her ladyship had addressed some comment to her and was waiting for a reply. In her extreme agitation she deliberately dropped her handkerchief, and as she bent to pick it up, she was relieved to hear Emma speak.

"Dear Mama is no doubt thinking of the problem which Papa expounded to us at breakfast. It concerns the fate of a family of beggars who strayed within the bounds of his other parish. I daresay you know, ma'am, that Papa also owns the living of Lower Downham. It is cared for most ably by his curate—"

"I have met the curate," interrupted Lady Augusta. "Lucy and I have attended morning worship on the three Sundays we have been resident in Lucy's property in Warmley. He gives an excellent, if somewhat prosy sermon, though that can scarcely be reckoned to be a fault. It is not the duty of a man of the cloth to be imaginative, but to interpret, as best he knows how, the wisdom of others."

Her ladyship paused and looked at Mrs. Waring, still awaiting a reply. Evidently a woman not thrown easily off the scent, decided Emma.

Once again she rescued her mother. "I meant to explain, ma'am, that Mama, being so concerned for Papa's dilemma, had allowed her attention to wander for a moment." Realizing that Lady Augusta was about to make a comment that would probably cause Mama further confusion, Emma hastened to answer the original question. "My sister, Sophia, is not yet out, wanting two months of seventeen."

"Which is why," said Mrs. Waring, hurriedly, "I was so distressed when it appeared that I would be unable to take dear Emma to London for her first Season. Sophia should not be brought out until Emma is properly launched into society. I do appreciate that one *could* bring out the two girls together, but it would not be thought altogether proper for a younger sister to be presented with an elder, especially if she should not be blessed with a suitable match. It would be particularly unfortunate if, by some mischance, Sophia should get betrothed first . . ."

Mrs. Waring's voice trailed away from an explanation that was being received by Lady Augusta with some displeasure. Not only did people seldom venture to make her long, involved speeches, but even less often did they fail to recognize her absolute knowledge of etiquette pertaining to the polite world. Also, she looked with disfavor upon anyone who drew observation, however obliquely, however unintentionally, to the sorry fact that Lucy, at twenty-one years of age, had graced two full Seasons with her comely face, her pretty figure, and her enviable fortune, and had not taken. If, in her third Season, she did not encourage an acceptable suitor, she might rusticate forever, for the *ton* would snicker behind their hands and declare her on the shelf.

"It is truly good of you, dear Lady Augusta, to offer to stand in my stead," finished Mrs. Waring.

"I am happy to do so, Mrs. Waring, though I have to confess I fail to comprehend why an outbreak of the measles among the younger members of your family should prevent your leaving the rectory. You have a trustworthy head nurse, I presume."

Mrs. Waring made a strangled sound and nodded.

Lady Augusta appeared to find nothing curious in this. Many people who found themselves in her company were quite frequently deprived of speech.

"Precisely! And she, I do not doubt, since I know your husband's fortune to be more than respectable, besides what his two livings bring him—although I feel bound to express my surprise at the quite unnecessarily generous stipend his curate tells me he is paid—has an abundance of assistance in the nursery.''

Seeing her mother's face color angrily at this censure of her husband and fearing she might say something they would all regret, Emma interposed, ''Mama is a most devoted parent, Lady Augusta, and feels she could not for any consideration leave little Amabel, who is scarce two years old and not robust.''

''Have they *all* succumbed to the disease?''

''Fortunately George and Frederick are at school at Eton College, but both Osbert and Patience are ill and Nurse believes that Amabel is about to fall victim.''

''I see,'' replied Lady Augusta, who looked as if she did not see at all.

In fact, she could scarcely be held to blame for her inability to understand. Anybody could have told her that the Warings' head nurse was dearly loved by them all and could easily have coped with a dozen children with the measles. The truth was that the attack was a heaven-sent excuse for postponing Emma's come-out. Her twin brother, Gerard, who was at Oxford University, had incurred yet another gambling debt, and this time one so large as to render his family scarce able to find the means to pay. Mr. Waring was forever dipping deep into his pockets to help the needy, and Mrs. Waring's savings from her own income of two hundred pounds a year had, of necessity, been breached and severely depleted. Try how they might, she and her afflicted husband could not find a way to send Mama and Emma to London, where they had intended to rent a respectable lodging.

''What does Mr. Waring intend to do about them?'' demanded Lady Augusta.

Mrs. Waring began to look distraught, and Sophia, who had been too awed to murmur more than a dozen words since her first introduction to her high-toned relatives, gazed imploringly at her sister. Emma did not let her down. Casting her mind back swiftly over the conversation, she concluded, correctly it transpired, that her ladyship was referring to the beggars.

''Papa will act with his customary charity—his *Christian* charity,'' she interpolated quickly as he saw that her ladyship was about to make another provoking observation, ''and will try to find work for the man and accommodations for the whole family. If he cannot, then he will give them as much money as he deems it essential to help them on their way.''

"You mean, of course, that he will subsidize them if the man should prove too idle to work, which would not surprise me. Your papa's liberality appears to be a byword for miles around.''

The entrance of the elderly housekeeper, who had been with Mrs. Waring's family since she was a scullery maid, followed by a young maid, each bearing refreshments which they placed upon a table, put a timely end to the conversation. Emma breathed freely again. Not for worlds would any of them desire to have a person outside the immediate family guess to what straits Gerard had reduced them. They loved him and would continue to do so, though Papa prayed nightly that his son would behave with more propriety and less selfishness.

A light nuncheon having been consumed, Emma and Sophia hurried upstairs to put on outdoor clothes, for they had been invited by Lady Augusta to accompany her on other visits in the neighborhood.

Sophia's fingers shook so much that Emma begged her to compose herself while she buttoned her sister's blue velvet spencer. She felt a little unsteady herself. In spite of Lady Augusta's imposing presence, she believed she would be able to hold her own. It was Miss Lucy Venables who troubled her. She appeared so impossibly tranquil, her smooth oval face giving not one hint of her feelings during the entire visit. She was, decided Emma, like a doll. And, she reflected a trifle enviously, a beautifully gowned doll. Emma and Sophia's clothes were cut out from patterns by Nurse, who could never be persuaded to permit any hint of décolleté, the seams sewn by a local sewing woman, and finished at home.

If the young ladies had not been guided by Papa in the tenets of humility and forgiveness, they might have found it impossible to feel charity toward a brother whose excesses prevented them from having their gowns made in Bristol, the nearest large city, or by Bath's fashionable modistes.

Sophia and Emma took the backward-facing seats in an elegant new carriage with a crest upon the doors, drawn by two high-bred horses and driven by a coachman dressed in

smart red and silver-gray livery. He looked older than her
ladyship and displayed obvious indication of his status as
ancient and privileged retainer by leaning down and giving
unnecessary instructions to the young footman, who assisted
the ladies up the steps, and adding stern directions to Lady
Augusta to take care.

"I am thankful we decided to use the closed carriage
today, Grandmama," said Lucy. "Although it remains dry,
the wind is somewhat keen."

She snuggled further into a fur travel rug and stared out of
the window, her face partially concealed by her ravishingly
decorative ruby-red velvet bonnet, lined with pale pink satin.
Her stylish pelisse was of the same red velvet and tied at the
neck with a pink satin bow.

Her tone had been almost without expression, and Emma
wondered if she came to life only in the presence of gentlemen. There were young women like that among Emma's
acquaintance, and she did not care for them.

Sophia, who had been gazing raptly at her cousin, said
abruptly, "You are so very stylish, Cousin Lucy, I wonder
that you are not—"

Sophia stopped, her face reddening to her hairline. The
word "married" had remained unspoken, but was nevertheless hanging in the suddenly frigid atmosphere of the carriage.

Poor Sophia had been searching her brain for something
pleasing to say and had, in a gauche, sixteen-year-old way,
hit upon the very words that should have remained unsaid.

Lady Augusta was looking at her with a basilisk glare that
brought mortified moisture to her eyes. The expedition looked
like proving a disaster before it had fairly begun.

Emma said, speaking in a breathless way that betrayed her
agitation, "I collect, Cousin Lucy, that such attractions as
yours may command any gentleman's attention. It is no
wonder to *me* that you have found it impossible to make up
your mind which of your suitors to favor."

Lucy stared at her with unwinking, brilliant dark eyes. Lady
Augusta subsided, and Sophia gave her sister's hand a grateful squeeze.

The carriage was being driven in a decorous manner along
the winding country lane that led to the manor house of
Squire Downham. The squire's son, Anthony, was also at

Oxford, and living life to the full in the manner of Gerard. The squire did not condemn his behavior in the least. Anthony had been sent to Oxford because his mama had insisted that her only son must enjoy all the activities open to a young gentleman of quality. His father paid his debts with an indulgent grin while Mrs. Downham, who had brought a large fortune to her marriage and joined it with that of her husband, could see no flaw in her offspring.

There was the sound of a vehicle coming up behind them fast and a loud call.

"Some young person in a hurry, no doubt," remarked Lady Augusta with a total absence of concern that was evidently shared by her coachman. The road widened where two farm gates enclosed opposite fields of grain behind the high hedges. There was room to pass if travelers were willing to accommodate each other. Lady Augusta's servant made no move to rein in his slow-moving animals.

Then, abruptly, there were shouts from the men on the box. A sporting curricle drawn by a matched pair of grays and driven by a man in a many-caped coat and a dark driving hat with a curving brim overtook them in the only place where it was possible. Somehow, with consummate skill, he guided his galloping horses around the coach and left them behind in his swirling dust.

"Young puppy," remarked Lady Augusta, though Emma gained the impression that she rather enjoyed such behavior.

"It was Kinver, Grandmama," said Lucy without interest. "I saw his crest quite distinctly for a moment. I could not fail to recognize it."

Lady Augusta turned her gaze upon the sisters. "Are you acquainted with Lord Kinver?"

"No, ma'am," said Emma, "though I have read of some of his exploits in newspapers."

Lady Augusta's eyebrows rose. "Do you read newspapers very often?"

Sophia, forgetting Mama's strictures regarding bluestockings, was about to reply and explain that her dear Emma was a most erudite young lady when she felt a sharp pain in her toe where her sister's foot pressed hers.

"I read aloud sometimes to Papa when he is tired," explained Emma. Her answer was true, but only in small part.

"A right and proper activity in a young girl," approved her ladyship, "though I wonder that your papa, a man of the cloth, should permit you to peruse accounts of the cavortings of one of our more outrageous young men when you are not even out. In my youth girls were kept in strict seclusion before they entered society. My mama would allow no reading matter save the Bible on Sundays and the sermons of worthy men during the week."

"How horrid that must have been," exclaimed Sophia. "Papa and Mama know that we read the magazines to which Mrs. Downham subscribes. Some of the romances in them are so delightfully Gothic they have me in a positive quake."

Lady Augusta directed a quelling look in Sophia's direction and she subsided, the ready color once more suffusing her face. She was saved from further unwelcome attention by Lucy, who said in her calm way, "I collect, Grandmama, that you believed your parents to be overstrict and were excessively gay during your first Season, possibly as a result of your earlier close confinement."

"Who dared to utter such a thing?" demanded Lady Augusta in a terrible voice.

"You did, Grandmama," replied Lucy, who appeared not to be in the least intimidated by her fearsome relative.

The horses were turned through a pair of wrought-iron gates opened to them by the gatekeeper's wife, who dropped a curtsy. Her ladyship was able to pursue an occupation in which she seemed to take great delight; that of comparing estates held by herself or Lucy with all other estates, to the detriment of most of the latter.

She was hard put to find anything derogatory to say about Downham Park. The broad driveway lay between a wide avenue of oak and elm, and the house, which had been extensively improved by the present Squire Downham, was large and immaculate. The ladies were shown into a spacious drawing room whose long windows could be opened onto a paved terrace from which a broad flight of stone steps led to well-stocked gardens.

Mrs. Downham rose to greet them, her hands outstretched in welcome. "Lady Augusta, how pleasant it is to see you. We have not met since I attended a rout at Lady Farley's. Of course, I was much younger then."

"So were we all," replied Lady Augusta.

She made for the most comfortable-looking couch wide enough to accommodate her voluminous skirts.

"Mrs. Downham, pray allow me to present my granddaughter, Miss Lucy Venables. I believe you are not acquainted."

"No, indeed, though I have heard of Miss Venables as must all who follow the doings of the *ton*. I am keenly interested, you know, although I do not care to go into society myself. My home and garden are quite enough for me, along with pleasant local pastimes."

"Indeed," said Lady Augusta, conveying in one word her incredulity at a woman who could be satisfied with so little.

Mrs. Downham's brown eyes held a laugh and Emma released a breath she had not known she was holding. Mrs. Downham was far too good-humored to care for set-downs.

"And how are you, Emma, and you, Sophia? I need scarcely ask. You are both in obvious health and beauty."

The ladies seated themselves, but had managed only a few sentences of polite converse when the door opened and the butler announced, "Lord Kinver."

2

Emma looked with curiosity at the man who had overtaken their carriage in such a skillful manner. This was the man of whom she had read much, whose life was passed apparently in the pursuit of pleasure. Viscount Kinver was a striking figure. He appeared about thirty years of age and was something over six feet tall, with dark hair cut in a Brutus crop. His expertly tailored coat of brown cloth did not conceal the broadness of his shoulders. His pale buckskin breeches were molded to muscular legs, while his black top boots could have been used as mirrors. He wore a small diamond pin in his white cravat, a plain gold ring on one hand, and a modest gold fob watch and chain on his white piqué waistcoat. He could not be faulted on appearance, decided Emma, who was prepared to dislike him. All she had read of him certainly did not make him her idea of a desirable companion, and his lack of consideration on the road outweighed, in her opinion, his brilliant driving.

He was introduced to the young ladies and swept each one of them a low bow, ending with Lucy, whom he favored with a smile that rendered his lean, austere face unexpectedly attractive.

He seated himself near her. "I hear that you are to grace the Season again."

Lady Augusta stopped speaking in midword. "She is, indeed, sir, and it is to be hoped that this time you will not be living a rackety existence in foreign climes. I should like to see more of you. I know that Lucy was disappointed, after losing what should have been her first Season because of a riding accident, not to have renewed her acquaintance with you.''

"I intend to remain in London throughout the Season,'' replied the viscount calmly, "though now I find my little cousin has grown so charming I fear I shall have a difficult time of it making my way through her many admirers.''

Lady Augusta sent him a mistrustful stare. "Am I to understand that you think Lucy has increased in looks since you first met, or are you spinning some Banbury tale to amuse yourself?''

Emma caught Sophia's agonized glance. Both girls wondered how Lucy could endure this blatant fishing for compliments, though Lucy did not look at all put out, even when the viscount continued, at her ladyship's insistence, to reiterate that Lucy's appearance had improved with maturity.

"She can scarcely be termed 'mature,' '' protested Lady Augusta.

Lucy's pale cheeks took on a tinge of color and Emma jumped into the conversation in a way she instantly regretted.

"I trust, Mrs. Downham, you received the copy of *The Lady's Magazine* I returned. I did not expect to be this way, and having learned you wanted the new pattern for a handkerchief, I sent it with our garden boy. He's a willing child, but if he meets his friends, he can be easily diverted into a tied-legs race or ring taw—marbles, you know—'' She broke off in the face of Lady Augusta's expression.

"I do *not* know,'' said her ladyship, her flush of annoyance deeper than her rouge. "I have no knowledge of street games . . .''

"No, ma'am, of course not.''

". . . and if I had, I would conceal the fact in polite company, as I trust you will do in London.''

"Are you to be in the capital this Season, Miss Waring?'' inquired the viscount smoothly.

Emma was grateful for his intervention until she saw that his eyes gleamed with satirical amusement. His gaze was so deeply penetrating she felt he could read her mind—probably any woman's mind—and only just prevented her lip from curling in disdain.

His lordship's exploits—often with women—were printed under a disguised, but recognizable name, and his own opinions, pronounced witty by many, were frequently published. Emma had long since judged his tongue to be cruelly caustic, though she had to admit that she had quite often laughed involuntarily at his revealing glimpses into society. But she envied the fact that a man could apparently do and say whatever he chose, while a woman was expected to be thoroughly discreet. Nevertheless, on no account must she allow him to believe her clever, for, according to Mama, who had been a decorative member of the *ton* until she met and married Papa, such a discovery would frighten away both men and women. "Except," had shuddered Mama, "certain females who dress and behave most oddly and delight in being called freakish."

Emma had no wish to have such a title bestowed on her.

"She is to accompany Lucy and myself," answered Lady Augusta for her.

"But how amazingly kind of you, dear Lady Augusta."

The viscount had replied to her ladyship, but kept his eyes on Emma. She ached to give him a set-down, but reflection made her cautious. She amused him, but to amuse a gentleman was precisely the right way to behave. If he believed her to be a trifle empty-headed and admired her looks, that must be exactly what Mama would wish.

She was searching her mind for a flirtatious remark that would intrigue such an experienced man when she became aware of the conversation between the others. She realized that they were discussing the puzzle in the latest issue of *The Lady's Magazine.*

"An Enigmatical List of Young Ladies in Bristol," said Mrs. Downham. "I own I could not work out several of them. How did you fare Sophia?"

"I—I managed to discover their identities . . . with Emma's assistance."

"What a clever young lady you must be," remarked Lord Kinver to Emma.

Sophia blushed. She was aware of Mama's severe strictures on the kind of picture a young girl should present to society. And she had not only made herself sound cleverer than Mrs. Downham, her hostess, but she had embroiled Emma, who really *was* very intelligent indeed and rightly fearful of revealing such a failing.

The viscount turned to look at Emma. "So Miss Sophia had help from you with the more difficult ones. Congratulations!"

"Oh, no, sir," Emma said mendaciously, managing to simper a little. "Mr. Treen, Papa's curate, came to visit and he it was who helped us."

The viscount stared a moment longer. "I see," he said, and turned away.

Squire Downham entered and greeted everyone in his bluff way and sat near his wife.

"Apologize for my late appearance. Been struggling with the acrostic in my *Gentleman's Magazine*."

Emma closed her eyes in momentary despair. This was turning out to be a nightmare morning, and if her stay in society was to continue in such a fashion, she would need to take plenty of hartshorn with her. She had been assured by her mother that it was excellent for faints, spasms, and hysterics, all of which were mercifully unknown to her—until now. She thought she could, at any minute, quite easily succumb to any one, or all three.

"Emma," boomed the squire, "when you see Mr. Treen ask if he has completed the puzzle, for I confess it has me all at sea."

Emma breathed again. Perhaps before it was discovered that she put all her quickness of perception to the credit of Papa's curate she would be safely married and able to be herself. Or would that be impossible? Was she destined forever to pretend to be something she was most definitely not?

She felt as if she were suffocating in the room, which was heated by a large log fire, and stood up. Both gentlemen leapt to their feet, looking surprised.

"I—I beg your pardon," she stammered. "I had not meant to move so precipitately. The truth is I would like very much to stroll in your pleasure gardens, Squire, and see how many flowers and shrubs are looking springlike."

"Of course," said Squire Downham, "and while you are gone, I shall ask little Sophia here how her brother does at Oxford. Young rascals both are my son and young Mr. Waring," chuckled the squire to Lord Kinver. "Forever kicking up larks and spending too much. Well, they will never be young again and—"

Sophia sprang to her feet and said a little too loudly, "If you would not mind, I also would like to walk in the garden."

"Good heavens," exclaimed Lady Augusta, who had been unusually silent, never having wasted time in solving useless puzzles. "You are like two jack-in-the-boxes! You must have a remarkable garden, Mrs. Downham. In my young day we would have needed to be dragged from such a personable man as Kinver."

Lucy said, as if her Grandmama had not spoken, "I will join Miss Waring and Miss Sophia. I am too hot," she added simply.

Lord Kinver bowed. "If all the youth, though not all the beauty," he smiled, bowing again in the general direction of the older ladies, "is to be found outside, I feel it incumbent upon me to offer my escort."

"Pray do not put yourself to any trouble, sir," said Lucy.

If looks could kill, she would undoubtedly have lain dead, slain by the one speared at her by Lady Augusta. "It is not for you to tell Kinver what he wishes to do, miss. You will accept his escort."

Lucy sighed softly, "Yes, Grandmama."

She rose to her feet with exquisite grace as Emma wondered how it was possible to appear so serene. Was she always so? Maybe, inside, she shared Emma's uncertainty regarding herself and her future. Emma hoped that when they became better acquainted she would discover a sympathetic friend.

The breeze on the terrace was quite keen, but as the small party made their way down the stone steps into a sunken garden sheltered by high box hedges, they felt the benefit of a warm sun.

"This is delightful," exclaimed Sophia. "So many flowers and such sweet scents."

Lucy looked animated for the first time since Emma had met her. "I dote on the countryside," she said in her well-modulated voice. She sighed. "We seem to spend so much of our time in towns, and although I walk and ride in the parks as often as I can, it is not the same. I was happy when Grandmama decided we should visit my Warmley estate. I am so fond of it, yet have seen it only twice before, and that when I was a child."

Sophia said in her ingenuous way, "Have you many homes, Cousin Lucy?"

"Lord, yes, and a great army of people to look after them. One day I shall have more from Grandmama's will."

Sophia's eyes grew round. She was astonished more by Lucy's casual reference to her grandmother's demise than by Lucy's riches.

Emma had been listening to their exchange, wondering how it must feel to be so wealthy. Papa had told her that she would receive her portion of one thousand pounds when she married. He had begun to apologize for the smallness of the amount, but Emma begged him to stop. With the expenses of the boys' education and three more daughters to bring out, and his merciful charity to those who suffered hunger and disease, she knew he must often be hard-pushed. When Gerard had thrown the family into such disarray with his recent debts, both she and Sophia had offered their portions to help, but Papa had utterly refused to accept them. He would go to the poorhouse before he would take their money. His sweet smile illuminated his face for a moment to show them he was joking, but Emma was not deluded as to the extent of his worry, and unhappy as it made him, Papa had been forced to reduce their pin money.

Emma helped her parents about the parishes and had seen real need and often dreadful suffering. Her life was heaven on earth compared with many; yet now, for the first time, she began to wonder exactly how she would fare in London. Meeting Lucy had given her doubts. The clothes she wore must have cost a great deal and the pearls in her necklace, though small, as befitted a young woman, were of pale pink, expertly matched and exceedingly costly.

Mama had explained that she must be clever in her purchases, ordering gowns that were plain and could be improved by the addition of knots of ribbon or lace trimming. Emma had agreed. She would have done so anyway, but when Mama spoke so kindly to her, she was rendered almost speechless by her sense of shame; and when Mama had raided her own small jewelry case and handed her all the pieces that would suit a young lady about to enter society, Emma had almost broken down and confessed. But she remembered how deeply distressed Mama and Papa were about Gerard, and she refrained from easing her conscience.

So she only knew that in London the sum of seventy-five guineas lay waiting in the bank of Mr. Palmer of Paternoster Row by St. Paul's Churchyard, printer, publisher, and seller of books and magazines. When she allowed herself to linger on the memories of how she had been pushed deeper and deeper into deceit as she discovered that her works of authorship sold every time, her joy and sense of fulfillment were almost destroyed. Almost, but never absolutely. For Emma, writing was a part of her very being, and the possibility of being forced to relinquish it could not be tolerated. From an early age she had been possessed of an urge to set down the ideas that poured into her brain.

She had begun by sending riddles and acrostics to local papers and then to London publications, but had found it increasingly difficult to prevaricate when, as this morning, her own work was openly discussed in her presence. So she had decided recently only to pen her novels, which she wrote in serial form for magazines. The more outrageously and adventurously gothic they were, the more they were begged of her by Mr. Palmer. Her parents never mentioned such reading matter. It probably never occurred to them to consider it. Emma was persuaded that they would disapprove strongly of tales that depicted ladies in horrid situations from which they were invariably rescued, after dreadful anguish, by rich and handsome men. Many times Emma had felt so consumed by guilt that she had fully resolved to give up such writing, but she feared she would be utterly lost without it. But if her beloved parents should ever learn the truth . . ."

"A penny for your thoughts."

Emma started and looked about her. She had failed to notice that Lucy and Sophia had left the sunken garden and were disappearing into the shrubbery beyond and she had been left alone with Lord Kinver.

She managed to produce a trill of mirth. "I—I beg your pardon, my lord. I had not realized . . . I did not know . . . I was far away in thought. Life poses many distractions, does it not? For instance, should I purchase pink ribbons or lavender for my new morning gown?"

The viscount looked at her, and an expression she found it

impossible to understand flickered briefly in his eyes. His face, she saw on closer inspection, bore lines. There were grooves running from his nose to the corners of his mouth and traces of many frowns between his brows. He's got a temper, decided Emma. Yet a network of tiny lines near his eyes showed an inclination to laugh. Altogether she found it an intriguing face and mentally filed it away for fictitious use, possibly for a villain, remembering his proclivities.

"I trust, ma'am, you have examined me closely enough."

If Emma had been prone to easy blushes, she would certainly have produced one. She had been staring most rudely at a man whom she had met only half an hour ago. Recalling Mama's instructions, she dredged up something to say.

"La, sir, if a man has countenance, why should not a young lady be allowed to study him?"

The viscount's surprised blink found a response in Emma. Good God, she thought, I sound like one of my more lunatic characters.

" 'La!' " repeated Lord Kinver, his eyebrows climbing. "I must assume you to be a devotee of novels, for surely no modern young lady would use such an expression."

Was the man a mind reader? Emma felt hot with mortification.

"I read novels," she responded, trilling another laugh, which sounded shrill and forced.

"I wonder that Mr. Waring allows it. I have it on excellent authority that he is a man of very high principles."

Emma was distracted by the emotions that afflicted her. If she admitted she read novels openly, she implicated her parents. If she did not, she might need to tell a real whisker of a lie, something which, so far, she had successfully avoided.

The viscount kept his gaze fixed on her, watching every expression that crossed her face, his own assuming a more caustic look with every passing second.

"I have not, er, mentioned the matter to my parents, sir, and must rely upon you not to do so."

The viscount took a step back and raised his hands in spurious holy horror. Then he laid one hand solemnly over his heart. "I swear," he said in tones melodramatic enough to be put in one of her books.

Emma gave a gurgle of laughter. Lord Kinver smiled in

response, and again she saw how his smile relieved the tense harshness of his countenance and rendered him almost attractive.

Almost attractive, Emma assured herself, because of course no woman of sense would be foolish enough to be drawn, however briefly, to a man whose reputation for committing practically every folly known to society reached all but the most remote corners of the kingdom. Emma was not sophisticated enough to know precisely the nature of the indiscretions perpetrated by Lord Kinver; she had only the veiled information gleaned from her reading and a sense of a disapproving atmosphere among many of the local gentry if his name was mentioned. But she had an exceptionally vivid imagination and a critical faculty induced by an education usually denied to a woman.

"Do you do it all the time?"

Lord Kinver's voice interrupted her and Emma looked up at him inquiringly. His face held a mixture of amusement and a hint of scorn. She had to force down a surge of anger. Why should he look at her so? They had met for the first time today and he knew nothing of her.

She managed to keep her voice cool. "You speak in riddles, my lord. Do I do what all the time?"

"Disappear into a world of your own. For minutes together I had the impression that I was not here at all."

"And that, I daresay, must be a wholly new experience for you."

Emma had not meant to sound abrasive; she had intended her response to be frivolously provoking, but she was not comfortable with such dissimulation and her true emotion showed. She was not surprised when Lord Kinver's brows drew together in a frown.

"Have I offended you in some way, madam?"

Emma was nonplussed. Since she had attained the age where gentlemen saw her as a woman, her beauty had commanded admiration tempered with respect among the local beaux. Now she was faced with a sophisticated man who had been out in the world for years, and she realized that she was vulnerable to attack. Her youthful worshipers would not have dared to risk her spleen. This man cared nothing for her reaction. Emma wondered if he thought her beautiful, before she crushed the idea as immodest and unworthy. She drew a deep breath and followed it with a simpering smile.

"Mama and Papa have sometimes had cause to reprimand me for my daydreaming ways, but I had not expected such a caution from a gentleman to whom I have been only just introduced. I declare, sir, you are far too direct."

If she had been holding a fan, she would have fluttered it, allowing only her eyes to be revealed. She began to feel uneasy. Had she written about so many heroines who discovered themselves in compromising positions, their only weapon their beauty, that she was not capable of rational reaction toward a member of the *ton*? Were all the men like this? No, this could not be. Lord Kinver was not any ordinary man. She felt his overpowering presence most keenly. She suspected that he was trying to goad her for reasons of his own. What those reasons were she had no notion, but she determined to show him that she was capable of playing her part in any situation.

"And I swear, ma'am, that you are a sad flirt. I wonder what your papa, a man of the cloth, would do if he discovered your guilty secret."

Emma felt suddenly cold. Guilty secret? The only one she had was that of her writing. Surely this taunting male could not have stumbled upon it.

"I do not understand you, sir." In spite of all her efforts her voice shook.

"No? Oh, but I think you do. A daughter of the parsonage without even one Season in London is ready to play the coquette with a man only just made known to her. Have you not been warned? I must confess to disappointment. Most mamas caution their virtuous daughters against me."

He was amused, and Emma's mouth almost dropped. The conceit of the man. How she ached to even the score between them.

She raised her brows. "Truly you flatter yourself, my lord. I take leave to doubt that you have ever been given a second's thought in my home." She continued reflectively, "Though, of course, there is time yet. When I take my leave of my parents perhaps they will summon me to their presence and hand me a list of gentlemen of whom to be wary. No doubt your name will grace the top. If it does, do you wish me to inform you of the fact? Such knowledge would surely add to your opinion of your consequence.''

She had forgotten her mincing attitude and gained the qualified satisfaction of seeing the viscount's face flush faintly.

"You're a saucy little minx, aren't you? But I assure you, Miss Waring, that my life is far too full of consequential matters for it to be the least disrupted by anything you could do.''

She dropped a small curtsy, laughing up into eyes that were coolly assessing her.

"My dear sir! 'Saucy minx!' That is nursery language, for sure. I do hope that the level of badinage in the polite world will prove somewhat higher.''

She rose from her curtsy and would have escaped to join Lucy and Sophia, but she found herself held in a firm grasp.

She glanced down in furious surprise. Long white fingers of astonishing strength, their only ornament the gold ring, were curled about her wrist. Such incidents quite frequently occurred to her heroines, at which point they cried in outraged tones, "Unhand me, sir!" Whereupon one of two things happened: a chagrined suitor fell to his knees to kiss the hem of her gown, babbling apologies; or a villain pulled the protesting, often half-fainting girl into his arms and planted a cruel kiss upon her mouth, stifling pleas for mercy made in an agony of fear.

Lord Kinver took the villain's part. He pulled Emma close to him and held her to his lean body. But there were some significant differences in the story from this point. To begin with, Emma was not the fainting kind. Second, she felt mesmerized by his lordship's expression, by his warm, glowing eyes, and by his gently teasing smile. He was going to kiss her, and every ladylike instinct so painstakingly instilled by Mama and Nurse was routed. A part of Emma, the rational part, watched disbelievingly. But the flesh-and-blood Emma was aware only of the hard strength of his lordship's muscles; of the desire, which she recognized, although she had never before encountered it; of the treachery of her own senses, which were responding to his overwhelming sensuality. She struggled to dredge up some vestige of good behavior, but Kinver's lips touched hers in a whisper of a kiss and she drowned in pleasure. Her whole body was alive with it; it became a fire that leapt about her senses and made her yearn for an experience she did not yet comprehend. Lord Kinver held her for only a moment while his mouth moved on hers, then he released her and Emma stood quite still, staring at him, the realization of how completely she had betrayed her emotions horrifying her.

"How dare you, sir!"

She knew as well as the viscount that her protestation carried no sense of outrage such as so grossly insulted a young lady should suffer. She prayed that he could not guess how much she wanted him to kiss her again. Her tortured wits became a morass in which she struggled to find a secure foothold.

"You—you are hateful, my lord. Hateful!"

"How odd, Miss Waring. I received quite a different impression of your response toward me."

Emma seethed. How she would like to strike that ironic smile from his arrogant face. No wonder he made so many female conquests if he found his prey so easy to subdue. She had prided herself on being a woman of strength, an emancipated woman who would follow a literary life and be admitted into the ranks of the bluestockings. And she had yielded herself to the first experienced man who had approached her. She was not a prude. She knew that a kiss between a man and a woman need not be considered so dreadful a crime. Once or twice she had permitted a youthful swain to touch his lips to her smooth cheek, but that had been different. The viscount had probed sensations so deep within her that she had not been aware of them until he brought them storming to the surface.

"You are doing it again, Miss Waring. Staring at me, thinking your own thoughts, while your beautiful eyes see into a scene I can only surmise."

Emma gave him the benefit of a full and searching look.

"You took advantage of my—my inexperience, my lord. It was despicable of you."

"So I did, and so it was," he agreed blandly.

"I suppose you have seduced many an innocent girl. You open your onslaught so well. It—it amused me to indulge you, sir."

"Fustian, Miss Waring. You *enjoyed* it."

"There is no shame in you!"

"None whatsoever."

Emma hated him. Her hatred rose until she thought she could taste its bitterness. She raised her hand and deliberately wiped her lips before she turned and walked away. Behind her she heard a gentle, mocking laugh, and while her mind raged against Lord Kinver, her body responded to his magnetism.

Miss Lucy Venables was moving through the pleasure garden with languid grace, accompanied by Sophia, who appeared ill-at-ease. She greeted the reappearance of her sister with obvious relief.

"Cousin Lucy knows a great deal about plants, Emma. Even more than Mama and perhaps as much as Tompkins. He is our gardener," she explained to Lucy.

"I have many gardeners in my various residences," said Lucy. "I try to speak to all of them when I am able, though that is not as often as I would wish."

"You seem so fond of country living, Cousin Lucy, that I wonder you should spend so much of your time in London," blurted out Sophia. She turned scarlet as Lucy subjected her to a long, considering gaze.

"At present I am subject to Grandmama's commands. It will not be always so."

She spoke in perfectly even tones and her face remained placid. Emma wondered what Lucy would do in an emergency. Probably survey it with her large dark eyes and make a solemn pronouncement. Much of her speech came out in the form of pronouncements. Maybe it had to do with living with Lady Augusta, and Emma wondered if she would return home talking in the same manner after her Season. By then she might be married or, at the very least, betrothed. She fell into a reverie as she contemplated the unknown who would love and cherish her, as in all the best novels, and whom she could love devotedly in return. To her surprise and annoyance she could not direct her thoughts with her usual facility, for the harsh features of Viscount Kinver insisted on intruding.

3

She realized that she was being addressed by Lucy.

"Cousin Emma, we are required to return to the house. I know that Grandmama has other calls to make."

"Has Miss Waring left us in spirit once more?"

Lord Kinver had joined them, and Emma was chagrined to be discovered yet again oblivious to her surroundings. The footman sent to summon them walked a few paces behind as they strolled back to the house, Lord Kinver at Lucy's side.

"When are you to be in London, Miss Venables? May I hope it is soon? I would like very much to pursue our acquaintance."

"How gratifying," responded Lucy impassively.

Lord Kinver remained undaunted by her manner and Emma wondered if all young ladies in polite society behaved in so dispassionate a way. She supposed she would need to learn how to do so, though it seemed an unattractive prospect. However, the object of her visit to London was to enable her to meet a man of honor and wealth—and, Emma hoped, charm and personal beauty—with whom she could spend the remainder of her life, and if it was essential to act with a certain ennui, she must strive to do so. The daughters of the rectory needed to marry men in comfortable circumstances. Lady Augusta had made plain only this morning what was expected of a lady of quality.

She watched her Cousin Lucy, who moved with exquisite languor across the scythed lawns, her clothes as perfect as her manners, her voice serene and perfectly modulated as she discoursed with Lord Kinver on various subjects. Emma absorbed the way the viscount reacted, placing his hand beneath her arm when they reached the terrace steps and assisting her to ascend. Emma felt a surge of resentment at his lack of decorum toward her, and of mortification at her helpless response. She considered writing a lampoon about him to relieve her feelings, savoring the words: "vanity," "arrogance," "presumption"—the list could easily be extended.

Lady Augusta watched their entrance with an approving look.

"You may escort us to our carriage, Kinver. It would also be civil of you to attend us to our next call, which is to be on Sir George Croft and his wife. One never meets them in society, but that is from their choice. They are very wealthy and well-connected. It does not do to slight such people. You won't forget that, Emma."

Emma had difficulty in biting back a retort. Sir George and Lady Croft had been friends of her family as far back as she could remember, and she did not need this ancient autocrat to instruct her in behavior toward them.

She glanced up to see Lord Kinver watching her with a derisive expression, and she controlled her wrath. When she realized that Sophia was about to make a remark that might prove less than tactful, she gave her a small pinch. It was discreetly done, but the appreciative gleam in Lord Kinver's eyes made her aware that he fully comprehended the situation. Why was the man so intent on provoking her? And why had he the power to do so? She was the acknowledged belle of the district and no man had ever had the slightest influence over her feelings.

He bowed in Lady Augusta's direction. "I shall be charmed, ma'am. I welcome the opportunity to pursue my acquaintance with the young ladies."

He included them all, but his eyes were on Lucy, and Lady Augusta was well aware of it.

"Did you enjoy your walk in the grounds, Lucy?" Lady Augusta turned to the assembled company. "My granddaughter dotes on country pursuits, but I tell her to her head that it will not do for her to languish unseen. When she is married, I shall no longer have jurisdiction over her, but a fashionable man will not expect his wife to renounce the pleasures of the polite world."

"I see no reason why Miss Venables should not be permitted to follow any pursuit that makes her happy," remarked Lord Kinver, and earned himself a small smile from Lucy.

"Do you not, sir?" snapped Lady Augusta. "Well, I trust you will cease from putting such quirks into her thoughts. I have to contend with this ridiculous notion that town life is tedious, but if she does not mix with the *ton*, she will never find a proper husband."

Emma squirmed inwardly. Had she been in Lucy's shoes, she could not have borne to hear such a personal subject so openly alluded to. Lucy remained apparently unperturbed.

"I agree absolutely." The viscount spoke softly with an encouraging glance at Lucy, who made no sign of acknowledgment.

"Well, that is good, at all events. It is a great pity you decided to absent yourself during my granddaughter's earlier Seasons. You might have prevailed upon her to accept one of the offers she received."

Emma caught Sophia's agonized glance and shook her head slightly. It was not for them to intercede in a conversation that embarrassed them, even if it was having no effect upon its center.

"It does not surprise me that Miss Venables had offers—" began Squire Downham in his bluff way.

He was interrupted without ceremony. "Why should it, indeed?" Even the squire was daunted by the glare he received from his despotic guest. "Why any man of sense should wish to be jaunting about the world when he might be in England is more than I can fathom. One goes to Scotland for the shooting—at least I do not, but those who care for such sport may do so without censure—and it is permissible to visit various watering places and sea resorts if one is so inclined, but for a single man of property to remain unavailable to the polite world for two years together is beyond my capacity to tolerate."

"I am here now, ma'am, and promise you I shall stay." The viscount was as unmoved by his elderly relative's fearsome aspect as was Lucy. Perhaps one became accustomed to it, thought Emma. She hoped so, or for the next few months her existence promised to be a series of alarms.

The viscount walked the ladies to their carriage. "Miss Venables, would you care to join me in my curricle?"

The maquillaged wrinkles in Lady Augusta's face deepened in a beaming smile, but it was wiped out when Lucy replied, "I thank you, sir, but I do not care to ride except in a closed carriage unless the weather is truly warm. Also I do not like the dust produced by the dry spell. In London it will be different. There one can drive in Hyde Park. Pray do not hesitate to ask me again."

Once more Sophia and Emma exchanged disbelieving glances. To ride in the viscount's curricle drawn by two such beautiful animals as his grays would have given them enormous pleasure. Lucy was an enigma.

Sir George and Lady Jane Croft greeted their visitors with their customary good welcome. Lady Augusta was conducted by Sir George to a padded compass-seated chair purchased by his grandfather.

"I think, ma'am, you will be most comfortable here. As you see, it will not crush your pretty gown."

Lady Augusta seated herself and arranged her embroidered skirts about her before replying, "Most thoughtful of you, Sir George. I cannot abide modern furniture. It is designed in the main for the new namby-pamby wisps of garments designated as fashion. Why our young ladies do not freeze to death I shall never know."

Another voice broke in before Sir George could reply.

"It is understandable that you are puzzled, your ladyship. I have heard it said, and I believe I also read in the newspaper— or was it *The Gentleman's Magazine?*—that quite a number of young ladies have contracted lung fevers and that some, as a consequence of so doing, have actually left this mortal coil. And all in the name of fashion. If I had my way—"

"I daresay you are right, Mr. Treen," interrupted Lady Augusta. "However, I would prefer you to keep your dissertations to the pulpit, where they belong."

Mr. Phineas Treen moved from a corner to stand in front of Lady Augusta. He bowed, not a whit affronted, his pale-blue eyes alight with a smile that illumined his fresh-complexioned face. He would have spoken further had not Lady Croft intervened in her gentle way to offer refreshment.

Glasses of ratafia were ordered for the ladies and sherry for the gentlemen, and Mr. Waring's curate seated himself at Lucy's side and engaged her in conversation.

Emma would have preferred to emulate the men and drink sherry, but she sipped the sweet drink considered suitable for the gentler sex. She had known the Crofts all her life, but only now did she truly appreciate that neither could be considered handsome. Sir George was quite short and thickset, his skin marked from an early attack of smallpox. Lady Croft's long, thin nose, heavy jaw, and undistinguished figure, which was thickening as she grew older, precluded all claim to beauty. All Lady Croft's preganancies had ended in miscarriages, the last only the previous summer, and it was a great grief to them that a long unbroken line was about to end and that the baronetcy would go to a distant cousin they did not like. It was well-known too that Lady Croft had not brought a fortune to her marriage, and folk had sometimes marveled at their devotion, for there could be no doubt that they lived for each other, finding in their home and estates enough to satisfy them. Emma felt a sudden chill. She was not vain, nor was she stupid. She had assumed that she would find the right husband because of her beauty, but it was not necessarily so. Lucy could afford to be choosy, while Emma must find a husband who would enable her to live respectably and assist her brothers and sisters to advancement. She was the eldest daughter, and the responsibility was hers. Even Papa, unworldly though he was, accepted this as a fact of life.

"Don't you agree, Emma, my dear?"

Emma almost spilled her drink. She looked up, mortified to have lost the thread of conversation.

"Miss Waring would seem to be in the clouds, again," remarked Lord Kinver.

Lady Croft spoke in her gentle voice. "I am sure Emma was thinking about her papa's worries. She is such a help to him in his work." Lady Croft's forgiving smile, her protective defense were a soothing balm. It was no wonder that Sir George remained in love with his wife.

Sir George's attention was compelled by Lady Augusta, who had been staring from the long windows overlooking the landscaped park and had decided that she could find ways to improve the view, and Lord Kinver was free to move to Emma.

"Were you truly thinking of your father, Miss Waring? He will miss you sadly."

Emma gave him a cool look. "I think it prudent not to reveal my thoughts to you, sir. You might insult me as you did in the garden."

"Such icy dignity!" Lord Kinver's mouth was twisted in a sardonic smile. "You need not worry, Miss Waring." He glanced around the drawing room. "I should not dream of making us the object of censure by kissing you in front of so many onlookers."

Emma forced out a tinkling laugh. "Indeed, I should suppose not, sir. A man who is held to be a sad rake should be careful to uphold his reputation by sly and secret methods, only making sure later that his admiring friends learn of his exploits. Tell me, my lord, which of the London beaux will be favored by your confidences regarding this morning? I must be sure to behave in a worldly way with them. On no account would I reduce your lordship's value among the *ton*."

Emma was interested to note that the viscount had to unclench his teeth before he replied in clipped accents, "I am *not* a man who discusses ladies, madam. You are pleased to force an argument upon me. Well, it will not serve. I have more important matters in my life than the provocation of—"

"A saucy minx?" Emma laughed again, though her heart was beating too fast for comfort as she noticed that Lord Kinver was flexing his fingers as if he ached to shake her. Or perhaps to seize and kiss her again. She was humiliated and surprised by the delicate wave of color that suffused her face at the idea. "So be it, my lord. And when we meet in London, I will hang upon your every word, waiting for a pause to add my small, female contribution."

"You have a waspish tongue at times, Miss Waring. It sits ill with your appearance. You are a beautiful woman, but you must take care not to alienate the great ladies if you are to make your mark in polite society. Through them you will attract the gentleman like honeybees to a flower. Only in that way will you obtain a husband to suit you."

Emma's color faded. So he regarded her as a beautiful flower, and himself, she supposed, as one of those honeybees who could, if he chose, sip at her and fly on to the next woman he fancied.

"Thank you for your advice sir. It is a sobering thought that I might have entered society without the benefit of your wisdom. Have you ever considered writing down your observations and publishing them as a guide to the *ton*?"

"I have written on a number of subjects, but not that. Most young ladies entering society have received enough strictures from fond parents and governesses. Were you not cautioned against flirtatiousness?"

"I can assure you, sir, I do not flirt." As if to belie her assertion, Emma smiled and lowered her long lashes for an instant, having recollected that the advice given her most frequently was that she must make every effort to please the gentlemen. She looked up to see the viscount regarding her with a provoking smile and she felt suddenly deflated. She longed to meet a man of wit and erudition who would revere her intellect. The memory of how she had felt when this one kissed her must be banished.

She demanded an answer to her earlier question, making it sound as frivolous as she could. "Well, Lord Kinver, would you give consideration to the idea of publishing your invaluable advice?"

"Well, Miss Waring, would you read it if I did?"

"Oh, I do not think I care for such prosy stuff."

"Ah, yes, I recall that your interests are novels and magazines. I must not bore such a pretty creature. Your head is filled with thoughts of new gowns, satin slippers, reticules and the like, and the number and grandeur of the invitations you will receive in London. Far more fitting subjects for you, are they not?"

Emma feared that if she ground her teeth much harder the sound would echo through the room.

She summoned a passable simper. "How well you comprehend the workings of a woman's mind, my lord. It must make life so—so amusing for you."

"And amusement is of paramount importance, is it not?"

The viscount turned to look at Lucy, who was discoursing earnestly with Mr. Treen. "That gentleman is your papa's curate, I collect. Miss Venables is behaving with her usual courtesy, but I believe I must rescue her. Pray excuse me, Miss Waring. I have so enjoyed our conversation.''

His words sounded utterly insincere to Emma, who observed his elegant, athletic figure as he strolled in a leisurely way across the wide room. His shoulders were perfectly encased in a coat without a single wrinkle; his muscular legs were displayed to advantage in buckskin breeches and shining black boots; his short dark hair was brushed into orderly disarray. She wanted to despise him for his conformity to fashion, but found it impossible. He was no foppish coxcomb. She tried mentally to berate him for his rakish life, but could recall only the stories of his fearless riding to hounds, his success in madcap contests between himself and his friends, his deadly accuracy with pistol and brilliance of swordplay; and she had seen for herself his control over his high-bred horses and sporting curricle. Added to which, she often, regrettably, had more liking for the villains in her stories than for the pure and blameless heroes the magazine readers demanded.

Lucy glanced up at Lord Kinver and showed neither annoyance nor pleasure when he seated himself on her other side and joined in the conversation. Emma was delighted to note that Mr. Treen, oblivious to his lordship's ire, still commanded Lucy's attention and there was nothing he could do about it. Mr. Treen was as well-born as Lord Kinver, being the youngest son of an impoverished earl whose wife had succeeded in presenting him with fifteen children, all but one of whom had survived. Mr. Treen's only faults were those of poverty and his need to work.

Lord Kinver felt Emma's eyes upon him and looked across at her before she could wipe the slightly acerbic smile from her lips, and she was gratified to see that she had managed to irritate him.

Lady Augusta had been watching Lucy relentlessly while continuing to converse with the older occupants of the room. Not for worlds would she have drawn Mr. Treen away from her granddaughter. In her ladyship's opinion, almost any gentleman's attention was better than none, but now Viscount Kinver had joined Lucy and she called imperiously, ''Mr. Treen, I wish to speak to you. There was a point in your sermon last Sunday that I could not quite comprehend. I desire that you come and expound it for me.''

Emma reflected that Lady Augusta would have no difficulty in finding something that needed expounding in one of the unfortunate Mr. Treen's sermons, for they were almost as remarkable in their obscurity as they were in loquacity, but Lady Augusta had no intention of permitting the curate to bore her. As soon as he seated himself at her side, she returned to her discussion with her hostess on the latest fashions. Lady Croft was familiar with the subject through her magazines, though she wore a comfortable loose gown with no pretension to fashion at all. Once or twice Mr. Treen made efforts to escape, but Lady Augusta kept him at her side with a look which had the effect of a ferret's at a rabbit, and a brief word to be patient.

Emma was content to sit and watch the other occupants of the room. She had lived all her eighteen years in the country, with the exception of rare visits to Bristol and Bath on modest shopping expeditions and, once, to Weston-super-Mare for fresh sea air after she, Gerard, and Sophia had contracted the whooping cough. So she was eager for any opportunity to observe human behavior. Her fictional characters were a potpourri of folk she had met plus her own imagination.

Lady Augusta terminated the call by announcing that she and Lucy wished to be at home in Warmley for dinner and must return Emma and Sophia to the rectory.

''There is no need for you to go out of your way, Lady Augusta,'' said Sir George. ''I myself will escort the young ladies home.''

Lord Kinver intervened smoothly, ''My curricle is outside and my horses still fresh. I should be most happy to deliver Miss Waring and Miss Sophia to the rectory.''

He makes us sound like parcels, seethed Emma, who ached to decline the invitation, but could not do so without appearing selfish toward Lady Augusta.

''A splendid idea,'' said Lady Augusta. ''Tell your parents that our traveling coach will call for you in three days' time for our journey to London. Give them my compliments and say everything to them that is proper.''

Emma caught the viscount's eye and saw that he fully appreciated her dilemma and was amused.

"Three days!" exclaimed Sophia. "It is so short a time."
At Lady Augusta's raised eyebrows she blushed. "My—my
sister and I are close, ma'am. I shall miss her."

"Then the soooner we find her a man of property to marry,
the better, for she will then be in a position to offer you frequent
hospitality and thus increase your own prospects."

Sophia was rendered dumb by this sudden incursion into
her private life. Emma glanced at Lord Kinver and surprised
a look of sympathy directed at her sister. It annoyed her. The
man was a debauched tormentor and she did not want to see
good in him. She would avoid him as much as possible in the
weeks to come, though this would be difficult if he was
intending to court Lucy. She refused to analyze the stab of
emotion this idea produced.

The whole party stood on the front steps to watch Lady
Augusta and Lucy climb into their carriage. A gracious wave
from her ladyship and a half-smile and a languid movement
of the hand from Lucy, and they were gone. The viscount's
curricle and horses were brought, and Lord Kinver handed
Emma up first—the privilege of being the elder, he murmured—
then Sophia. He walked to the horses' heads, touched each
one in a gesture of affection, and joined the ladies on the
driving seat.

"It is fortunate that we are none of us large in person or we
should be sadly crowded," remarked the viscount. "Let 'em
go!" he called to Sir George's groom, and as the man sprang
back, the horses leapt into movement. For a few moments the
viscount was engaged in negotiating the turn into the driveway and seemed oblivious to the fact that three people in a
curricle ensured that they should sit in closer proximity than
might be thought seemly. Emma, in the middle, was very
conscious of the movements of his lordship's body and held
herself rigid, staring ahead.

4

Once the horses were in the driveway Lord Kinver allowed them a fast pace, and as they bowled into the road, which was well kept by the local gentry, he said in conversational tones, "How attractive the hedges look filled with spring flowers."

"How many do you recognize, sir?" asked Sophia, trying hard to remember her social drill, though her voice quavered.

"Absolutely none," replied the viscount blithely. "My interests have never lain in gardening or the naming of rural vegetation. I come into the country only to hunt and shoot and to examine the running of my estates."

"Have you one nearby?" asked Sophia. "I have never heard of it."

"A small property to the west of Bristol. I drove over here today to renew various acquaintanceships."

Emma was becoming cramped by her endeavors not to brush against the viscount more than absolutely necessary, and she was forced to move a little.

"You need not be nervous," advised Lord Kinver in kindly tones. "I have complete command over my animals."

"I did not doubt it," replied Emma. "Your skill in driving is known, though it was not necessary to take us up into your curricle. We should have had more room had we traveled in one of Sir George's larger vehicles." She remembered belatedly that she had already crossed swords with a man who probably knew all the right people in polite society, and softened her tones. "However, my lord, it was most kind of you to offer your escort."

"I saw how surprised you were when Miss Venables declined my offer," explained Lord Kinver in bland accents. "Disbelief was writ plain on your faces, and I assumed that you would not dislike to drive with me. Was I not right?"

Emma found herself unable to reply. How this man goaded her. A part of her wanted to say with honesty that she relished the experience of bowling along in a sporting vehicle drawn by beautiful thoroughbreds, but she had become cautious in the past couple of hours. Lord Kinver seemed to take one's words and twist them to suit his own warped sense of amusement.

Sophia, oblivious to the seething tensions in her sister, answered, "Yes, indeed, sir, you are quite right. Papa and Mama keep a gig that might go quite fast if only our horses were not so plodding. But animals such as yours must cost a great deal and . . ." She stopped, realizing that she had allowed her tongue to run on too far. Her parents' financial limitations were not an outsider's concern.

Lord Kinver released her from her embarrassment. "Do you think you will enjoy the company of Miss Venables in London, Miss Waring?"

"I hope so. Have you known her long?"

"Since we were children. My great-grandpapa was cousin to the Earl of Abbotsbury, father of Lady Augusta."

"Why, that means that we also are related," cried Sophia, "for our grandmama, Lady Lavinia, was sister to Lady Augusta. I never knew that you were a . . . What are you, Lord Kinver?"

"Alas, I do not know the ramifications of cousins, first, second, third, or removed, but I collect we are among them somewhere. Shall I call you Cousin Sophia? Would that please you?"

Sophia hesitated, turning to look at Emma, who said in a deliberately roguish voice, "I think, sir, that it would be as well to consult Papa first. He does not approve of undue familiarity, especially between males and females. A distant relationship need not necessarily lead to closeness. After all, sir, you address Cousin Lucy as Miss Venables, so why should you expect more from us?"

"I have already had more from you than ever I hope to obtain from Miss Venables, unless we should wed," said Lord Kinver to Emma in such low tones that, above the sound of carriage wheels and the horses' hooves, Sophia could not quite hear him.

Emma set her lips, and for the rest of the journey maintained silence.

Mrs. Waring was divided in her reaction when she understood that her girls had not only met Lord Kinver, but had been driven home by him. His lordship had declined an invitation to enter the rectory, reminding Mrs. Waring that there would be no moon and he preferred to get his horses back to their stable by dusk.

She acknowledged that fortune and position such as were held by Lord Kinver would be an enviable prize in the marriage mart, but he had shown no inclination to settle, and if a woman allowed her name injudiciously to be coupled with his, she was finished so far as acceptance in polite society was concerned.

"I am persuaded," she said hopefully, "that his lordship treated you with all due respect. The viscount is a rake. His father died and he inherited the title and great wealth and possessions while still at Eton. His mother," she paused, "his mother is—is a sad invalid. His grandmama tries to restrain him. Strong-minded though she is, she does not succeed. You must understand, Emma—and it is not too soon for you to learn, Sophia—that although you must not fail in courtesy toward such men, you must never permit an opportunity for familiarity."

As Emma removed her hat and pelisse in her room, endeavoring not to mind that they were of plain brown stuff and not very stylish, she reflected that Mama was a little late in her warning. Not only had Emma permitted herself to be discovered by Lord Kinver unattended in the shrubbery, she had also been kissed by him and worse, much worse, she had enjoyed it. She resolved to put the disgraceful episode behind her and behave in future with greater caution. After all, it scarcely mattered what the viscount thought of her, and he had assured her he did not kiss and tell.

Descending the stairway to dinner, she met Mr. Treen, who was ushered into the hall by the footman.

"Ah, Miss Waring, I decided that being in the neighborhood I would call," he explained unnecessarily. "Is your papa in his book room?"

"Probably," answered Emma, stifling a groan.

Mr. Treen disappeared into the book room and Emma heard him greeted by her father with civility before she entered the dining room, where a maid was adding an extra cover to the table. Everyone in the household knew that when Mr. Treen arrived he would not depart until he had been fed.

Emma strolled to the window. Already it was growing dark and the trees cast long shadows over the lawns and flower borders. The gardener and his young assistant were gathering weeds and taking them to the back of the rectory to burn.

Lord Kinver won't arrive home before dark, she mused, then berated herself for thinking of a man who cared only for his own pleasures. When she was in London, she would not consider him at all, for there would be hosts of young men only too eager to pay their addresses to a beautiful woman, or so Mama had assured her. Yet, thinking of Lady Croft, Emma wondered. Clearly beauty was not of paramount value, and according to Mama, men never looked for brains. "A gentleman likes always to feel superior to his wife in this respect," said Mama, vociferously backed by Nurse, who constantly deplored Mr. Waring's habit of allowing a daughter to sit in on his lessons with pupils who needed a crammer to help them enter university, extra work undertaken by Mr. Waring to increase his income. An added advantage to Emma in these arrangements was the large quantity of writing paper always in the book room from which she was able to extract undetected what she needed.

During dinner Mr. Treen held forth on a number of subjects. He appeared to possess a measure of knowledge of anything under discussion. The Warings found him tedious, and if he had not been a son of one of Papa's foremost friends from university days, he might not have been given the curacy of Lower Downham. Fortunately there was nothing in his character or behavior to make the decision impossible for the idealistic Mr. Waring, and although his discourses rambled, his parish visits were undertaken diligently and the people liked him. Mr. Treen was almost six feet tall, thin and angular, with straight fair hair, pale-blue eyes, and a rosy complexion. He was in demand among the young ladies of the district who had almost all been warned not to fall in love with him, since he possessed no fortune. The only girls who were instructed by their parents to encourage him were the unfortunate plain ones who could bring him a dowry and for whom a husband must be found somehow. However, any man was better than none at all to stand up with in the small dances got up by the gentlefolk, and Mr. Treen was never short of partners.

The following morning Emma rose to pursue her complicated routine. For almost two years she had insisted that she needed a constitutional walk early in the morning, and she kept it up regardless of the weather until her family accepted it as harmless, if eccentric. It was fortunate that Emma was blessed with robust health, since she often wrote far into the night and obtained little sleep. She did enjoy her morning walks—well, most of the time—but in truth they were absolutely necessary. When she had completed a manuscript, she gave it, along with any family mail, to the local carrier, who went every day, except the Sabbath, to Bristol to buy provisions to sell. He left letters and parcels at the post house, from where they were delivered. Mr. Palmer, the bookseller and printer, wrote to Emma, and his letters were collected, with others, from the post house very early in the morning and brought to the villages through which the carrier passed. Emma met him and brought the Waring mail home, concealing her own beneath a heavy cape. At first she had been so transported by excitement at her success that she had regarded her subterfuge almost as a game, but as time went by, the secret had begun to weigh heavily on her conscience and now she failed to see how she could ever tell her trusting parents how grossly she had been deceiving them.

The carrier handed her several letters, one of which was for her. The morning was fine and the sun warm and Emma stopped and leaned on a stile leading to a footpath through a field in which cows were contentedly grazing.

Mr. Palmer said how delighted he was to know that he was soon to meet the authoress of *The Horrid Haunting of Chesney Abbey*, *The Unfortunate Lady Joan*, *The Secret of the Priory*, and other such admirable Gothic works. Emma suppressed a small shudder at the thought of her parents' reaction even to the titles as she went on to read that Mr. Palmer would keep all monies due to her until she called for them. Letters still arrived from subscribers begging the true name of his most popular authoress, but of course he had not divulged it. He had laughed mightily at her lampoon of His Highness the Prince of Wales. He remained her devoted servant, etc., etc.

Emma had momentarily forgotten the verses she had sent regarding Prince George. She had penned them impulsively and posted them to Mr. Palmer because she wanted someone with whom to share a joke. They had relieved her disappointment when she was told by her tearful mama that her London Season must be postponed. Now that she was actually going to town in three days' time she remembered the lampoon uneasily. It must not get into the wrong hands. If ever it became common knowledge that she had composed verses which his Highness would consider unflattering, if not downright insulting, she might as well say good-bye forever to her chances of acceptance by the *ton*. She must recover them as soon as possible after she arrived in London.

The Prince, who had once been popular everywhere, was regarded with disapproval now by many, but there could be no doubt that he still held strong sway over much of the highest society.

Phrases from the lampooning verses floated into Emma's brain. She had left out nothing. There were references to Prince George's secret marriage to Mrs. Fitzherbert, his official wedding to Princess Caroline of Brunswick, and the fact that, to the disgust of many, he had left her as soon as she became pregnant and returned to the welcoming arms of his mistress. She had introduced the matter of his extravagant alterations to Carlton House, using borrowed money which it seemed unlikely he would ever repay, and ended with his love of food. More biting wit than hers had devised verses about the royal family and there were political prints, notably by Mr. Gillray, which were far crueller than anything Emma could produce. But surely no other young woman in need of a marriage partner of note would be shortsighted enough to risk being socially ostracized.

In the rectory all was bustle as Emma's portmanteaus were packed. "You absolutely must have new gowns soon after you arrive," said Mrs. Waring. "Lady Augusta, or someone she appoints, will conduct you to the best emporiums to purchase muslins, silks, and the like, and to the right establishments for hats, slippers, reticules, and fans. Papa has given Lady Augusta one hundred guineas for your purchases—"

"A hundred guineas! I cannot need a quarter so much."

"Indeed you will. You will be hard-put to make it stretch far enough. And here is a purse from me. It contains twenty guineas more for pin money so that you will not be needing to run to her ladyship if you fancy a few new ribbons or a box of bonbons. It must also cover vails to the various servants so always keep something by you."

Emma felt like sinking through the floor. She had never come closer to confessing her misdeeds as she did in that moment. "How did Papa manage so much?" she asked, her voice choked.

"Hush, now, my dear. It will all be worthwhile as long as you enjoy yourself. And if you should meet an eligible gentleman whom you can like enough to wed, Papa will be repaid a hundredfold. I am exceedingly relieved that Lady Augusta is to take you under her wing. She will be a formidable chaperone and lacks for nothing. In a way, it is lucky that I cannot go with you."

Sophia paused in her folding of a pale-green muslin gown in silver paper, "It is like you to say so, Mama, but I am persuaded that you must be very disappointed. You told us you enjoyed London life."

"When I was a girl, I did. Now I am content to live quietly with Papa."

Sophia sighed. "I do hope, Emma, that you make a good match. I see no hope of Gerard's reform and I long to have my Season next year."

"Do not speak so of your brother," commanded Mrs. Waring, but her reproof lacked force. There were times when she wished that Gerard was still young enough to be whipped.

The two days of preparation passed with amazing speed, and on the morning of the third day an imposing traveling coach drew up outside the rectory. Behind it was another coach containing an astonishing amount of luggage, considering that the two ladies had been absent from home for only three weeks; two ladies' maids; Lady Augusta's dresser; a quantity of sheets and cutlery for use at posting inns; and a footman in livery.

The two coachmen also wore the Abbotsbury livery of red

and silver-gray as did the grooms and two outriders. Sophia watched from the window as the entourage crowded into the rectory driveway.

"Emma, what grandeur! You will never be the same again."

"You cannot think it, dearest Sophia! How I wish we could be going together. I am sorry now that I did not wait for you until next year."

"Oh, no, that would not do at all. Next year you will be nineteen. Cousin Lucy is twenty-one and very nearly on the shelf."

A tap on the bedroom door heralded the entrance of Lucy. Emma had been content with her deep-blue cloth pelisse and hat, but the minute she looked at Lucy she was aware that there were subtle but very important differences in the cut of their garments. Lucy's pelisse of amber-colored cashmere with two capes trimmed with fur and her close-fitting matching hat with a simple spray of pale-gold feathers made Emma remember that her own hat was over a year old and had been refurbished with one sweeping feather brought by her mother from a trunk in the attic, and her pelisse sewn partly at home.

She greeted Lucy with a smile that was a trifle forced. Her newfound cousin was so unmistakably wealthy. Even had Lucy possessed a rackety brother, there would have been no problem in paying for his excesses. Emma pulled herself up short. She must continue to love Gerard as she ought.

Lucy looked at herself in the cheval glass in a detached way, as if, thought Emma, she was so well aware of her consequence she had no need to assess herself as she and Sophia were wont to do, probing their appearance and speculating on their situation and prospects.

"You—you look as well as always," stammered Sophia, in an endeavor to break the lengthening silence, Mama having gone downstairs to supervise the loading of Emma's baggage.

"Thank you, Cousin Sophia."

Emma supported her sister's efforts at conversation. "It is exceedingly generous of you not to mind that Lady Augusta is allowing me to share your Season."

"Yes, indeed," agreed Sophia, "for Emma is very pretty, is she not, and you are still a single young lady and—" She stopped, her ready blush crimsoning her face as she realized that again her wayward tongue had betrayed her into a remark that must be considered uncivil and could be interpreted as spiteful.

Lucy's composure remained unaffected. "Oh, you are afraid, Cousin Sophia, that Cousin Emma may outshine me, but Grandmama says I need have no fears on that score, for your sister's looks are not fashionable. Red hair is not, you know."

"Emma's hair is not *red*," cried Sophia. "It is a beautiful golden color with auburn gleams!"

"But gold hair is not fashionable either," said Lucy calmly, "while dark hair is the thing. And besides, your sister has no fortune."

Mrs. Waring hurried in. Anxious to return to the nursery, where Amabel was showing increasingly fretful signs of taking the measles, she failed to notice anything strained about the atmosphere.

"Come along, Emma, and you, too, Lucy dear. Lady Augusta is impatient to be away."

For the first few miles of her journey Emma could not forget the sight of her parents, Sophia, and Nurse waving from the rectory door and was silent in her grief at leaving her family for the first time in her life.

Lady Augusta, enveloped in a large wool cloak and wearing a hat adorned with feathers, ribbons, and silk fruit, leaned back against the squabs with closed eyes. Had she been a lesser personage, one could have sworn that occasionally she emitted a little snore as she compensated for her early rising. Lucy merely gazed through the window, her face expressionless. Emma had been allotted the seat with her back to the horses and she stared out until the dear, familiar landmarks were gone and the coach carried her into unexplored country. But she was an optimist and began to consider the advantages of her trip.

She interrupted Lucy's reverie impulsively. "Cousin Lucy, I rely on you to show me how to go on in London. I have previously known the guests at parties and small dances and am unused to meeting many strangers."

Lucy turned a bland gaze upon her. "You will soon learn the way of things, Emma."

"I shall instruct you in the ways of polite society." Lady Augusta's voice startled Emma.

"I thought you were asleep. I hope I did not waken you, Great-aunt Augusta."

"I most certainly was not asleep. I never can sleep in a confounded carriage. I heard every word you said. And you will please refrain from addressing me as great-aunt. It makes me sound like a monument. I shall be Aunt Augusta."

"Yes, Great—I mean, Aunt Augusta."

Emma was suddenly desperately homesick for the company of her family. At home there was always someone to talk with, to laugh with, even to weep with if occasion demanded. Lucy had returned to gazing from her window, Lady Augusta had closed her eyes again, and Emma reflected that great ladies clearly possessed the ability to snore gently while awake.

At first she found the changes of horses of interest as the ostlers raced out to meet such a magnificent procession, vying with one another as to who could work fastest, and within moments of arriving at the posting inns they were on their way again.

"How astonishing to find horses always of such excellent quality," Emma remarked.

"They should be," was Lady Augusta's daunting response, "since they all belong to Lucy and have been stabled awaiting our return, though for what we are being charged one would think a whole cavalry regiment had been stationed. The cost of travel nowadays is scandalous."

Once more Emma subsided. When Mama had told her that she would have her London Season after all, and with relatives, she had been delighted. Now she began to wonder if her joy had been premature. It was one thing for her to conjure up rich people from her strong imagination and put them in stories, but quite another actually to experience such wealth. Her parents were often hard-pressed for money, yet never grumbled, while Lady Augusta had no hesitation in commenting on any expenditure and even arguing about it with unabashed vehemence at the post houses. This was a vastly different world from hers. She resolved to collect a good store of material for future writing. This brought her thoughts back to the problem of Mr. Palmer, her secret money, and, not least, her lampoon on the Prince of Wales. She resolved to try to put it all out of her head and live for the moment. Somehow she would find a way through the tangle.

5

After six changes and only two brief stops for refreshment, the stately pace ordered by Lady Augusta began to pall and the inns lost their novelty. Emma looked coveteously at dashing curricles, gigs, and phaetons that appeared to fly along the road. Once they were even passed by the heavily laden mailcoach, the driver and guard and even the passengers inside swaying and clutching whatever they could for security.

Her thoughts returned abruptly to the ride she had enjoyed—hastily she altered the word to endured—with Lord Kinver, that insolent man who had dared to kiss her without permission. She wondered what she would have said had he asked.

In spite of their dignified progression they covered many miles in the fine weather and arrived at Speenhamland in Berkshire, where beds had been bespoken at the George and Pelican Inn. Emma was to share a room with Lucy, and she wondered if during the quiet time between climbing into bed and sleeping they might talk and become a little closer. She was disappointed. As soon as Lucy's maid had assisted both young ladies to undress, supervised the bringing up of cans of hot water for their ablutions, and settled them into feather-beds between Lady Augusta's fine linen sheets, Lucy blew out her candle, wished Emma good night, closed her eyes, and composed herself for sleep.

Emma woke to windows streaming with rain and a damp chill in the air, and she shivered in the coach despite the fur lap robes unpacked by the maids. Lady Augusta's dresser placed a hot brick wrapped in flannel at her mistress's feet, but evidently her ladyship was of the opinion that the feet of the young did not need such cosseting. Lucy seemed impervious to any human condition.

The coach jolted its way into ruts that the teeming rain had turned into quagmires, and slid along patches of road that farm animals had rendered as slippery as ice. Emma became weary as change of horses followed change. They rested once at the Castle Inn at Salt Hill, where a nuncheon was produced. Emma felt unable to eat as the well-sprung carriage had begun to make her feel nauseous.

Lady Augusta regarded her with disfavor. "The food has been spoke for and must be consumed. I cannot abide waste."

Emma resignedly helped herself to fruit, and contrary to her expectation, it made her feel a little better. She faced the final twenty miles of the journey with fortitude.

They arrived in London at four o'clock and she forgot discomfort in her excitement. Nothing had prepared her for the size of the city and the constant noise and interesting bustle. The street vendors crying their wares half-blocked the thoroughfares. There were knife grinders with their portable machines; and women of all ages, their skirts short enough to reveal sturdy bare legs, their feet thrust into heavy shoes, carrying spring flowers or new laid eggs with an exhortation to "crack 'em and try 'em"; a young man in knee breeches and white stockings with a cage of singing birds, which saddened Emma who preferred birds to fly free; and many others—all adding to the cacophony and congestion.

The scenes held no novelty for her companions, but Emma, try as she might to show some town polish, gave up the effort and stared this way and that.

As they approached the heart of the district where richer folk lived, the cries were more vociferous and became a chorus in her head. "Three rows a penny pins"; "Fine writing ink"; "Milk below, maids"; "Songs, penny a sheet"; "Cat's and dog's meat"; "Buy a doll."

The carriage stopped as the coachman exchanged a lively series of insults with a young man trying to drive a phaeton in the opposite direction. With blood-freezing clarity, Emma heard a male voice booming above the others, above the rattle of wheels over uneven cobbles, above the barking of dogs and the shouts of children: "Ballads! Who'll buy my ballads? Here's a new one for your delight, men and maidens all."

The ballad-monger's voice grew more raucous as a grinning crowd gathered around him and with many a theatrical gesture he declaimed, "Great Florizel with princely form expanded. / A Brunswick fish his rod and line hath landed. / He looked not for his wedded comfort there, / But princes all must needs beget an heir. / He, fainting, groaned, 'To give Britain her heir, I must depart the perfect mansion where, my heart hath settled and doth linger still, / With she who pines and yearns on Richmond Hill . . .' "

The young man gave way, recognizing Lady Augusta's imposing cavalcade to be impassable, especially as the occupants of the principal carriage made no effort at all to intervene. He began slowly—agonizingly slowly, it seemed to Emma—to back up his horse while the man bawled on until Emma was sure that either her great-aunt or Lucy must surely remark on it.

To encouraging shouts from the crowd the ballad-singer bellowed, "His duty done a daughter forth was brought, / And hapless Florizel was heard to groan, / 'A halt!' " Here the ballad-seller stopped quoting and yelled, "Come, lads and maids all, housewives and goodmen, who will learn the behavior of he who shall be nameless, but unmistakable? Who will read of the sad fate of the lady of Brunswick?"

Mercifully for Emma's fast-disintegrating composure, the way was cleared and the procession rolled on. She had no need to purchase a ballad sheet to learn the fate of the lady of Brunswick, for those were the verses she had written in a fit of boredom when several consecutive evening engagements had kept her from her bed until she was too tired to work on her latest serial. She had never thought to warn Mr. Palmer that they must not be made public. No proper young lady would admit to knowing the irregular details of the Prince's amorous arrangements. She had assumed that Mr. Palmer would understand this, but she had failed to consider the fact that he had never met her and had no notion of her status. Somehow she must stop him from allowing the ballad to be hawked around the streets.

The carriages moved into the grandest part of London. There were houses larger than Emma could have believed were in a town, some of them enclosed by walls and set in pretty gardens. Ladies and gentlemen strolled together in animated converse. Maids, footmen, and pages—some, tiny black boys in gaudy dress—were on errands for their employers; if they worked for a person of uncertain temper, they hurried along, for life for servants in many great houses was comfortable in a land where there was much poverty and crime, and such positions were not easily come by. Some young women in fine gowns and fashionable hats lingered to flirt shamelessly with menservants and tradesmen, and Emma guessed them to be ladies' maids.

Tucked into corners of grand streets and squares were shops of all kinds. A butcher stood outside in a dark apron, his steel dangling from a string, a dark round hat on his head, his fat legs in stockings, and buckled shoes on his feet. A bakery and cook house sent out savory smells. There were tobacco and snuff sellers, their discreet shops painted as brown as their wares, the leaded windows full of jars.

The entourage turned into Hanover Square, where Lucy owned a town residence. The cobbled roads were so spacious that several carriages might go side by side. In the center was an iron-railed expanse of grass where nursemaids watched children at play. A high-perch phaeton dashed by, rattling over the cobbles, its body hanging several feet above the wheels. It was driven by a lady accompanied by her groom, who sat, apparently impervious to peril, with his arms folded, his tall, cockaded hat swaying with the movement of the large, curved springs.

"I had not supposed ladies to drive themselves in London," said Emma, "especially in such a carriage as that. Can it be safe? How I should like to try!"

Lady Augusta turned a stern gaze upon her. "There will be no opportunity for you to drive such a ridiculous equipage while you are under my chaperonage. And, Emma, although I have said nothing of the matter of your turning this way and that and staring at everything you see, I must impress upon you before we leave the coach that such behavior will not do for a lady of quality. However unusual things may appear to you, I must ask you not to act like a country gapeseed, but with perfect decorum, affecting even ennui."

Emma refrained from defending herself. "I beg your pardon, ma'am. I will behave, I swear I will."

Lady Augusta smiled. "That is being a sensible girl. I can see we shall do well together."

Emma by no means shared her ladyship's opinion. She felt exceedingly unsure of herself and wished that Mama had been able to bring her to London. Mama knew how to go on and would not make her daughter feel buffleheaded.

She conceded that it was as well she had been cautioned when the coach stopped and the groom leapt to open the door and put down the steps to allow the ladies to descend. Immediately the great front door of Lucy's large mansion swung back to reveal a butler, an under-butler, and behind them, several footmen in livery and a number of maidservants.

Emma followed her hostesses into a hallway into which one might have fitted an ordinary dwelling. To a girl raised in a country rectory run by a modest number of female domestics, the waiting platoon was daunting.

"Welcome home, your ladyship, Miss Lucy," said the stately butler.

"Thank you, Bardsea," murmured Lucy.

"I trust you found Warmley agreeable, madam."

Lucy became animated. "I did indeed. The gardens are filled with most delightful blossoms and shrubs and the countryside—"

"We have brought Miss Waring with us," announced Lady Augusta, cutting short Lucy's eulogy. She spoke to a plump woman in black from whose waist hung a massive bunch of keys. "You received my instructions to prepare the blue bedchamber, Mrs. Overton?"

"Yes, your ladyship. All is in readiness."

Mrs. Overton glanced at Emma and curtsied, and Emma smiled. Lucy had subsided into her customary lethargy. The footmen bowed and the maids bobbed curtsies, their lace caps snowy against their severely dressed hair. Lucy's and Lady Augusta's personal maids joined them in the hall and bustled about, looking incongruous in their finery among the other soberly clad females, giving orders and making demands for their mistresses' welfare and comfort. Miss Wheeler, her ladyship's dresser, had marched upstairs immediately. Bardsea made a gesture with one hand and the servants turned to file away. They were halted by Lady Augusta, who demanded to know the whereabouts of Alphonse.

Bardsea sighed a little and looked at the ceiling. "He is being very French, your ladyship, *very* French indeed. He refuses to leave a special sauce that is in preparation for dinner tonight. He insists that it will be quite spoiled if he allows a kitchen menial to tend it. 'Kitchen menial' were his words, your ladyship. He also said other things, but as they were in French, a language I have no wish to speak, I don't know—"

"That will do, Bardsea. Alphonse must be permitted a little license."

One of Bardsea's eyebrows lifted a fraction to display his opinion of temperamental foreign cooks. He dismissed his domestic army save for two footmen and a page, the continued presence of whom he evidently considered imperative to keep up the standards to which his employers were accustomed. The hall porter reseated himself in his high-backed chair to continue his watch.

Lady Augusta called for refreshments, Bardsea took the ladies' outer garments, and the footmen opened the double doors leading into what was described as the small parlor. It was larger than the Waring drawing room, furnished in a mixture of styles. The walls were hung with paper painted with Chinese design and there was an Oriental rug in the center of the polished oak floor.

Lady Augusta sank into a large chair, Lucy seated herself on a sofa, and Emma chose a chair by the window from which she could watch a nurse girl throwing a ball for her young charges. They reminded her of the rectory nursery, and homesickness overtook her once more. But she must endeavor to remain as calm and tranquil as Lucy, for apparently remorseless ennui was the behavior expected of young ladies.

The doors were thrown open and Bardsea led a procession into the room. He directed the first footman to place a tray of glasses and bottles on a table, a second to add to it dishes bearing macaroons, cheesecakes, and gingerbread, and a third to contribute a platter of very thin bread and butter and one of toast. Her lack of sustenance on the journey caught up with Emma and she heard her stomach give a definite and very unladylike gurgle. She prayed that no one would notice, while at the same time she was almost overset by a terrible desire to giggle. She accepted a porcelain plate and was helped to a cheesecake, a piece of gingerbread, and two slices of toast. She sank her teeth into the melting butter with a sigh of delight, feeling suddenly so ravenously hungry that she was sure she could have demolished half the refreshments and had to bring restraint into play to eat slowly.

"Will you take wine or tea?" asked Lady Augusta, who presided over the table.

"Tea, if you please, ma'am," answered Emma, adding, "It is so refreshing."

"That is your opinion," remarked her ladyship with asperity. "I find the habit of tea-drinking during the day quite extraordinary. Pour me a glass of wine," she ordered Bardsea.

Lucy took tea and one slice of bread and butter, refusing everything else, making Emma feel like a greedy pig, but she consumed the contents of her plate and two macaroons, and began to feel that she might survive this seemingly endless day.

Her optimism was shaken when, the refreshments having been removed, Bardsea reentered to announce, "Lord Kinver, your ladyship."

The viscount advanced toward his elderly relative, who stared at him as if he had been a species she had not hitherto encountered.

"Good God, Kinver, we have scarce set foot in the house and you are calling!"

Lord Kinver bowed and took her hand in a courtly manner to his lips, a gesture that softened Lady Augusta's attitude.

"Well, well, I must suppose you to have a sufficient reason for disturbing us when we are enervated by a most tedious journey. The weather today was atrocious and the roads practically impassable in places. It is high time the government took steps to induce folk with estates adjoining the highways to ensure that they are kept in good order."

"Would not that be somewhat expensive for you, dear Lady Augusta, since your principal estate marches with one of our most frequented roads? I mention it only in your own interest, you comprehend. I would not wish you to declare in public something that might be acted upon," he added deprecatingly, but with a wicked smile in his eyes.

Lady Augusta was torn between her annoyance at the truth

of his words and her gratification in being thought to possess influence over the government.

She took refuge in attack. "Why are you here, sir?"

"I returned to London yesterday and came only to leave my card, but finding you at home, decided to see you and, naturally, to inquire after Miss Venables." He smiled warmly at Lucy. "Oh, and Miss Waring, of course. I believe you are unaccustomed to long journeys, Miss Waring, and perhaps found it trying."

"Certainly not, sir," replied Emma coolly, instantly putting aside the memory of the jolting, swaying, nauseating hours. "My health is excellent and I have no difficulty in combating fatigue."

"How fortunate." Lord Kinver turned again to Lucy. "And you, Miss Venables? You have said nothing."

"There is nothing to say," replied Lucy. "One becomes used to travel. I visit my properties whenever possible to ascertain that all is well with the land and with my tenants. I find pleasure in so doing."

"Excellent! How delighted your tenants must be. So many estate-owners care nothing for their unfortunate dependents."

Lady Augusta permitted a few more remarks before she rose. "Come, young ladies, we shall retire to our bedchambers now to rest before dinner. It will be served at seven o'clock, Emma. You must adjust to town hours for meals. I have requested Mrs. Overton to assign a suitable maid to you and she will apprise you of our customs."

Emma would not have chosen to receive such counsel in Lord Kinver's presence, though what he thought of her could scarcely matter. She wished Lucy joy of him. The memory of his kiss in the Downhams' garden rose to taunt her as she recalled her involuntary response. She had best put it down to her inexperience of rakish gentlemen and forget it, as Kinver had. Then she caught his eyes upon her and knew at once that he was remembering too and found the recollection droll. She seethed with longing to give him a set-down. Thoughts of a lampoon came into her head again, but after the ghastly experience with the ballad-singer in the street, she had learned too late that words penned in the security of her room were actually enjoyed by strangers. She had seemed remote from the outcome of her endeavors—until today. And that reminded her that somehow, at the very earliest opportunity, she must get secretly out of this house and find Mr. Palmer and request him to stop publication of the lampoon. The consideration that it could come to the attention of Prince George that an unknown female from a country rectory had made him a laughingstock gave her a shuddering sensation of doom.

Lord Kinver opened the door for them and they left the room in order of precedence. Lady Augusta first, naturally, followed by Lucy. Emma had meant to behave as serenely as her cousin and pass by Lord Kinver without a shadow of emotion, but in spite of her resolve, her lashes lifted and she found herself staring in a mesmerized way into his glinting hazel eyes. He found her amusing, yet she felt powerless to retaliate. Ladies simply did not demand of gentlemen, especially those practically unknown to them, what lay in their minds.

Then, defying all her practical understanding, she heard herself say, "A penny for your thoughts," echoing his own words to her, and bringing back with relentless clarity the scene that had followed.

"My dear Miss Waring, you do remember! I could have staked my life you were trying to forget our previous meeting. I must confess I recall it with delight. You are bound to enjoy London. You have such a way with you."

Emma could have shrieked with vexation as he continued, "My thoughts were precisely those I have just expressed, and now that you have granted me an opening, I feel at liberty to say that I think you are exceedingly pretty. I am persuaded many men have already told you so. And many more will do so in the weeks to come. I felicitate you in advance on your conquests. Believe me, Miss Waring, I do not doubt that you will secure just such a gentleman as you and your hopeful family desires."

His final words could mean anything. Was he paying her a compliment, or offering an insult? Inwardly she fulminated, but against what? Did he imagine she cared nothing for a man's character so long as he had wealth? To even attempt to deny an accusation he had not made would embroil her in exactly the tone of discussion that would afford Lord Kinver most merriment. To her horror she felt tears stinging the backs of her eyes, and with an incoherent murmur she escaped. Her thoughts as she ascended the wide stairway behind Aunt Augusta and Cousin Lucy were regrettably unladylike, and as she felt the eyes of Lord Kinver boring into her back, she had an infuriating certainty that he was aware exactly of how he had provoked her and was pleasurably gratified.

6

Viscount Kinver stepped from his bath to be wrapped in a large towel by Kidwelly, his valet. As he dried himself, his friend Mr. James Exford, who had been a companion of his lordship through Eton and Oxford, looked at him enviously.

"How d'you do it, Kinver? Not an ounce of spare flesh anywhere. I have the devil's own job to keep weight off."

Lord Kinver glanced at James, his face filled with humor. "Is it true that you are trying a diet of potatoes and vinegar?"

Mr. Exford sighed. "I did, but to tell truth, I could not stomach it. And besides," he grinned, "meals became excessively boring."

Kidwelly produced a moderately frilled white shirt and held it for Lord Kinver to insert his arms.

"You should take more exercise, James. Remember the time when you hunted half the day, sparred with men like Jackson or the Brewer, and went on to dinner and cards half the night? No fear of your putting on excessive weight then."

"I was younger."

Kinver gave a shout of laughter that disarranged his shirt, causing Kidwelly to frown at his master's guest. In his opinion, no callers should be allowed until a gentlemen was perfectly ready to receive them. "You are but nine and twenty now—barely a year older than I. No, the trouble is you prefer to use your fortune to roister away the days and nights."

Mr. Exford looked suitably glum. "You are right, Kinver." He brightened. "However, I am exceedingly glad that when my unknown uncle in Italy kicked the bucket, he cut up so warm and left me his money. I daresay I am now almost as wealthy as you."

"I daresay you are, James."

All speech was halted as Kidwelly eased his master into a pair of the newly fashionable buckskin trousers. They fitted so perfectly that the muscles in Kinver's legs were shown to great advantage, causing yet another envious sigh from Mr. Exford. Silence of a reverential nature continued as the valet pulled on his lordship's hessian boots, which sported modest black tassels, but it was as nothing to the hush that prevailed as Kidwelly laid out a number of stiffly starched white neckcloths.

Exford watched, as he had watched often before, trying to discern the secret of Lord Kinver's excellence with cravats, but he was still unable to follow the swift movements of his friend's long fingers as he spoiled only two before tying the third into a perfect arrangement.

Mr. Exford's slow exhalation coincided with Kidwelly's at the sight of the snowy folds that reached a third of the way up Kinver's neck. Not for him the inability to move one's head sideways because of the extreme height of his neckwear.

"What do you call that, my dear fellow?" asked Mr. Exford, hoping to receive some guidance in the name.

Lord Kinver stared at his reflection for a moment longer. "I call it 'a minor puzzle within a vast enigma,' " he stated blandly. "The appellation is perhaps a little clumsy, but what is one to do? It is so difficult to describe perfection."

Mr. Exford grinned. "All right, sharpen your wit at my expense. I've known you too long to take offense. In any case," he added frankly, "I wouldn't dare. Only think if you should call me out. I should quake in my shoes."

Kinver's eyebrows rose. "But of course you would. Just as you did when that rakeshame Lowther challenged you because you defended with fisticuffs a tradesman's daughter whom he was attempting to violate."

Exford went pink. "Couldn't stand by and see the poor little soul hurt."

"Exactly so. I was one of your seconds and do not recall one trace of nerves when you met Lowther, and I was well aware of your skill when you got off without a scratch and pinked your opponent."

Exford shrugged. "The fact remains, dear old fellow, I'm not the man you are with either sword or pistol."

"We have returned full circle, James. You should practice, and that would give you exercise."

Kidwelly, who had left the room, now returned to say that breakfast was ready in the morning parlor and would the gentlemen be pleased to partake as Mr. Hardy was waiting for them.

Kidwelly melted away to resume his inspection of his master's clothes ready for the coming Season. He was thankful to know that it would be passed in London, where he had been born and would never think of leaving, he told Mr. Hardy, the butler, were it not for his devotion to his master.

Kinver and Mr. Exford walked downstairs together and Kinver muttered, "One of the things I most enjoy about traveling is the absence of the vast retinue I am obliged to keep."

Mr. Exford was shocked. "It is obligatory in your position. I can only thank God that since the demise of my uncle I no longer have to make do with a cook and a couple of maids. If you had suffered as I have in the past, you would never deplore the early possession of your fortune."

His countenance went a deep shade of red as he recalled too late that Kinver's inheritance had preceded the immediate return of his mother, Viscountess Kinver, who, by the blatancy of her sexual intrigues, had scandalized even the promiscuous society of her day. She had finally decamped with a handsome French *groom de chambre* when Kinver was an infant. Worse, she had actually had the effrontery to return to London on her husband's death when Kinver was fourteen. She had been shunned and would have fared ill if her son, accustomed to having his way during his father's long, wasting illness, had not intervened and insisted on her being given one of the family estates and an adequate income. Mr. Exford knew that Kinver visited her, but he never discussed her. Since his early manhood, no one had dared to raise the subject in his presence. He had fought two duels with men both senior to him who had spoken ill of his mother. One had been with pistols and one with swords, and only the magnanimity of his nature permitted his opponents to escape with their lives. Mr. Exford attended as his principal second on both occasions. In fact, Lowther had been the most insolent of Lady Kinver's detractors, and her son had conducted their duel of swords with controlled fury, playing him as one would a fish on a rod and line. Other men had got wind of this rare treat and an appreciative audience had witnessed Lowther's humiliation. He was generally disliked and became a butt for a good deal of caustic wit. He had hated Kinver ever since.

The viscount proceeded downstairs as if his friend had not spoken, and the two gentlemen went into breakfast, where Kinver dismissed two footmen, a parlormaid, and his butler, who, with eyes raised heavenward, walked out looking affronted, though the scene was enacted every morning.

The gentlemen helped themselves from dishes on the side table. Kinver ate a plate of cold meat and a buttered egg, and Mr. Exford, whose appetite had been subdued by his social solecism, remained content with a dish of fricando of beef, four slices of toast and preserves, and two hothouse peaches. The food was washed down by ale.

Kinver spoke so suddenly that Exford started. "Exford, there is no need to look like a kicked dog because you happened to touch upon the past. I am aware that I can trust my honor to you."

Exford grinned thankfully and immediately rose to help himself to bacon and ham and three eggs.

After a few succulent bites he asked, "Have you heard anything about the Season's new crop of beauties? Are there any of note?"

Kinver shrugged slightly and his lip curled. "I've no doubt that London is filling rapidly with any number of simpering misses enjoying their first come-out and anxious young ladies eager not to spend yet another Season waiting for the right husband . . ."

His words recalled Miss Lucy Venables to mind. He knew she had refused marriage proposals and deduced that she would give her heart and hand only to a man she considered worthy. He also knew she had not taken in the polite world, but he held this to be in her favor; he despised the average young woman who was clasped to the undiscerning bosom of society. When they were married, he would enjoy watching the toadying of folk who had once disregarded her.

Mr. Exford had been watching his friend. "Do not tell me you have someone in mind for yourself." He ceased to masticate in his amazement. "I thought you were past being ensnared by marriage."

"Very well, then, I won't," declared Kinver. "Is that how you regard marriage—as an ensnarement?"

"No, I do not. I wish to set up my home—not to mention my nursery—with the right woman, but you are always so cynical about women. Some who have set their caps at you have been exceedingly handsome and often wealthy and always well-born."

"I would agree with that. Yet I have never yet met one to compare with Sybilla."

Mr. Exford tried to conceal his exasperation. Lady Sybilla had been dead these ten years, yet the viscount retained his youthful idealistic view of his first love and held her as a pattern. Mr. Exford had not considered Lady Sybilla to be anything out of the ordinary, but it was not often that two men saw eye to eye about women they wished to marry. This accounted, no doubt, for the way in which male friendships suffered when a man became bogged down in domesticity. One had the choice either of neglecting one's family and continuing to racket around with equally rackety companions, or of turning into a model husband and father. Although the polite world would have hooted with mirth at the conception that Lord Kinver belonged to the second category, Mr. Exford knew that he did.

"Of course, Lady Sybilla was exceptional," agreed Mr. Exford, half-despising himself for uttering sentiments he felt to be exaggerated, "but as it was heaven's will that she should succumb to illness so tragically young, you would be advised to consider some other lady to be mistress of your estate and mother of your heir."

"It is not essential," asserted Kinver. "The title will pass to a cousin who is already the proud father of a hopeful brood."

"Kinver, you can't consider *him*! He is a red-faced country squire, and always will be."

"You are speaking of my cousin, sir," said Kinver in mock-heroic tones.

Exford grinned. "Impossible to believe that such a bucolic man could be related to you." He studied his friend. His own clothes were as exclusive and well-cut, but he did not fill them with such distinction as Kinver.

"You failed to answer my question about the present crop of girls, Kinver. Have you heard anything?"

"You will see for yourself soon enough. In no time at all we shall be plunged into an endless whirl of gaiety that must satisfy even a man so recently in possession of a fortune."

"It's all very well for you! You don't know the horrors of penury."

His lordship gave a bark of mirth. "Penury! What nonsense! You had a most adequate income."

Mr. Exford looked closely at Lord Kinver. "I would almost swear that you are avoiding my question. What young woman has taken your eye?"

Lord Kinver hesitated, then asked, "D'you recall Miss Lucy Venables?"

Mr. Exford apprehended that his friend was roasting him again. He almost gave vent to a disbelieving laugh when he realized, just in time, that Kinver was serious, and he forbore to mention that he had always placed Lucy Venables in the category of dull women to be avoided whenever possible.

"Of course I do. *I* have not spent years junketing around foreign parts. I have attended all the right soirees, routs, and grand occasions for several consecutive Seasons."

"Naturally, I shall not ask for your opinion of her," said Lord Kinver decisively, which caused Mr. Exford to feel almost faint with relief, "but I have to say that having met her again when I was in the country, I was surprised. She has become a woman of quiet distinction and grace. And I was gratified by her reflective conversation."

Mr. Exford managed to conceal his horror with difficulty. "Quiet distinction and grace and reflective conversation," he repeated, feeling dazed.

"I intend to get to know her a great deal better."

Mr. Exford took refuge in sounding hearty. "Splendid, old fellow! Absolutely splendid! No one, I am sure, will presume to try to cut you out. Indeed, no one could succeed."

"You overestimate my value, James, and it is clear that Miss Venables has command enough of her own to repel the attempts of undesirable men to become acquainted with her."

In Mr. Exford's view, Miss Venables had no need to make

any effort to repel any man; to spend time in her company was to invite boredom. However, it sounded as if she was destined to make the match of the year, for no woman would turn down an offer from Viscount Kinver. And, in any case, that guardian dragon of hers, Lady Augusta, would have her married to Kinver before Miss Venables knew what had happened.

Mr. Exford pulled his wits together. "So what are you leaving for the rest of us?"

"It depends upon what you require. Lady Augusta is bringing a new girl out. A Miss Emma Waring."

Mr. Exford waited for more. A note that puzzled him had crept into his friend's voice. As he seemed reluctant to continue, Mr. Exford became even more fascinated.

"Is Miss Waring a frump? Perhaps she has freckles? Pimples? Pockmarks? Why do you hesitate? Tell me the worst and I shall be forewarned."

"She is one of the loveliest creatures I have met. She is around five feet, four inches tall, slender, yet with a perfect form; she has flawless creamy skin, speaking eyes that merge from blue to gray and back, depending on her mood. Her conversation is lively."

Exford gasped. "Has she no flaws?"

"One only as regards appearance. Her hair is gold with titian gleams—most unfashionable. As for the rest, she has no fortune and no expectations so far as I am aware. She is by way of being a distant cousin of mine, but I have so many I cannot possibly know them all. Her most unredeeming point, so far as I am concerned, is her tendency to play the coquette."

Mr. Exford was puzzled. Kinver had just described a veritable goddess. It was regrettably true that her lack of wealth would make her ineligible for a poor man, but she sounded exactly the type of young woman who would be greeted by the male members of the *haut ton* with delight.

"Is she forward? Will she put up the hackles of the first-rate hostesses?"

Mr. Exford noted that Kinver hesitated for a fraction of a second. Only a fraction of a second, but a multitude of memories flashed across Lord Kinver's consciousness. He was in a dilemma. He considered that a young woman who allowed herself to be found alone in the shrubbery by a bachelor and who behaved so flirtatiously that she practically asked to be kissed must be considered forward. Yet, knowing how much power he commanded in the polite world, he hesitated to condemn her to the horrors of ostracism because she had once forgotten the rigid discipline required of her. He had no proof that she was always so frivolous. He recalled the sweetness of her beautiful mouth; the faint scent of damask rose that had drifted from her; her submission, followed by anger, which he must assume had been simulated because she had responded to his kiss in a way that had excited him.

He frowned. Such a woman could never compare with Lady Sybilla, who, even after their betrothal had been announced, had permitted only a chaste touch of his mouth on her cheek, and that only in the presence of her mama. After her tragically early death he had been brokenhearted and had plunged into the excesses that had made his name a byword for reckless behavior. His mistresses had been taken from many levels of society, and his gaming had threatened at one point to rival Mr. Fox's. He had been pulled up here after an acrimonious interview with his man of business, who asked him if he intended to insult his ancestors and beggar his tenants by his profligacy. The viscount played thereafter for stakes that drew respect from his opponents, yet never threatened his fortune. But he continued to consort with women who took his fancy in a desperate effort to satisfy a deep need within him, while oldsters shook their heads and declared that he must have too much of his mother in him, and dowagers groaned over the waste of so eligible a husband.

"Did you not care for this paragon?"

"You know full well that I abhor women of extreme levity. Miss Waring appears to have no sensible thoughts in her head. She is one moment behaving frivolously and at the next allowing a quite waspish tongue to set one down."

Mr. Exford's face creased in a smile, which he hastily wiped from his face when Kinver looked up from his plate. "I can't believe she gave you a set-down. You are always in command of any situation."

"Of course she did not." Lord Kinver applied himself to his breakfast and, when he had finished, leaned back and picked up *The Morning Post*, leaving Mr. Exford *The Morning Chronicle*.

The two gentlemen read for a while, only the sound of rustling paper disturbing the companionable silence, until Kinver was startled by the sound of a great shout of mirth from his friend.

"I wish you would not do that, James. It is far too early."

"It is almost twelve o'clock, and in any case, I could not help myself. Here is an account of a lampoon that has been printed as a ballad sheet and is being shouted abroad. The author is anonymous, and I hope for his sake will remain so. It concerns the affairs of our dear Prinny, who will have one of his spasms when he reads it. A devoted acolyte will be sure to point it out to him."

"There will be a copy in any coffeehouse or club. I must read it." The viscount's mind roamed over the names of men who dabbled in writing. "It would be amusing to discover the reckless author. Possibly an elderly Tory who cares nothing for the junior members of the House of Hanover."

The day being fine, they elected to walk about their business: Mr. Exford to St. James's Coffee House and later to oversee improvements being made to his newly purchased residence in Manchester Square, and Lord Kinver to his favorite literary club. Here he found his acquaintances perusing several copies of the latest ballad sheet to astonish the London residents.

He was accosted the moment he appeared. "Come and see, Kinver. Or have you already read the ode to His Royal Highness?"

He shook his head, read, and grinned appreciatively. "Not brilliant, but amusing, definitely amusing—and witty."

An elderly buck suggested that Lord Kinver himself was the author, and Kinver shuddered in mock horror. "Far be it from me to antagonize the Prince."

Speculation continued for a while until frivolity was abandoned for a discussion of Lord Kinver's "Essay on Traveling in Greece," published in *The Gentleman's Magazine*.

Mr. Exford stepped out of his house at five o'clock and viewed his friend's equipage with less than enthusiasm.

"A Highflyer!"

"Not afraid, are you?" taunted Kinver.

Mr. Exford surveyed the dauntingly delicate lines of the phaeton, whose seats hung high above the ground, and a restive gray horse that Kinver held in check. "Yes," he said simply.

"Rubbish. Come, up you get. From so high a position you will have plenty of opportunity to survey the ladies."

"True," agreed Mr. Exford, swinging himself resignedly into place. He sat there and endeavored to appear as unconcerned as his friend, as the carriage swayed and jerked before Kinver's strong, experienced hands brought the horse under control.

He maneuvered through the streets with consummate skill and turned into Hyde Park, where he allowed the thoroughbred to have its head for a while. When he was satisfied that the horse would not cause havoc among the driving and promenading *haut ton*, he joined the fashionable company enjoying the early-evening sun.

The arrival of two personable and exceedingly eligible bachelors was a signal for every lady, and not a few ambitious fathers, to take stock of the appearance of any marriageable female among their party. Young widows out of mourning smoothed their gowns and adjusted their hats; mothers hissed instructions to daughters; chaperones gave muted orders; quite a number of women who were studiously ignored by the majority, being members of the demimonde, tried openly to entice them to their sides; and one or two who had been already in keeping by Lord Kinver, waved shamelessly.

Mr. Exford, his status so magnificently improved since his last Season, was hard-put to appear unconcerned. In the event, he gave up trying as he found himself recognized and smiled upon by people who had once treated him with distant courtesy.

"What a time of it I intend to have," he said to Kinver, bowing to a dowager with a bevy of youthful beauties around her.

Kinver looked bored, as befitted a man who had been wealthy all his life, until his eye fell upon a party that sauntered along a grassy walk beneath an avenue of trees. Lady Augusta, gowned in blue brocade and wearing a hat with five tall feathers, was shepherding Miss Venables and

Miss Waring among the crowd. They were followed by a groom who carried three parasols and an extra shawl.

"Good God," exclaimed Mr. Exford, "is that the goddess you described?"

Kinver's eyes met Emma's. For a long moment he was unaccountably disinclined to look away. "Miss Waring," he confirmed, before his gaze passed beyond her to Miss Venables.

7

Emma's first day in London was a bewildering mixture of pleasure, astonishment, and anxiety.

Never had she envisaged, even in her most imaginative stories, the number and variety of domestics considered essential by Lady Augusta and Lucy to maintain a comfortable establishment. She could scarcely conceive the possibility of her slipping quietly away to visit Mr. Palmer's bookshop.

And even if she did, she could not see how on earth she would ensure enough privacy to continue the further installments she owed him. She had yielded to his pleas and was actually writing two serials, and had not found it easy in the privacy of her small bedchamber at home. But here . . . ! And not only would she lack privacy—the servants got everywhere—she wondered how she would ever find the time.

After being awakened at ten with tea and a slice of paper-thin bread and butter, which left her wanting more, the ladies went out to shop. Confronted by the glories of Oxford Street, she let her worries fade into the background for a while. They passed the pyramids of fruit, the stands of china and glassware, and the bowls of sweetmeats, and swept into a shop selling fans. Emma purchased a simple white lace one with slender ivory sticks as being suitable to use with any color gown. Lady Augusta added one embellished with painted country scenes and another in Portuguese gilded filigree. When Emma murmured that Mama had bade her not to be extravagant, she was subjected to a disbelieving stare from Lucy and ignored by Lady Augusta. From then on, she simply followed and obeyed. It was, she admitted, not diffi-

Eileen Jackson

cult to be compliant as they rode in Lucy's town carriage from milliners', where creations of straw, lace, feathers, and silk were ordered for daytime wear and delicious confections for evening headdresses, to gown shops, where bolts of cloth were inspected and approved and styles decided. Lady Augusta held up pieces against Emma, and she and the dressmakers conferred and exclaimed until Emma felt that they believed her to be as insensate as one of the small dressed dolls sent in previous times to enable distant buyers to choose their garments.

They entered yet another linen shop. Its windows were adorned with cloth cunningly allowed to flow in graceful folds that any passing stroller might admire. Lady Augusta insisted Emma purchase a piece of celestial-blue gauze to be fashioned into an overdress above white tiffany. Six pairs of white kid gloves were pronounced to be indispensable, and Emma lost count of the yards of ribbon and numbers of feathers purchased.

She became the owner of a burgundy velvet cloak edged with satin. She climbed into the carriage behind Lucy and Lady Augusta, believing that at last they were returning to Hanover Square, only to discover that they were on their way to be fitted with shoes and reticules to match the various outfits. She dragged up enough courage to remind Lady Augusta that she had limited means and simply could not plunge Papa into debt.

Lady Augusta said dismissively, "I am not quite a babe on the town, miss, and know what I am about."

Not a word about payment had been mentioned, and Emma had no means of assessing her expenses. Lucy had simply looked around in her languid way and waved a hand at anything she desired, flipping through the pages of fashion plates to point out her choice of garment as if she had been purchasing papers of pins. She had tried on hats and ordered at least a dozen, and now followed this by adding shoes of every color and texture. Emma contented herself by choosing three pairs of white silk pumps—essential, she was informed by Lady Augusta, for dancing—two pairs of white kid pumps, and half-boots for walking in the park. Lady Augusta accepted that Nurse's hand-knit cotton stockings would do for daytime wear, but was adamant in her assertion that Emma should purchase four pairs of white silk for evening from the draper's shop where the expedition ended. Here Emma heard a price mentioned for the only time and tried not to show her disbelieving horror when the sum of ten shillings the pair was apparently considered reasonable for a lady of quality.

Arriving back at Hanover Square, ravenously hungry, to partake of a cold collation, she was touched to be handed a parcel by Lady Augusta and informed that the beautiful Norwich silk shawl it contained was a gift.

"We must change now for our walk," announced Lucy. "It is almost five o'clock."

Emma looked up inquiringly.

"All the world and his wife promenade in Hyde Park at this hour," said Lady Augusta, "though the town is almost empty at present." This was a surprise to Emma, who had felt half-stunned by the noise of people and traffic. "But I like to bring Lucy up a few days early so that the business of buying new gowns may be dispensed with before the Season proper begins. I have found that at this time the dressmakers are anxious for work and one receives one's clothes quite quickly."

Emma's eyes flickered quickly over her ladyship's attire. Lady Augusta had bought little for herself.

"You are wondering why I choose to dress in styles of my earlier years, are you not, Emma?"

Emma blushed. "I—I would not presume. I mean—"

"There is no need for embarrassment, miss. If all mature ladies followed my example, society would not be full of elderly women dressed like chits. These newer fashions with the high waist make many of them look as if they are permanently with child."

"Grandmama!" protested Lucy, whose resigned tones proclaimed that she had heard the sentiment before.

"You will see," continued Lady Augusta, addressing herself to Emma as if Lucy had not spoken, "women as old, indeed, older than myself, tricked out in garb more suited to their granddaughters. I have heard, though I can scarce believe it, that some of them even tried to leave off their stays, as is the custom now with you young women, but my dresser told me—servants always know all the gossip—that when they looked at themselves in their mirrors, most of them were

forced to admit that such sights would probably terrify even
the horses into fits. No! Such antics are not for me. I wear
my stays and petticoats, and thank God for my good sense.''

Emma walked into her bedchamber to find a maid laying
out garments across the half-tester bed. The girl looked young,
about seventeen, Emma guessed, and rather nervous.

Emma smiled encouragingly and the maid curtsied. "I'm
Betty, miss. I'm to be your personal attendant.''

"I scarce expected . . . I am used to caring for myself.''

Betty's face crumpled and for an awful instant Emma
thought she was going to cry.

She asked hastily, "Did Lady Augusta send you? If so,
then, of course . . .''

Betty was shocked. "Lady Augusta, miss? Oh, no, I doubt
if her ladyship's ever heard of me. Mrs. Overton ordered me
to come to you. She's Miss Venables' housekeeper. I think
her ladyship gave orders to Mr. Bardsea.''

Emma blinked. In her plan to marry a man of substance
she had not taken into account the necessity of running a
large staff of domestics. The belowstairs life in such an
establishment was evidently far more complicated than she
had imagined.

Betty spoke again, "Ma was a lady's maid and she taught
me and my sisters so that we could rise in the world. You're
my first lady, miss. If you give a good report of me there's
no telling where I could end. Maybe even a lady's dresser. I
can read, too,'' she said with simple pride. "Ma made sure
we could all read and count our numbers.''

Emma was fascinated. "Do you like to read, Betty?''

"Oh, yes, miss, love stories, mostly, especially ones that
make my flesh creep. That's what happens to the heroines in
the stories I like. Their flesh is always creeping. And they are
in danger from wicked uncles and guardians, and then a
wonderful, handsome hero comes along and in the nick of time
saves them and they marry and live happily ever after. Them's
the kind of stories I like, miss.''

Emma gazed at the maid, who could have read one of her
serials. "I'm so glad you enjoy reading. I would like to talk
about it, but there is no time.''

"Indeed not, miss. It won't do to keep her ladyship waiting. I heard tell she's terrible if she gets cross.''

Emma allowed Betty to assist her out of her gown and washed herself in the basin of hot water in the basin stand. She liked her ingenuous maid, but realized with a sense of despair that she would make it even harder for her to conduct her secret literary life.

Betty held up a gown. Emma was puzzled. "That is not mine."

"Yes, 'tis, miss. Lady Augusta bought it today. Miss Wheeler is sure the gown will fit you perfectly, and suit you too. It was made up for a young lady who died." Betty clapped a hand to her mouth. "Ooh. I wasn't supposed to tell you that!"

"I'll not tell," Emma assured Betty, whose homely face split in a wide grin of relief, "but I wonder if her ladyship realizes . . . I mean, I cannot—"

She stopped. The impropriety of seeming to be critical to a servant of anything done by Lady Augusta struck her forcibly. Betty would never understand that a young lady about to embark on her first Season, sponsored by a wealthy aristocrat, could be short of money. She looked at the gown properly. It was of pale-green muslin with long lace sleeves and adorned by darker-green velvet bows and a froth of lace about the low-cut neckline. She had never owned anything half so beautiful.

Betty coughed, "The time, miss . . ."

Emma stood obediently as Betty eased her into the gown and dealt with tapes and buttons. The greens were perfectly matched to the hand embroidery on her white Norwich silk shawl, and when she had put on one of her new hats, a confection of straw, lace, and little pink and green silk roses, she felt sure she had never looked finer. She descended the stairs.

"Oh, there you are," said her ladyship. "We must go at once. One accepts that to arrive a little late is conformable, but not so late that it is noticeable. Folk will make gossip out of nothing, you know, Emma. You look very modish, child."

Emma stammered her thanks for the gown.

"Phoo! 'Tis nothing. Your Papa can well afford to dress you properly."

Emma felt horrified. Was Lady Augusta running up debts she would present to Mr. Waring? She could not ask here.

The hall porter was standing by his chair, Bardsea waited to watch the ladies go, a footman was about to open the door, and Miss Wheeler hovered, tugging Lady Augusta's garments into the order she thought desirable.

"Enough, woman!" said her ladyship. "Have done."

Miss Wheeler was unmoved by her mistress's peremptory manner. She too wore clothes of an earlier age and had probably been with Lady Augusta forever. She looked older than her ladyship, though that might be because her thin face was devoid of artificial aid. Lady Augusta's skin, however, was whitened and rouged, her eyebrows drawn fine, her mouth reddened, and she wore a brown wig beneath her large hat. Also, Miss Wheeler's sunken cheeks told of many missing teeth while Lady Augusta—in public, at any rate—sported several white porcelain teeth. They were somewhat incongruous wired to her own yellowing ones, though she appeared to be indifferent to the fact.

Lucy's embroidered muslin promenade gown was of the palest pink, and she had chosen to wear one of the new spencers. It was a rich crimson, and her jaunty red bonnet sported ostrich plumes. Everything looked perfect and expensive, as, indeed, did Lucy. Emma tried hard not to be glad that she was prettier than her cousin. Papa would be saddened could he see into his daughter's mind. But then, Papa would be *horrified* if ever he discovered that she had been secretly writing and selling lurid love tales for almost two years and had entered into a conspiracy with an unknown bookseller-printer. And what would be his reaction if he learned that she had written a lampoon that not only betrayed more knowledge of the Prince of Wales' amatory affairs than could be considered proper for a young unwed lady to admit, but that was now being bruited abroad in the streets, threatening to bring her down in society before she had even made her come-out?

The ladies traveled by coach to the park, where they alighted and began to walk. They had covered only a few yards, greeted by everyone of any consequence, when Lord Kinver's carriage appeared.

His lordship instantly reined in and raised his hat, as did Mr. Exford, his eyes exploring every line of Emma's face and form.

Emma was endeavoring to conceal her unexpected confusion as she realized, as soon as she saw Lord Kinver, that he had never been out of her mind since the time he had kissed her in the Downhams' garden. The knowledge mortified and angered her. It also frightened her. She knew that no properly brought-up lady ever entertained even the remotest consideration of a man until he had proved beyond all doubt that he was interested in her. Emma had always found conformity difficult and was forever being scolded by Mama and Nurse for her high-spirited disregard of the behavior expected of a young lady, but she could not be sedate and proper and always speak softly and sit quietly and hem handkerchiefs. She had never accepted that men were a superior breed, although this was a heresy she had never dared to voice. Her reticence was induced by her conviction that if she made any such radical remark, her mama would prevail finally upon Papa to forbid her to sit in on the lessons he gave to the young gentlemen he taught. Now she was being made to understand the reasons for her mother's apprehension as she gazed with more than friendly interest at a man who barely acknowledged her presence.

In her anxiety to prove that she cared nothing for Lord Kinver's indifference, she gave Mr. Exford a dazzling smile that made him dizzy.

He turned to his companion, grinned, and said softly, "My thanks for bringing me to the park, Kinver. She is truly a veritable pearl." Then he leapt down from the phaeton and stood before the ladies, hat in hand, bowing gracefully from the waist as he offered them his escort.

Lady Augusta accepted graciously enough, though the look she shot at Kinver expressed clearly her opinion of a man who came to the park without an attendant groom to take the reins while he did the proper thing and joined Lucy.

Emma glanced once at the viscount and decided he was annoyed at Mr. Exford's freedom. She was glad. She would be delighted to discover anything that irritated Lord Kinver. He was monstrously encroaching, and she would never forgive him for the kiss. It was a burden to know that her senses insisted on recalling the way he had stirred her. She favored Mr. Exford with another smile.

Lady Augusta put aside her pique at Kinver and beamed upon Mr. Exford and her protégée. Last Season she would have depressed his pretensions with a frown, but that was last Season, when he had been attractive, but poor. Now he would make an excellent catch for almost any woman, and especially for a girl from a rectory who had no fortune.

Kinver leaned toward her and said, "Good day, your ladyship. I trust you and your fair companions will soon grace my residence. I am giving a ball."

Lady Augusta stared at him over her impressive nose. "A ball!" she repeated. "And who will act as hostess, since you have not yet seen fit to do your duty and marry? Will your grandmama venture out?"

"Lady Kinver will please herself," said the viscount smiling. "My Cousin Anne is already established in my home."

"There has not been a grand entertainment there since . . . heaven knows when." Her ladyship ended abruptly, recalling that the last person to entertain on any scale had been Kinver's mother. "Who will be there?"

"Why, everyone," his lordship replied blandly, "just as soon as news gets around. Town is filling fast. My invitations go out tonight."

Lady Augusta was caustic. "You scarce return to England before you expect all society to tumble over itself to flatter you."

"Flatter me? I am impervious to flattery, ma'am, but I do not pin all my hopes of a success on my own attractions. His Royal Highness the Prince of Wales has returned from his latest experiment in sea-bathing, and Carlton House is being reopened. One would not wish to be backward in showing him every courtesy. As for entertaining, I intend to fulfill my obligations at last. In more ways than one." Kinver's eyes flickered for an instant over Lucy.

This was not lost on her ladyship, who nevertheless answered composedly, "I shall consult my engagement book, and if it is at all possible, we shall accept."

The viscount bowed and his voice held spurious humility as he thanked her, since both knew that only death would prevent her from chaperoning Lucy and Emma to Grosvenor Square on the night of the ball.

Kinver bowed. "With that I must rest content, ma'am."

Lady Augusta took immediate exception to his manner and dug him in the ribs with her long, beribboned cane. "And you, sir, will be pleased, I trust, to attend a small party I shall hold in Hanover Square where guests will meet dear Miss Waring.''

Kinver's eyes strayed to where Emma and Mr. Exford were conducting what was obviously a highly flirtatious conversation, and the humor died momentarily from his face. ''Naturally I shall be there. I look forward with great pleasure to renewing my acquaintance with you, Miss Venables.''

Lucy smiled and Lady Augusta gave her a surreptitious poke from behind. ''Thank you, sir,'' said Lucy with a modicum of animation. ''I shall look forward with pleasure to conversing with you. I shall question you on your recent travels and shall show particular interest in forms of flora and fauna that are strange to me.''

Lord Kinver looked impressed by this evidence of Miss Venables' inquiring mind. His eyes flickered once more to Miss Waring and Mr. Exford before he gave his horse the command to move on.

Lady Augusta and Lucy joined Emma and Mr. Exford. ''Lady Anne Harvey is playing hostess for Lord Kinver,'' she informed them. ''There, young ladies, is an example of what may happen to a female who disobliges her family. She was ill-favored in the matter of looks, yet she received an offer from an exceedingly rich and highborn man and had the temerity to defy her family and refuse him. She imagined herself in love with a penniless curate, but of course her parents were not so foolish as to countenance such a mésalliance. They shut her in her room on bread and water for an age until it was discovered that her curate, far from languishing after her, had married a woman with five thousand pounds.'' Lady Augusta's diatribe was directed straight at Lucy, who received it calmly. ''Have you nothing to say, miss?''

''The rich man was thirty years older than Lady Anne . . .''

''And what has that to say to anything? A disparity in age should be acceptable to an unappealing woman.''

''He was also bowlegged, ugly, and—''

''Are looks everything?''

''No, ma'am, certainly not, but he was steeped in all manner of excesses and generally reckoned to be unpleasant in the extreme.''

''Who told you that faradiddle?''

"Wheeler," replied Lucy. "She recalls it all clearly."

Lady Augusta breathed hard, her flush of fury warring with her white maquillage. "I vow I will dismiss that woman. She is altogether too free with her opinions. And in any event, no excuse could be found for Lady Anne to fall in love with so unsuitable a man."

"Perhaps she was not so in love as she believed, or she would have made bold to find a way to escape and reach her curate."

Lady Augusta looked ready to burst with indignation, and Mr. Exford intervened. "I daresay Miss Venables is right, your ladyship, though one accepts that she should have been guided by her parents. Perhaps, after all, she did not wish to wed anyone."

"Not wed anyone! My dear sir, can you be serious?" Lady Augusta continued to expatiate on the impossibility of a woman enjoying life without a husband. "Look at me. Did I *love* Mr. Brancaster? Of course I did not. I would, quite correctly, have deemed it vulgar to allow myself such an emotion before marriage. A young girl knows nothing of love, but I esteemed him and affection grew between us."

"But, Grandmama, I understood that you cared deeply for Grandpapa from the day you met, that your appetite suffered and you positively languished because your parents would countenance only a titled nobleman as husband for an earl's daughter, until they understood that Grandpapa was the younger son of a baron and his fortune was twenty thousand pounds a year. That was very fortunate for you, was it not, Grandmama?"

Lady Augusta stared at Lucy with malignant fury. "I must suppose that Wheeler told you that also."

"Yes, Grandmama."

"That woman is pushing beyond endurance. This time I will dismiss her."

"She will not go," said Lucy. "I well recall the time you purchased a puce-colored satin gown and she refused to robe you in it because she said the color was not right for you. You dismissed her then, but she ignored you."

Lady Augusta breathed hard.

Mr. Exford bent his head to Emma. "Do you think fire will emerge from her nostrils?"

Emma suppressed a giggle with difficulty. She forced her voice to remain steady. "Dear Aunt Augusta, pray do not overset yourself. Our housekeeper came to Papa with Mama, whom she had known since she was in leading strings. I vow Mama is sometimes exceedingly vexed with her, but hardly dares raise her voice, and our gardener was with Papa's uncle. Servants who have been an age with one's family can be such a trial, can they not?"

While the party talked, they had moved slowly along a grassy walk into a shrubbery.

"Is that your considered opinion?"

Emma started. Lord Kinver's voice was the last she expected to hear, having seen him drive off at a spanking pace that indicated his frustration.

Lady Augusta scowled. "Must you spring upon us from nowhere?"

"I did not mean to, ma'am. I heard your voices and joined you, since that was my intention when I gave my horse in charge of Lord Pembridge's groom."

"That ninnyhammer!"

"I assure you, ma'am, he is experienced with horses."

"You know full well I referred to Pembridge."

"But he has not taken charge of my horse." The viscount's brow was puckered, though his eyes held a devilish gleam.

Her ladyship breathed hard as she ignored this. "Is Pembridge still in the park? Will he not need his groom?"

"His lordship was about to return home to change for another evening of rioting on the town. He had a pair of very young bloods with him. They look ripe for any mischief."

Emma was seething with vexation. She had loved the family housekeeper since she was a baby and the gardener was a friend. She had spoken only to cool Lady Augusta's wrath against Lucy. She wished very much that Lord Kinver had not overheard. She wondered why it should matter what he thought. He was a rake, impossibly haughty, and she disliked him.

8

Emma watched Lord Kinver join Lucy, and they walked a little in front, Kinver speaking animatedly and Lucy bending her head in its elegant bonnet to listen, once or twice interpolating an answer.

"They make a handsome couple," pronounced Lady Augusta with great satisfaction. "There's a man who won't allow himself to be ousted by anything or anybody. You thought you had scored over him, Mr. Exford, did you not?"

Mr. Exford laughed. "I hoped I had, ma'am, but it makes no odds, since he is Miss Venables' admirer and I am Miss Waring's."

Emma enjoyed Mr. Exford's company. Like his friend Lord Kinver, he was conservatively dressed in light, well-fitting pantaloons and hessian half-boots, a waistcoat, a dark cloth coat with long tails, and a gray felt hat with high crown and narrow brim. The only difference lay in their choice of embellishments. Lord Kinver's gold watch chain crossed the white of his waistcoat and his boot tassels were of black silk; Mr. Exford sported a pale-blue waistcoat, his watch chain was elaborate, and his silver boot tassels were larger.

There were personal differences. Lord Kinver's muscled legs were clearly emphasized by his pantaloons; he was tall and his carriage held the grace of a born athlete. Mr. Exford's pantaloons were a little strained about his person, and he was shorter. He appeared to be about the same age as Kinver. It was impossible not to enjoy his company, even had he not been showing in every way permitted to a gentleman on first meeting a lady that he believed her to be utterly fascinating. His conversation was both amusing and sensible, his manners perfect, and as Lady Augusta was showing her varicolored teeth in a smile of approval each time Emma glanced at her, she must suppose him to be a man of substance. In fact, reflected Emma, he was precisely the proper kind of husband her parents would wish for her, and she felt instinctively that he was not a man who would demand that a woman should bring him money.

Their small party had joined the folk thronging the wide walks and Mr. Exford glanced up at the sound of hooves and harness. "Here come Pembridge and his friends."

Merriment was implicit in his tone and Emma looked up, expecting to share it. Instead she was struck with horror. Driving toward them in a brightly painted barouche drawn by two chestnut horses were three young men. They were garbed in the height of extreme fashion, though she saw only one of them clearly. He wore lemon-yellow pantaloons, an apple-green waistcoat from which dangled several chains and fobs, and a bottle-green coat that fitted him like a second skin. His boots were of black, highly polished leather and sported gold tassels that dwarfed Mr. Exford's. His hair, gleaming with pomade, was visible beneath a tall, pale-gray hat with a large gold buckle. He was making a great to-do, talking and laughing loudly with his equally noisy friends, and all three were bowing to every pretty young woman they saw. He was her brother Gerard, who should have been in Oxford pursuing his studies.

Her glance flew to Lord Kinver, who was regarding the trio with a measure of derisory amusement, and she had never come nearer to resenting Gerard with real bitterness.

Lord Pembridge pulled his horses to a halt and raised his hat. " 'Servant, Lady Augusta, Miss Venables, Kinver, Exford. May I make you acquainted with my good friends, Mr. Anthony Downham and Mr. Gerard Waring." His eyes went straight to Emma, who endeavored to form a coherent remark.

Lord Pembridge took the problem from her. "Pray, Lady Augusta, won't you introduce us to your fair companion?"

Gerard, who had been regarding Emma with an astonishment that matched her dismay, intervened. "Lord, Emma, are you here, then? I had thought you unable to come to town because of the young 'uns' measles."

Emma stammered, "L-lady Augusta was good enough . . .

and Miss Venables . . . I am staying in Hanover Square. But, Gerard, did you not receive Papa's letter telling you my news?''

"No! I ain't been in Oxford for two weeks. Anthony and I were, er, requested to leave for a while, and only because of a prank.''

Lady Augusta said, ''Am I to understand that you are Emma's twin brother? You must be. You resemble her, though I perceive that your hair is quite red, while hers, thank the Lord, is mostly gold.''

Gerard bent his full attention on her ladyship, who continued, ''I am Lady Augusta Brancaster. If you are indeed Emma's brother—and neither of you has denied it—it seems we are related.'' She looked as if the realization gave her no particular pleasure.

Gerard was unembarrassed by her haughty demeanor. He leapt lightly from the carriage, revealing that his form was sturdy and lithe and that he was about the same height as Mr. Exford. He bowed to her ladyship. ''You are my Aunt Augusta. I have heard my parents speak of you.''

''Indeed!''

''Indeed, yes. Papa has told us of your great triumphs in the *haut ton* and of how you were sought after by many men of great quality and wealth, but that you chose to ally yourself to a plain mister whom you esteemed and admired. Delighted to know you, ma'am. Good of you to take my sister in tow.''

This was a view of her marital decision that had never been so ingenuously propounded to her before, and Lady Augusta almost preened herself. She held out her gloved hand and Gerard held it lightly for a moment.

''Your manners are as pretty as your sister's. You will do well in London.''

''What was the prank for which you were rusticated?'' Lord Kinver asked.

''Lord, it was funny,'' said Gerard. ''We dressed a dancing bear in a gown and cap and I gave a dinner for it. We weren't to know that it would seize upon a quantity of wine and drink it and get quite out of hand and wreck my rooms. Of course the noise gave us away.''

"A prank indeed," said Kinver. "I trust you later sobered up the wretched animal."

Gerard looked taken aback. "It came to no harm, sir. We paid its master well and I've left a sum of money to repair the damage."

Emma felt even more dismayed. More bills for Papa, she supposed, and how was Gerard able to afford to racket around London yet again? And it did not increase her composure to know that she was in agreement with Lord Kinver's implied censure.

"We got up to pranks in our day, Kinver." Mr. Exford's voice was mild and he looked amused.

Kinver merely bowed.

Lady Augusta bestowed her attention on the third member of the trio.

Mr. Downham blushed and climbed hastily out of the carriage. He bowed. "Anthony Downham. Your servant, ma'am."

"Why, you are little more than a child. You should be at your studies. How old are you?"

"Eighteen—almost, ma'am."

"Seventeen years of age and on the town with older men. Do your parents know?"

"I have written to inform them. Papa will not mind it, though Mama may be anxious."

"I should think so, indeed! You should return instantly to Oxford."

"He cannot," pointed out Lord Kinver in caustic tones.

"Then he should go home."

Mr. Downham went redder. "Prefer to remain in London, ma'am. I have not been here before. Papa will send money. He expects me to see the world before I settle to become a country squire."

Lady Augusta said, to no one in particular, "If he is not to return home and he cannot go back to Oxford, he should be taken in hand by an older man." She looked at Kinver.

"No, I thank you, ma'am," he responded promptly. "I am no bear-leader."

Lord Pembridge laughed heartily. "A very apt phrase. You was ever a wit, Kinver."

"Be silent, Pembridge," ordered her ladyship. She turned

to Mr. Exford. "You, then. You will keep an eye on young Mr. Downham."

Mr. Exford made a deprecating sound, which her ladyship ignored. "Where are you staying, Mr. Downham?"

"Waring and I are with Lord Pembridge in his house in Brook Street. He was kind enough to—"

"Good! You must all three come to the party I am giving. I shall send invitations."

"You may be positive that we shall be there," Lord Pembridge assured her. He swept Emma a deep bow. "Looking forward to having the pleasure of meeting you again, Miss Waring. You really Waring's twin? Should never have guessed. She ain't much like you, Waring. You ain't near as handsome."

Lady Augusta raised her eyes momentarily heavenward. "You have not changed, Pembridge."

"No, ma'am. Did you think I would? Always been like this." He looked puzzled. "Did I do something to annoy you, ma'am?"

Her ladyship sighed. "No, not at all. You remind me of your late father. You behave in similar ways."

Lord Pembridge gave her words his full attention, decided that this was a rare compliment, and thanked her. Lady Augusta turned, indicating that the interview was ended. The three young gentlemen climbed back into the carriage to resume their drive, although Emma was thankful that they had been subdued enough by the encounter to behave with more decorum—at least until they were out of earshot.

The stroll through the park was continued. Lady Augusta was absorbed in staring at her many acquaintances and saw one of her chief rivals in what she described as a "positive quiz of a hat." To judge by the way the lady in question had looked at her ladyship's headgear, the opinion was reciprocated. Her ladyship's day was crowned by meeting an exceedingly stout dowager duchess in the very latest gown.

"Good God, she resembles one of those flying balloons," muttered Lady Augusta before giving her hand to the duchess and congratulating her on her excellent looks.

Lord Kinver appeared to regard everything that occurred with a mordant cynicism, making Emma long to utter a remark that would succeed in provoking him, but he remained annoyingly at Lucy's side and engaged her in conversation, which appeared most often to emanate from him. She wondered how he could be satisfied by the companionship of so listless a female, then censured herself for her pettiness. At this rate her character would be ruined before she had been in town for a week. She was thankful when the promenade was concluded and they returned to Hanover Square for a quiet dinner and an early night.

"Rest while you may, Emma," ordered her ladyship, "for once the Season is properly under way you will need all your energy."

Emma could not rest. She was certainly fatigued enough, but when she was finally able to rid herself of Betty, who insisted on performing all that was proper for a budding lady's maid, she took out her paper, pens, and ink bottle and settled herself to finishing the last episodes of the two serial stories. And tomorrow she must contrive a way to take them to Mr. Palmer. She had scribbled a hasty note to him as soon as she had discovered Lady Augusta's plans, but he must have the episodes in time to print. And if she did not let him know definitely that she was in London, he might send a letter to the rectory.

She wrote far into the night, finished the required work, and tumbled into bed to fall into a deep slumber from which she was aroused with difficulty by Betty, who brought tea and bread and butter at nine o'clock.

"A lovely morning, miss. Lady Augusta says please to be ready to shop by ten o'clock."

Emma groaned and put a hand to her head.

"Have you got the headache, miss?" inquired Betty solicitously. "I daresay you're not used to such a busy life."

She fussed about the room, talking as she took out a morning gown and matching accessories. "When you go to balls and masquerades and the theater and the like, you won't rise till noon. Ladies always lie abed till noon in the Season. When Ma told me this when I was very young I couldn't imagine such a thing, me always having to get up at five o'clock to milk the cow and set the dough to rise and other things, but I understand now I've lived in a gentlewoman's residence. Ladies and gentlemen keep very different hours from country folk, though you was in the country, wasn't you, miss? Did you rise early in the country?"

"Yes," said Emma, her acerbic voice indicating her lack of desire for such a volume of information. The little maid's face fell and Emma was remorseful. "I do not mean to be short with you, Betty, but I am not the thing this morning. Not at all. Be so good as to ask Miss Wheeler to request Lady Augusta to excuse me from shopping."

Betty's eyes widened. "She won't like it."

Emma wanted to scream with frustration. "Please do as I say."

Lady Augusta made the smallest of taps on Emma's door before she sailed in, gowned in sprigged brocade and wearing an immense hat with ruffles and ribbons. "What is this, Emma? You *must* go shopping. We have not yet purchased stuff for your presentation gown. It is essential that it be ready in time for the Queen's Drawing Rooms."

Emma clutched the sheet to her. "Please, ma'am . . ."

Lady Augusta walked closer and peered at her. "Hm, you do look out of spirits. Not *sickly*, are you? I did not bargain for a languishing female. You know why you are here. It is important that you find a well-to-do husband so that Sophia may have her proper chance next year. Imagine your remaining unwed and seeing a younger sister cut you out with the gentlemen. You will be mortified, Emma, I assure you, and Sophia will not care for it. It does no good to a younger sister to have an older one hanging about."

"I apologize, ma'am. I swear I am not usually ill. I think perhaps all the excitement—"

"Well, you may remain in your bed this morning. Tonight we dine in a member of Parliament's house and you will meet influential and wealthy men there. Kinver will be present, of course, and Mr. Exford. Would you like it if I ordered hartshorn jelly for you?"

"Good God, no, ma'am. I mean," Emma's voice resumed its die-away tone, "I shall be perfectly well by tonight, I assure you. I simply need to sleep awhile."

As soon as the carriage had borne Lady Augusta and Lucy away, Emma got out of bed and threw off her nightgown. She washed hastily in water that had grown cold, and began to dress. The door opened and Betty walked in.

"What ever are you doing, miss? Lady Augusta said you was not to be disturbed."

"Then why are you here?" snapped Emma, her overwrought nerves betraying her.

"I was sent by Mrs. Overton to see if you needed anything. Now, miss, don't you let Lady Augusta push you into thinking you have to go shopping."

"She has not. I—I have to meet someone, that is to say . . ."

Betty's eyes widened. "An assignation, miss? Have you got an assignation? With a secret lover? Oh, miss, may I be hanged and drawn before I betray you. May I be tied to a stake and—"

Emma held up her hand for silence. If she denied her secret lover, she would need another valid excuse for going out. She wondered which would be considered worse by her hostesses: a lover, or a clandestine meeting with the man who had published her lurid gothic stories. She wondered which Betty would prefer. She wondered if any young lady without fortune had ever landed herself in such a morass.

She sighed. "Thank you, Betty. Now if you will just tie these tapes for me and fetch my brown pelisse and hat, I shall endeavor to leave . . ." She recalled the hall porter and groaned, "Though how it may be contrived—"

"Don't worry your head, miss. I can take you down the back stairs and out through a small door. All the other servants have sat themselves down for a cup of chocolate. They do that when the ladies go out. The senior indoor ones, that is, not the ones working in the laundry or the scullery or like places." Betty shuddered. She looked doubtfully at Emma's garments. "Shouldn't you wear something a bit different, miss? In the stories I read all the heroines go to meet their lovers in flowing velvet or satin dominos and masks over their faces."

Emma gritted her teeth. She had previously had no idea that gothic tales exerted such an influence over their readers. Perhaps she should turn to writing sermons instead.

"Such clothes would bring me to the notice of folk on the streets, Betty. It is bad enough that I am going unaccompanied—"

"Unaccompanied?" Betty's voice was shrill. "That you are not! I shall go with you."

By this time Emma was unsurprised to see that Betty clasped her hands before her bosom in an extravagant gesture denoting her willingness to share in her newfound heroine's activities, however hazardous. Emma, casting her mind back into stories she had written and read, decided that if she left Betty behind, her next move would be to totter into the servants' room and throw a fit of hysterics because her young mistress had gone untended into the evil streets of London. She decided against futile arguments.

Betty succeeded in smuggling them out undetected and the two girls hurried from the square into Holles Street. Betty's drab servant's cloak drew no attention and Emma had heeded her advice to drape a small shawl over her hat to partially hide her face. Betty called up a hackney cab, the driver of which looked askance at them.

"Show us yer money!"

Without answering, Emma pulled out one of the guineas given her by her mother.

The driver, a short red-faced man who had not shaved for days, whistled. "A gold finch! The gentry folk must be paying high wages these days. You be honest serving maids, I s'pose."

He gave an exaggerated wink and Betty recommended him to stow his gob-box. He grinned, displaying several discolored teeth. "Well, so long as you pay me! Where to?"

"Pasternoster Row, by St. Paul's Churchyard," replied Emma, who was thankful to escape from the stares of people whose attention had been drawn by Betty's forthright advice. The maid took the seat opposite her mistress, the hackney driver bellowed to his horse, and they moved off.

9

The hackney coach had once been owned by someone rich. Long ago, if the dilapidated state of the interior was anything to go by. There was straw on the floor and Emma preferred not to speculate on exactly what was causing its unpleasant odor. It rattled over cobbles, maneuvered its way between traffic, paused to allow a herd of cows to pass while exchanges of a clearly defamatory nature were bandied between cowgirl and driver, and narrowly missed a handcart pushed by a fat farm woman. In ordinary circumstances Emma would have been hugely diverted by all the sights and sounds, but she was too anxious to absorb anything other than the fact that the journey seemed farther and was taking longer than she had expected.

When the coach finally stopped, the driver demanded three shillings and Betty was deeply affronted.

"Three bob! You've never earned that much! You needn't think we're greenhorns, no, nor corkbrains neither. You could've driven a quicker way."

The driver stared down belligerently from his height on the box. "Oh, yes? P'raps you'd liked it better if I'd gone by way of the country and took you through a few turnpikes. Then you could've paid them too."

"Betty, be silent," ordered Emma, aware that once more the maid was attracting attention.

She handed the guinea to the man, who bit it, leered knowingly at her, and handed her the change.

"Please wait," said Emma. "We shall not be long."

Paternoster Row was evidently the place for bookshops, and feeling too nervous to give more than a glance to the splendid dome of St. Paul's Cathedral looming over them, she and Betty began to examine the names displayed. They reached a door leading into a small shop and through a grimy window saw a trade card advertising the information that Mr. Palmer printed and sold all manner of literature. Emma and Betty entered. A youth was stacking piles of magazines ready for distribution and a man was inserting columns of figures into a ledger. Two elderly scholars in frayed clothes were reading manuscripts. All looked at them curiously and a reader got down from his high stool.

"What can I do to help you, ma'am?"

Emma was relieved that he sounded respectful and cultured.

"Mr. Palmer?"

"Who, me? No, ma'am. He is in the printing house. I'll conduct you there."

Betty was told to wait, which she did with good grace, liking the looks of the youth, and Emma was led through another door into a noisy workshop. She breathed deeply in undeniable pleasure of the scent of ink and paper that permeated the air in the print room. Men in aprons and round caps were engaged in their various tasks—inking, placing the pages ready to print, drying and assembling them—and for one heady, carefree moment she felt glad to be a part of it all.

The reader spoke to a thickset man who stepped forward and looked at Emma. "This young lady wants to see you, sir."

"Name?"

"I did not give it," interposed Emma.

"No name given. But you want to see me."

He nodded a curt dismissal to his employee and subjected Emma to a searching look she did not altogether like.

"I—I wrote to advise you of my arrival," stammered Emma. "I am Miss Waring. Miss Emma Waring," she said as he looked puzzled. "You have been publishing my stories these eighteen months. You *are* Mr. Palmer!"

"Are you truly Miss Waring?" An expansive smile spread over his rubicund, fleshy face. He held out a hand, which was large and ink-stained, and Emma took it and returned his smile, trying to conceal her nervousness.

"I am astounded, ma'am. I had not thought you so young. Your stories . . ." He glanced around at the men, who were gazing interestedly and attempting to listen to the conversation through the noise. "Get on with your work! This is none of your business!"

Emma was startled by his abrupt change of manner and tone. He turned back to her and invited her in a smooth voice to step through to the back room. "We'll be able to talk in peace there, Miss Waring."

The back room proved to be Mr. Palmer's private parlor. He held a chair for her and she sat down, her legs feeling suddenly weak. Now that she was face to face with her publisher, she felt extremely agitated. She had pictured an elderly, kindly man with whom she could conduct business in a genteel manner. She had sent her work out and received praise in return, and had never connected it with a man who was so obviously from a much rougher station than she was used to. She pictured him actually reading her words and felt her face grow hot with embarrassment as she recalled some of the rapturous phrases from her pen.

"Now, don't you be bashful, miss. I'm forever reading tales that ladies write for me. My romance magazines are nearly all filled by ladies, you know, who have a proper understanding of what some other ladies want. In their secret hearts, of course. It don't follow that a young lady like yourself would really do anything like what her heroines get up to, nor yet even wish to. Not a young lady like yourself."

Emma did not like Mr. Palmer. She answered him as composedly as she was able. "No, indeed not! Mr. Palmer, I have little time to spare and must come straight to the point. I have brought you the final instalments of both serials."

"First rate! I can always depend on you. You wouldn't credit it if I told you some of the excuses I've had from persons not delivering work in time. My readers expect their stories at the right time, you know, Miss Waring, and I don't mind telling you, because I'm a straight-talking man, that your sort of stories are what they particularly like. I've already got an advertisement ready for the next issue telling them that two more serials will be coming from your pen shortly. You write fast, Miss Waring, and that's another advantage."

"Mr. Palmer, pray do not insert the advertisement. I cannot write—at present, I mean. I had no idea that the Season would be so strenuous and I shall find it near impossible to find time to myself. I know you will understand.''

Emma almost shrank back in her chair at the expression in the bookseller's eyes. "I'm afraid I don't understand at all, madam, not at all. My readers expect your stories. They'll write complaining letters to me if they don't appear. They may even cancel their subscriptions.''

"But it will be only for a little while! When I return home—"

"Oh, ho! Return home, is it? I thought young ladies of quality came to town to catch themselves a husband, and supposing he don't want you to write? What, then? No, Miss Waring, I have to insist that you go on working for me.''

Emma was appalled by his vulgarity. "Mr. Palmer, I can only repeat that it will not prove possible—"

"Miss Waring, I can only repeat that you must make it possible!''

Emma was silent for a moment. She would gain nothing by arguing. She would take her money, and if he chose to mislead his subscribers, it would be his own misfortune. She would never write for him again. She said evenly, "You have money for me in your bank. I wish to have it.''

"Ladies don't go to banks.''

"No, sir, but men do. My expenses are growing and my papa is not a wealthy man.''

If she had thought to touch a soft spot in his heart, she failed. "No, I know that. Ministers of the church are often quite poor. I take it you are the rector's daughter, miss, though your letters were sent care of the rectory only. I can see now I've met you that you are a proper young lady.''

"Yes, Papa is the rector.''

"And I take it he don't know of your writing and perhaps wouldn't approve?''

When Emma said nothing, Mr. Palmer continued, "If he approved, I reckoned you'd have had your letters addressed to him and there wouldn't have been the need to hide your money from him. Papa will think you a very naughty young lady if he finds out what's been happening behind his back.''

Emma felt her anger at this detestable man rise within her, but she maintained her even tones. "Papa would far rather hear of my writing than expect me to submit to your threats.''

Mr. Palmer spread his large, ink-stained hands. "Threats! Now, is that nice? I haven't a notion what you mean."

"I think you have, sir. You imply that if I do not continue to write for you, then you will inform my papa of what has been happening. I call that a threat, Mr. Palmer. In fact, I call it extortion. I think the penalties for that crime are quite dreadful."

Mr. Palmer's face went a deeper hue of red. "You're a cheeky puss, and no mistake. Well, if you hadn't got a good spirit, you couldn't write the way you do, and if you weren't full of bottom, you would never have dared send me your stuff."

Emma kept her tongue between her teeth. The more she protested, the more familiar this man became.

Mr. Palmer thought for a moment, then said, "Look here, Miss Waring, it don't do for us to quarrel this way. Tell you what I'll do. I'll change my advertisement and say that you'll be writing only one serial story for me. How's that?"

Emma considered. Perhaps she could manage one serial. Then this obnoxious man would give her her money and she could finish with him.

"Very well, if you will do that, I will begin a new story at once. And my money?"

She was vexed with herself. She should have let him think she cared nothing for the money, but the truth was that she wanted it badly. She had meant to give it to Lady Augusta—she imagined one could get a bank draft—and say it came from Papa. The details of such a transaction were vague to her, but she was sure it could have been arranged by a sympathetic person. Mr. Palmer could definitely not be cast in that role.

"Ah, yes, the money. We'll see about it later. Just you concentrate on your writing and leave the finances to me."

Emma was forced to comply with him. She was sincere when she said she would prefer to confess to Papa than succumb to Mr. Palmer, but second thoughts had reminded her that her brother's latest escapade would grieve and worry him and that Gerard's current mode of life would present yet another financial burden. She felt trapped, but it would not be forever. A time must come when she could refuse to work ever again for Mr. Palmer, and if she lost her money, well, she would endeavor to bear it with fortitude.

"You'll get your earnings, my dear young lady. I'm a very busy man, but as soon as I've time, I'll go to the bank. Would you like cash?"

Emma nodded.

"That's the style." Mr. Palmer made to rise, but Emma remained seated.

"I have something else to say. I sent you a lampoon—"

He laughed raucously. "Oh, yes, you did, and very amusing we found it to be sure."

"We?"

"Me and a clerical gentleman who makes a living buying and selling such things."

"A *clerical* gentleman?"

"Indeed, yes. You mustn't judge all such by your papa, who I'm sure is a real Christian, Miss Waring. When you've been about in the world a bit, you'll know that some clerical gentlemen differ from others. I showed your verses to him and he bought them immediately. They've been printed and—"

"I know," Emma interrupted, "and I have to say I find it intolerable. Surely you must have realized I did not intend them to receive publicity. They were for you to read and—and enjoy." She stopped as the remnants of her dream of a kindly old gentleman expired.

"Oh, but you should have said."

"I did not think it necessary."

Mr. Palmer remained cheerful. "It's too late now. The lampoon's public property. You'll get a portion of the profit."

"I don't want it! I want those verses withdrawn!"

"I've told you, it's too late. They're in all the coffeehouses and taverns."

The door from the printing shop opened and a man walked into the room. He was thin with a sallow countenance, and his pale-blue eyes roamed over Emma in a way she found distasteful. His clothing was dark.

Mr. Palmer smiled expansively upon the newcomer. "Ah! Miss Waring, here is the reverend gentleman himself. Mr. Clarence Rowley—Miss Waring, the talented young lady who writes her stories under the name of Delicia."

Mr. Rowley bowed from the waist. "So appropriate a name, dear ma'am."

Emma, who had believed her chosen nom de plume a pretty one, thought it sounded both ridiculous and overfamiliar on the tongue of Mr. Palmer.

"Delighted to meet such a clever and successful author. And your verses! Remarkable! They are selling well in the streets, and I assure you, ma'am, little else is being discussed in London since they were published."

"Miss Waring don't care to hear that, Mr. Rowley. She didn't mean them to be made public."

"But, ma'am, the verses are too amusing to remain hidden. Oh, no, that could not be. It would have been a sin not to publish."

"And no doubt you are making a profit!" Emma was unable to resist the taunt.

Mr. Rowley was unmoved except to further expressions of delight. Emma rose. The meeting had proved a nightmare and she wished only to leave.

"Going?" said Mr. Palmer. "You'll let me have the first installment of the new serial within a week."

It was a command not a request.

"It is not easy to—to get away from the house." Emma felt humiliated beyond words at the necessity of entering into further deceitful negotiations with Mr. Palmer. "Could I send the work to you by post?"

"Not necessary, Miss Waring. Mr. Rowley here will be pleased to meet you—just state your time and place."

The prospect of clandestine meetings with the unsavory cleric revolted Emma, but she appeared to have no choice.

"I know little of London."

"Where do you reside, ma'am?" asked Mr. Rowley.

"In Hanover Square." If she did not tell them, they could easily find out simply by following her. "I will meet Mr. Rowley in—in Holles Street, one week from today. It must be early."

"Yes, I understand," said Mr. Rowley in a confidential manner. "Ladies of quality do not generally rise before noon, or even later, so you can slip out first thing in the morning without letting on to your relatives."

"I will try to meet you at eight o'clock," promised Emma.
"If I am delayed . . ."

"I'll wait," promised Mr. Rowley, his face and tone
intimating that to wait for her would give him pleasure.

He opened the door to allow Emma to pass through, and
both men followed her. Betty had clearly been having an
enjoyable flirt with the youth and they wiped large grins from
their faces.

"Come, Betty, we must make haste." Emma hurried into
the street, but to her dismay Mr. Rowley seemed bent on
accompanying her and willfully ignored her expostulations.
He held out an arm for her, and as by this time they had an
interested audience—Emma was amazed at how swiftly one
could be surrounded by a crowd of rambunctious seekers-
after-sensation in London—she placed her gloved fingertips
upon it and walked away from Mr. Palmer's shop. They were
followed by an ecstatic Betty, who believed that this interest-
ingly pale young man was her mistress's secret lover.

At any other time Emma would have been fascinated by
the many booksellers' and printers' shops in Paternoster Row,
but all she could think of now was to escape as fast as
possible from Mr. Rowley. He passed pleasantries, and she
answered shortly.

Their hackney had not waited, and Emma spoke to Betty.
"Please procure us a vehicle at once."

"Pray, dear ma'am, allow me."

There was apparently no other way to shake off her unde-
sired escort except to comply, so Emma nodded. She could
not afford to antagonize anyone connected with the matter of
her secret writing. She had turned her head to him, only for
an instant, but it took her attention from the uneven flag-
stones and she tripped and would have fallen if Mr. Rowley
had not caught her in his arms. She leaned on him unavoid-
ably, her nerves jangling, and at that precise second Viscount
Kinver walked out of an interesting-looking bookshop. Their
eyes met and Emma blushed crimson.

She prayed that Kinver would just go away, pretend he had
not seen her, forget her existence, anything but regard her
with raised eyebrows and a sardonic look.

In her agitation she failed to disengage herself from Mr.
Rowley's arms as rapidly as could be thought feasible, and

he, misunderstanding her sentiments, grinned and hugged her closer. "So, my dear Miss Waring, you enjoy a little dalliance."

The street noises were insufficient to cover Mr. Rowley's insolent words and the viscount heard them with dreadful clarity. Emma wished she were the swooning sort; she wished the paving stones would open up and hide her forever, but all she could do was pull herself free, a flush on her face that could be interpreted as anything, including excitement.

Lord Kinver raised his beaver hat and executed a small bow. "Good morning, Miss Waring. You are abroad early. I trust you left Lady Augusta and Miss Venables well."

"What? Oh, y-yes, thank you, sir."

Kinver was looking at Mr. Rowley, obviously awaiting an introduction. Emma performed it and both gentlemen made their bows, Mr. Rowley's obsequiously low, Kinver's absolutely correct. His eyes went from Mr. Rowley, who was clearly what Emma's parents would term a half-gentleman, to Emma, and her spirit shrank from their flicker of disgust.

"Mr. Rowley is trying to obtain a hackney coach for us," she said.

"But of course, Miss Waring. And you were taking a farewell from him. So trying for you both to need to meet so early."

His words were ambiguous, his tone collected. Emma turned away, signaling Betty to walk with her. Mr. Rowley offered no explanation. The truth as to why Miss Emma Waring was discovered perambulating with an ill-bred fellow at a time when she should be with her guardian, could only land her in further complications.

The viscount joined her. "There is no need for you to remain," he said to Mr. Rowley. "My carriage is close by and I will escort Miss Waring home."

Mr. Rowley was not entirely impervious to rebuff, however impeccably given, and his sallow countenance took on a dull red. "I assure you, sir, Miss Waring is *my* concern. I am perfectly capable of attending her."

Kinver's answer was to place a firm grip on Emma's elbow and propel her forward quickly, leaving Mr. Rowley glowering after them. Betty followed, her face a study in amazement. It seemed that her mistress had more than one string to her bow. Life as a lady's maid held as much excitement as her reading had led her to expect.

"You should not put yourself to any inconvenience, my lord. Betty is quite capable of—"

"My carriage will be more comfortable and a great deal less odorous than a hackney," interrupted his lordship.

Emma was silent. To continue to argue with him could give the events of the morning even greater significance. She wanted to explain herself to the viscount, but nothing acceptable occurred to her. It was none of his business, she decided defiantly, her anger hot at his peremptory conduct.

An elegant town barouche was being driven toward them by a liveried coachman who stopped when he saw his master and touched his whip to his cockaded hat. A groom leapt from the back, opened the door, and let down steps. Kinver handed in Emma and Betty, whose delight was growing by degrees. Wait until she told her mother that she had been handed into a carriage by a viscount! Her sister, in service in the country, had never enjoyed such a privilege.

The groom folded up the steps, closed the door, and resumed his stand behind the carriage, which moved off as well as the heavy traffic would allow.

In an effort to keep the conversation away from herself, Emma said the first thing she thought of. "Were you buying books, my lord?"

He replied urbanely, "Not today, Miss Waring. I was handing in my latest essay to my publisher."

"You write?"

Kinver found something curious in her tone and turned a surprised look on her. Emma had never before met another author and would have been enchanted to spend hours talking to him.

"I do, though I would not for worlds bore a lady like you with such trivialities."

"Oh, but—" Emma stopped, biting her lips, then managed a rather strained coquettish smile. "Lord, no, sir, for I am sure you write on such subjects and in such a manner that only gentlemen would care for."

"But you enjoy novels."

"Yes, indeed. I told you so, did I not?"

"Indeed you did, ma'am, and I have kept my vow never to disclose so shocking a lapse."

Emma turned to the window, recalling that the subject she had introduced had first been discussed by them in the garden where he had kissed her. She glanced back at him and he gave her a bland smile, and she could not be certain in the half-light of the carriage if there really were demonic glints in his eyes.

"You find novels about romance shocking, my lord?"

"Not at all. Some are tedious, but the bookshops and circulating libraries would soon run out of business were it not for romantic novels and magazines. A veritable flood has descended upon us and ladies immerse themselves in it. I rather fancy that it is mostly women who read these things."

"Why so, sir? Surely men enjoy a little relief from worldly cares sometimes."

"Of course. I do myself."

His answer could mean anything, and while Emma was searching for a response that would not stamp her a blue-stocking, yet prove that she was not completely witless, the viscount spoke again.

"Since I have told you my business in Paternoster Row, Miss Waring, perhaps you would tell me yours."

As his tone plainly indicated that he already believed her business was to meet a questionable young man, Emma floundered for an instant before her lively mind asserted itself.

"I have heard Papa speak of the London bookshops and wanted to see some of them. It was a fascinating experience. So many books . . . so much printing activity." She forgot to sound flirtatious as it became increasingly difficult to conceal her enthusiasm, and Lord Kinver shot her a brief, uncertain look. For a moment Emma felt a curious sense of recognition as their eyes met.

Then he spoke and threw her into confusion. "And literary gentlemen can be so interesting, can they not?"

Emma breathed hard before she plunged in to defend herself. "I collect you refer to Mr. Rowley. I met him only today."

The viscount's gaze grew more interested, his brows rose. "Only today? Good God! I had thought I was beyond astonishment, but you prove me wrong."

10

Emma's memory of how she had permitted herself to be kissed on her first meeting with himself, of how she had lost control in his arms and had involuntarily encouraged his kiss, mingled with her sensitive awareness of his having surprised her in what must have looked like an embrace—and far worse, one performed in the public street. Naturally he took her for an accomplished flirt who was undiscriminating in her choice of men. She looked unseeingly at the passing panorama of London and felt very close to tears, which she held back, pulling around her the remains of her dignity, forcing out commonplace remarks to which Kinver replied with impeccable politeness. Then they were turning into Hanover Square and Emma said quickly, "Oh, pray, my lord, stop the carriage here. If Lady Augusta should see me out with you . . . That is to say, I, er, failed to tell her—"

"There is no need to continue, Miss Waring. I fully understand."

You do not, Emma cried inside herself as she saw the curl of his lip. She fled with only a murmur of farewell, followed by Betty, who succeeded in smuggling her back into the house. Emma scurried to her bedroom, dismissed her maid as soon as possible, and finally succumbed to the dammed-up tears of fury and frustration. She did not weep for long. It would not do to greet her hostesses with the marks of misery visible. Emma's life until now had been happy and she had seldom wept, but if ever she did, she was left with swollen eyes and a red nose, quite unlike the heroines of her stories, over whose lovely rose-tinted cheeks the tears tragically flowed, making them appear even more beautiful and vulnerable.

She glanced at her fob watch and saw with disbelief that she had been absent for only two hours. It seemed like weeks. Betty had already helped her to undress and slip back into her nightgown, and she climbed into bed thoroughly exhausted and fell asleep.

Lord Kinver directed his coachman to take the road to Hampstead and leaned back at his leisure as his horses were driven with careful consideration up the steep hills that lay to the northwest of London. He usually enjoyed this ride, but although the heath lay pleasant in the sun, which illumined the yellow-green spring foliage, turned the stone walls of imposing dwellings to gold, and even softened the customary disorder where new houses were being built, he was too deeply immersed in thought to notice. He was passed by several London-bound vehicles whose occupants he knew and whose greetings he returned absentmindedly, inducing his acquaintances to enliven their journeys by speculating on what was producing his lordship's even more than usually laconic air.

The carriage turned into a driveway lined thickly by shrubs, and pulled up before a house whose existence was obscured from outside view by evergreen trees.

He was welcomed by a rotund butler who took his hat and coat and said in lugubrious tones, "Her ladyship is expecting you, my lord."

"Is she indeed? I sent no word."

"Her ladyship is always expecting you, my lord."

"That's gammon, Yardley, and you know it."

The butler permitted himself a small smile that aptly conveyed his recognition of the truth, yet maintained his loyalty to his mistress. "As your lordship pleases."

He announced the guest and the dowager Lady Kinver looked up from her embroidery frame. Kinver crossed the room and bent to kiss her. When his mother had left him and his father had fallen so seriously ill, his grandmother had taken on a large part of his rearing, giving him love without sentiment, discipline without harshness, and instruction without humbug. She remained a strong foundation to his life and loved him more than any being on earth.

One would never have guessed as much when she glared

frowningly at him. "It is an age since you came. What have you been doing? You know I rely on you for all my news."

The viscount seated himself on a tapestry bench he pulled near, looking with approval at the dowager. She was dressed in a pale-blue morning gown whose flowing Grecian lines had been adapted by her sewing woman to suit her years, though her slender figure showed to advantage in anything. She wore a white lace cap decorated with lace daisies beneath which her silver hair curled naturally. She was assessed by society to be the same age as Lady Augusta, although, as she, like her contemporary, altered it to suit herself, no one was definitely sure what it was.

"You astonish me! We both know that you have several newspapers and journals delivered here every day at vast expense."

"Are you making mock of me?"

"Grandmama, as if I would!"

"Hm!" She jabbed her needle into her embroidery. "Papers do not tell one the kind of things one really wishes to know. Who is making up to whose wife? Who is with child? What is the latest crop of beauties like?" She looked up at him and her hazel eyes, so like his own, gleamed hopefully.

"Town is quiet at present because, as you well know, the Season is only just beginning. Soon I shall have much more news for you, though I hope by then you will have left here and opened up your house in Upper Brook Street."

"I would willingly sacrifice the fresh air of Hampstead for the odiferous streets of London had I any expectation of meeting a woman you believe good enough to wed."

"That is practically impossible, my dear, as there is only one of you."

Lady Kinver's eyes betrayed her amusement before she said, reflectively, "*Practically* impossible? Does that mean you have seen someone you like?"

"I believe it might be so."

Her ladyship laid down her tambour frame on her sewing table, folded her hands in her lap, and waited.

"Lady Augusta is in town," said Kinver.

The dowager's mouth opened and closed.

"She has brought with her two young ladies, Miss Lucy

Venables, whom you know, and a Miss Emma Waring, daughter of a country rector."

"Waring? That was the name of Lady Augusta's sister's husband. Is the girl related?"

"Lady Lavinia was her grandmama."

Lady Kinver's eyes gleamed. "A good family—excellent blood on both sides. Not much money, but that need never weigh with you. An affectionate bride and a well-bred mother of your children is what you need most. Is she pretty? Is she conformable? Do you care for her?"

"Is Miss Emma Waring pretty? Yes, exceedingly so—very beautiful, in fact."

Lady Kinver's eyes shone even more hopefully. There was a note in her grandson's voice she had never heard before, but she managed, with a great effort, to keep her tongue between her teeth.

"Conformable?" he mused. He recalled the circumstances under which he had met Miss Waring this morning. "I fear she is headstrong and—"

"And what? *Tell* me! Don't just sit there with that faraway look on your face."

"I was not aware that I—"

"Oh, do not trouble to climb your high ropes with me, Kinver. Is Emma Waring suitable or is she not?"

"It makes no difference in either event, Grandmama, since it was not she of whom I wished to speak."

"You exasperating man! If you were younger, I would box your ears. Of whom *do* you speak, then?"

"Of Miss Lucy Venables, ma'am."

This time her ladyship could not conceal her astonishment. "Lucy Venables? But you have known her forever. You met her when she was growing up. And she has had two Seasons already and has not taken."

"You forget I was away during those years."

"I most definitely do not forget. Two very lonely years they were for me, in spite of your many letters."

The dowager's voice had trembled for an instant and Kinver's irritation at her reception of his disclosure died.

"I assure you, ma'am, that Miss Venables is exactly the kind of young lady I would wish to see installed as mistress of my homes and mother of my hopeful brood. She is quiet, genteel, thoughtful, and converses with proper attention. She enjoys country living and will never grumble at spending a good part of each year out of town."

"What a catalog of virtues!" Lady Kinver had much trouble keeping her voice even. "And do you esteem her? Do you like her? Damme, Kinver, do you love her?"

"Love is not generally believed to be essential for marriage, ma'am, and certainly not by me. You should know that. It was love that my mother insisted she felt for her many amours. It was love that induced her to run off with a man who was not even her equal in rank. I thank you, madam, but that is an emotion I shall never consider when I view my prospective bride."

"I daresay you give it to your lightskirts and cyprians and that ladybird you have in keeping."

"What I give them could never be exalted by the name of love. Love was what I gave to my dear Sybilla. I cannot hope to find another such as she, but Miss Venables comes close. And I thought you heard the *on-dits* only from me, ma'am. I do not recollect ever having been indiscreet with you on the subject of, er, petticoat pensioners."

"Do not make sport of me, sir."

Lord Kinver saw that the dowager was more than a little upset, and he laid one of his strong hands over her frail ones. "Pray, Grandmama, believe me when I tell you that I shall never enjoy what the world calls love. I have seen it cause too many awful disasters. No! Respect and esteem are far the wiser. Why, you are not even fashionable to talk of love."

He had hoped to tease her into making one of her apt comments, but he failed. She pulled her hands away and placed them about his face, gazing into his eyes. "You must be sure, Kinver. If I were speaking to anyone other than you, I would follow society's way of making mock of love, but it sweetens marriage wonderfully."

The viscount smiled and kissed her, but made no reply, and she leaned back in her chair. "Lucy Venables! You are proposing to wed Lucy Venables. Have you declared your intentions? Have you sounded out the girl? I say nothing of Lady Augusta. She will leap at you. She begins to believe that her granddaughter will die an old maid, but if you make her an offer, there can be no fear of that. What girl could resist you?''

''Why, not one, I am sure, Grandmama.''

He was laughing at her and she glared at him, wanting to pick a quarrel. ''What a somber outfit, sir! White buckskins, a cravat with a pin so small one can scarce see that it is gold, and a white waistcoat and a dark-blue coat, and all cut so plain! And only a watch chain across your breast! How I sigh for the days when your Grandpapa was alive. *He* dressed in silks and brocades and rainbow colors, wore wigs and a sword, and looked handsome beyond belief. I suppose next you'll be carrying an umbrella.''

''Only if it rains, ma'am.''

She laughed unwillingly and ordered him to ring for refreshment, and they enjoyed some conversation before he took his leave. ''Can I hope that after hearing my news you will be spending the Season in Upper Brook Street?''

''I may—or I may not. I will inform you.'' He bent to kiss her and she said suddenly, ''When you spoke of Miss Emma Waring I thought you sounded as if she attracted you. Was I wrong, Kinver? Do not, I implore you, wed Lucy if you are enamored of another woman.''

''Enamored of Miss Waring? Good God, what an idea! She is the silliest butterfly imaginable. She has no serious thought in her head. I want a woman to talk to as well as make love to. And besides—''

''Yes,'' she prompted gently.

''I am not sure she is altogether discreet.''

''Discreet, is it? What have you discovered?''

''Nothing of import, ma'am. Not to me, in any event, since I view her merely as an acquaintance and a distant relative.''

''It may be nothing of import to you, but I should be sorry to see Lady Augusta embarrassed by unacceptable behavior.''

''You surprise me, ma'am. I should have sworn that nothing would have delighted you more.''

''Then you would be wrong,'' she snapped. ''Lady Augusta is one of my dearest—''

''Enemies?'' he supplied.

''What a wretch you are! What has Miss Waring done? It must be something disastrous if it shocks you.''

"Thank you, Grandmama. If you must know, I seized a kiss from her, and not only did she fail to resist, she actually enjoyed it."

"Is that all? Heavens, is no young woman ever to be kissed?"

The viscount frowned. "Lady Sybilla would not have permitted it."

Lady Kinver vouchsafed no reply to this unassailable truth, and he bowed, touched her hand with his lips, and walked out. She pondered on why his voice had assumed so significant a cadence when he spoke of Emma Waring and what it was that he had not told her. She also thought of Sybilla, whom she had secretly designated a "dead bore." No one could be glad of her early demise, but she had been heartily relieved that she had not needed to pretend to welcome her as a granddaughter-in-law. She picked up the latest issue of her favorite magazine and settled to enjoy the serial. The viscount returned to London even more thoughtful than before, wondering why he had bothered to keep the secret of Miss Waring's rendezvous with that jumped-up mushroom Rowley. He wondered why, when he had kissed so many women, he could not free himself from the memory of the soft sweetness of Miss Waring's mouth; of the slender beauty of her body, which he had molded for an instant to his; of the golden sheen of her hair and those expressive blue-gray eyes, which one could almost swear held intelligence—until, that is, she spoke, and wrecked the illusion. If only she had been a light-o'-love whom he could enjoy and leave when he tired of her. She would not have suffered. Viscount Kinver was known for his financial generosity to his discarded mistresses.

Lady Augusta and Lucy returned from their shopping trip and entered the house followed by two footmen and the groom laden with boxes and parcels. Emma greeted them in the morning room, where a cold collation waited.

Lady Augusta looked sharply at her. "Are you recovered?"

"Yes, thank you, ma'am. I am sure I shall soon become quite used to town."

"Good! You will be pleased to know that I have bespoken the muslin and chosen the style for your presentation gown. I knew you would wish me to do so, for the gowns are all similar in design—all requiring hoops, of course, as commanded by the Queen—the differences lying in how costly the lace and how many jeweled ornaments one uses. Since I know you do not wish to overspend, I decided upon a modest amount of lace and a few spangles; one cannot leave its ordering too late. You have a good figure, Emma, and will show to advantage.''

"Thank you, ma'am. I—I am relieved that you have not paid out too large a sum. Papa—''

"He gave me money for you.''

"Yes, I know. One hundred guineas, and by my reckoning there surely can be little left.''

"Tush, girl! What do you know about it? Your parents will not expect you to enter society looking like a dowd. And only consider, Lucy's gown will cost more than four hundred guineas.''

At the mention of such a sum for a single gown Emma lost her breath, which scarcely signified, as nothing she said would impress her aunt. She had noticed that wealthy people had no real appreciation of any necessity for economy.

"Did you happen to see my brother?'' she asked.

"We did, miss. We visited Atkinson's excellent shop in New Bond Street to buy perfume and wash balls. Your brother was strolling with his two friends and several other fine dandies, all engaged in ogling ladies. It is impossible to traverse that part of town these days without such insult. Make sure that you never enter Bond Street on foot, Emma, and never after midday.''

Emma flushed. "I am sure that Gerard would not intentionally be impolite, ma'am.''

"He is following the fashion of all other Bond Street loungers, Emma, and it is not your fault. He should have remained in Oxford.''

Emma could only agree with this as she reflected miserably on the realization that, while Gerard seemed intent on bankrupting his family, she was embroiled in a web with the unpleasant Mr. Palmer playing the part of spider. They were both deceiving and in high danger of disgracing Papa and Mama, and Emma could not decide which of them was worse.

"Do not look so lugubrious, Emma. Lucy has purchased a bottle of lavender water for you, have you not, Lucy?"

"Er, oh, yes, indeed. Grandmama was good enough to point out that you would like it, Emma." She produced a prettily wrapped bottle.

Emma thanked her cousin and assured her that she liked it very well, marveling that Lucy seemed unable to dissimulate on the slightest subject, even when such mild deception was socially desirable. Presumably Viscount Kinver preferred such unimaginative honesty. If so, he deserved all he would get, and she certainly did not propose to burden her mind with such a triviality. She had far more to concern her, and she went to her bedroom that night resolved to work on the promised serial as fast as possible and disengage herself from her unpleasant publisher forever. In consequence of which she sat up until the early hours and hoped, as she fell into bed, that she would not doze or yawn at the party planned by Lady Augusta for that evening.

She was inadequately refreshed when she rose in the morning, thankful that the only activities planned during the day were fittings for gowns, for which seamstresses came to the house, and a promenade during the fashionable hour in Hyde Park, where Lord Kinver was nowhere to be seen.

"He is most probably pursuing some such sport as gentlemen like," said Lucy without visible disappointment. "He enjoys fisticuffs and practices fencing. He also has female friends of a certain order whom he visits."

"Guard your tongue, madam," commanded Lady Augusta. "It is not seemly for a young woman to make such observations."

"But, Grandmama, Emma asked me to enlighten her in the ways of the world, and when she gets a husband, she had best know how gentlemen behave when not in company with their wives."

"A lady closes her eyes and ears to such matters."

"How can she close her eyes and ears to them if she does not know that they exist?"

Lady Augusta breathed hard through distended nostrils.

Emma said pacifically, "Lucy means to be helpful, ma'am, though I cannot help wishing I will find a man who does not seek other females after we are wed."

"There's no harm in wishing," conceded Lady Augusta.

"Did Grandpapa have cyprians?" asked Lucy.

Lady Augusta glared at her granddaughter. "That is a most improper question."

"Why must women always behave like ignorant simpering misses?" asked Emma.

"Because men like it that way. Have not your parents instructed you thus?"

"Yes, Aunt, but I—"

"Men enjoy a woman who shows wit, but not erudition. If a woman is clever, she should keep it a secret."

"Even after marriage?" Emma was beginning to feel desperate.

"*Especially* after marriage. You can influence your husband without his knowing of it. A large number of gentlemen follow their wives' dictates while imagining that they rule the roost."

Emma said disconsolately, "That seems dishonest."

Lady Augusta's penciled eyebrows rose sharply. "I have never heard that society matters were conducted honestly. How tedious that would be, to be sure! One would be deprived of so much amusement."

The park was thin of company of the kind her ladyship had hoped to find, for what use was a walk unless one could make adverse comments about the complexions and gowns, bonnets and morals of one's rivals? So they returned quite quickly to Hanover Square, and Emma was dispatched to her room to prepare for the evening.

11

The seamstresses had finished the first of Emma's new evening gowns and it lay on the bed. She touched it with sighs of delight, stroking the soft folds of silk gauze.

Maids entered carrying cans of cold and hot water for her bath, to which Betty added a generous dash of the new lavender water. The lesser domestics cast sidelong envious glances at their colleague, elevated gloriously to the status of lady's maid.

Later Emma regarded herself in the cheval glass with a satisfaction that Papa would have deprecated. Over the pale-green underdress, whose long sleeves buttoned at the wrist and whose décolletage would have had Nurse reaching for a yard of concealing muslin, was an open dress of leaf-green gauze. Betty had brushed her hair into shining perfection and pulled it back into a green velvet ribbon, allowing tendrils of curls to fall over her ears, with two studiedly wanton ones caressing her white forehead. Her only ornament was a pearl necklace. Her shoes were of white kid and her stockings silk.

Betty clasped her hands in delight. "Oh, Miss Emma, you look beautiful! There's no other lady will compare with you."

Emma descended the stairway to the first-floor drawing room, where she found Lady Augusta and Lucy waiting. Her ladyship was splendid in red brocade, high-heeled red shoes, and many rubies, while her hair had been piled over a sheep's-wool pad to give it height and volume. Her maquillage was uncompromisingly white and pink.

She made a striking contrast to Lucy in her gown of cream satin. A rose-pink gauze overdress fell from her shoulders to a short train, the hem of which was embroidered with tiny silk roses. Diamonds sparkled in her ears and around her throat, and there were two slender gold bracelets on her wrists. Her dark hair had been expertly dressed and was pinned up with a delicate filigree spray of gold with tiny diamonds. Her shoes were of rose and cream satin. She would never be a beauty, Emma thought, but she looked wonderfully attractive and attractively wealthy. Emma had to recall her mirror image to boost her courage for her first London dinner party.

The ladies had not long to wait.

"Lady Anne Harvey," announced Bardsea in precisely the correct tone for an unimportant member of a noble family, and Emma looked with immediate interest at the woman who had dared to defy her parents and been imprisoned by them for weeks. No one would know it, she decided regretfully. Lady Anne was a dab of a woman with no claim to fine looks. She hurried to Lady Augusta, by whom she was greeted with a peck on the cheek. Lucy shook hands with her and Emma had just been introduced when Bardsea made his second announcement.

"Lord Kinver and Mr. Exford."

Emma's heart gave a little leap. The viscount strolled across the drawing room to Lady Augusta, who held out her hand. He kissed it.

"Enchanted to be here, ma'am."

He greeted Emma with a bow and a handshake and went at once to Lucy and seated himself beside her on a pale-blue upholstered sofa that was a perfect backdrop for her appearance. Emma realized suddenly that Mr. Exford was addressing her.

"I am so happy to see you again," he said. "Please permit me to tell you that you are looking exceedingly beautiful."

Propriety demanded that Emma should behave a trifle coolly to a new male acquaintance who complimented her so blatantly, but at that moment the viscount, evidently sensing that he was being watched, looked across and caught her eyes. Instantly she gave a trilling laugh and answered Mr. Exford in tones clearly heard all through the room, "Why, sir, you make very pretty speeches. I thank you for your compliment. You are in excellent looks too, I vow."

As if possessed by a will of their own, her eyes darted over again to where Lord Kinver sat so close to Lucy. It was his turn to look quickly away, but not before she was aware of his odious derision. Damn the man! She renewed her flirtatious behavior with Mr. Exford.

Other guests arrived, including Gerard, Anthony, and Lord Pembridge in high spirits, all having won a bet that day.

"I've never seen anything like it," declared Gerard. "Imagine, if you can, three fleas drawing tiny chariots. We went into this booth near the Strand and saw a flea circus. Of course, we had to wager on a race and our flea came first by miles."

"No," said Lord Pembridge.

"I say it did."

"Not by miles. Stands to reason. Couldn't. Whole race was only six inches."

"A figure of speech," said Gerard kindly. "I meant only that we won handsomely."

This contented Lord Pembridge, who subsided. Anthony did not speak. His fresh young face and brown curly hair would have looked more in place at school.

"I trust that none of you have brought any of the contestants with you tonight." Lord Kinver's voice was cool, his dark face sardonic.

The three choice spirits looked at him inquiringly before Gerard broke into a loud laugh. "That's a good one, sir. Very amusing."

"Not brought anyone here but ourselves," explained Lord Pembridge. "Stands to reason you'd see 'em if we had."

"He means the fleas," explained Anthony, blushing.

"Why should one wish to bring fleas to a party? Not the thing to do. Plenty of the little creepers about a few years ago. Heard m'mother say so, but not the same now. Not so many. Not about the *haut ton*. Not the thing at all to—"

"Enough!" said Lady Augusta.

Lord Pembridge looked surprised. "Enough?"

"Her ladyship would prefer you not to continue to speak of fleas," explained Lord Kinford.

Lord Pembridge subsided once more.

Mr. Exford said quietly to Emma, "He's as rich as anyone in the kingdom, and practically witless. He went to Oxford University, but was asked to leave. His father was much the same. The son inherited his mother's good looks and his father's brain, such as it was. Now if he had inherited his mother's wits and his father's looks . . . well, we cannot choose what we will be." His voice resumed normal pitch. "Tell me, Miss Waring, do you resemble your mother or your father?"

As Emma hesitated, Gerard spoke for her. "She's got qualities from 'em both. I have to say she's devilish pretty, even if she is my twin sister. As for brains, she—"

Emma had not thought she could ever feel indebted to Lord Pembridge, who chose to interrupt. "You twins?"

"Yes," replied Gerard. "I told you so."

"Did you?" Lord Pembridge pondered. "I forgot. Often forget things. Thing is, you ain't much alike. She's in better looks than you, Gerard."

"Well, she's a girl, ain't she? Stands to reason—"

"Dinner is ready, your ladyship," announced Bardsea, ruthlessly cutting across the conversation, knowing that if his mistress were forced to choose between offending Alphonse, the temperamental French cook employed at vast expense, and her guests, the former would win.

Lady Augusta commanded a willing Lord Kinver to lead the way with Lucy, Emma placed her fingertips on Mr. Exford's proffered arm, and the others sorted themselves into couples, Anthony bringing up the rear with Lady Anne.

Emma was seated between Mr. Exford and Lord Kinver, and her emotions became a mixture of dismay and pleasure. She was finding it increasingly difficult to deny her attraction to the dissolute rake, who obviously believed her to be totally lacking in decorum. She blamed him. If he had not kissed her, she would not have given him a second glance, she assured herself before honesty compelled her to admit that Lord Kinver was the epitome of all the heroic men of whom she had dreamed and had not thought existed outside her imagination. He was a man with many facets who lived his life as he chose.

But he was male. He required a wife who behaved with dignity and certainly not one who crept out of her guardian's house to meet a man in secrecy. She realized that Lucy had begun a conversation with her other neighbor and that Lord Kinver was addressing her.

"Your brother is as lively as you, Miss Waring. I feel sure he will be a welcome guest in all the fashionable houses."

"Do you think so, sir? He would be flattered to hear you say it."

"Would he, in truth?" His lordship studied Gerard, who was flirting conspicuously with a young lady in white muslin and a feathered headdress. "Does the propensity to dally run in your family, Miss Waring?"

Emma was angry. "I am the only female member out at present, my lord. I have found that men are surprisingly easy to attract. One simply flutters the eyelashes, smiles a trifle provocatively, utters one or two verbal pleasantries, and any gentleman is captivated." She sighed. "It is so simple it becomes a bore."

"Do I bore you, Miss Waring?"

Emma turned the full gaze of her large, brilliant eyes on him. "Why, sir, surely you can have no doubt of your effect on ladies."

She had the gratification of seeing his eyes darken with vexation.

"And you, Miss Waring, must be aware of the effect you have on gentlemen. Exford has been talking of nobody else since he first saw you. He becomes tedious on the subject."

"Indeed!" Emma spoke coldly. "I regret that you find Mr. Exford so irksome."

"You must know that I enjoy Mr. Exford's company, but I have never before seen him so bewitched by a woman. It is on that subject he causes me to yawn."

"I *never* find him tedious."

"You would not, in the circumstances," agreed the viscount blandly, "and you make it only too evident, madam."

"Do I so?" She sought for some remark that would put down this infuriating man.

"It is your turn, Miss Waring," prompted the viscount.

Emma turned from her soup to slay him with as angry a look as she could conjure, only to find his eyes filled with such genuine, teasing mirth that she laughed aloud. It was the first time Lord Kinver had heard her natural, melodious laugh, and he stared at her.

"One would swear . . ." He stopped and Emma held her breath. "Are you exactly what you seem, ma'am?"

Emma turned back to her meal, her heart beating so fast she knew she could not swallow. She laid down her crested silver spoon. "It is a female tendency to perplex a man, sir," she replied in as flippant a tone as she could muster.

The viscount said nothing for a moment. "So it is all playacting with you, is it?"

He sounded sincerely disappointed and she made to speak, scarcely knowing what she wanted to say, except that it must be something that would dispel his first mistaken impression of her. All Mama's and Nurse's strictures were forgotten as she felt his magnetic power drawing out an honest response.

Then Lucy addressed him and instantly he turned away from Emma, leaving her feeling more desolate than she could have thought possible.

Mr. Exford had succeeded in breaking his conversation with his neighbor. He said softly, "Why, Miss Waring, you look downcast. Has something overset you?"

Emma gave her cultivated trilling laugh. "Certainly not, sir. I was thinking. Is this not a splendid party? Lady Augusta says it is in my honor, you know. I vow I was never so proud."

"How sweetly unsophisticated you are! So many of the young ladies who are brought out each Season enact an ennui they consider fashionable."

"Oh, Miss Waring could not be bored." She had Lord Kinver's attention again. "She finds very varied pursuits to fascinate her in London, is not that so, ma'am?"

Emma was sure he was referring obliquely to his chance meeting with Mr. Rowley and herself. There was nothing she could say in her defense, so she allowed the remark to stand, but her eyes showed a little of what she felt.

The viscount's brow furrowed. He wished he had not gone so far. Why did this infuriating, foolish girl have the power to make him feel regretful? It was not his lordship's way at all. So far he had lived in the manner prescribed by himself and he allowed no one, especially not a female, to interfere.

Emma turned her back to him and Lord Kinver resumed his talk to Lucy, the equable, sensible, eminently conformable girl he intended to marry. She had not engaged his deepest sentiments, but he had long accepted that the harrowing experience with his erring mother and the loss of his perfect betrothed had shattered irreversibly his ability to love.

Lady Augusta had said the meal would be simple, though Emma found it prodigious, consisting as it did of two courses with about fifty different main and side dishes, but inevitably it ended and the ladies followed their hostesses into the blue drawing room.

At the dining-room door Lady Augusta turned. "Gentlemen, I do not expect you to sit long over your drink and conversation. We ladies shall be waiting for you with anticipation." She deliberately allowed her glance to fall on Lord Kinver, who acknowledged it with a small bow and a smile.

As soon as the door closed, wineglasses were replenished and the men began to discuss sport and politics. Lord Kinver, an informed essayist on both subjects, remained unusually silent. His fellow guests railed humorously at him, speculating aloud on what ailed him. Kinver wondered also. He had discovered at last a woman he could take to wife, a suitable mistress of his estates, a serene mother of his children, yet every time she left him, her image faded, to be replaced by that of a slender girl with red-gold hair, stormy eyes, a quick temper, and a lack of decorum. He thought of the unpleasant young man he had surprised her with in Paternoster Row. They had actually been embracing and she had not minded, any more than she had minded his own embrace. Far from it. She had returned his kiss, and at the memory he felt the stirring of desire. He prided himself on being able to divide women into types. He had been forced into such learning from an early age. The viscount stared into his brandy glass, visualizing his future, and his friends wondered why he frowned.

Morosely he studied his fellow guests. Gerard Waring, his red satin quilted waiscoat contrasting with a sky-blue coat, his face alight with glee, was recounting a cockfight he and his companions had attended.

"I was badly dipped," he informed them, "but the sport was good, wasn't it, Pembridge?"

Lord Pembridge started, "Eh? Oh, splendid sport, Gerard. Splendid," he agreed.

Young Downham said nothing of his own volition. Anthony realized that he was being surveyed, and a blush suffused his face and neck. The viscount contemplated giving him some timely advice, but only for a moment. He would not be thanked for it and Downham would ignore it. Kinver had never listened to admonitions in his turbulent youth. Pembridge was three and twenty in years and God knew what in brains, but he could be left to his trustees.

The gentlemen waited a bare half-hour before joining the ladies. Even if her ladyship had not commanded it, Lord Kinver's lugubrious attitude was enough to damp them down, thought Mr. Exford. He wondered if his friend was in love with Lucy? He found her unappealing, and Lady Sybilla had been like a little brown mouse. His lordship's mother had a great deal to answer for, he decided sadly. Her son would always want a wife whose behavior was predictable. For himself, he enjoyed a girl with a little more liveliness. One such as Emma Waring, in fact, though, however spirited a wife might be, a man would require her to be absolutely above reproach in all things, before as well as after marriage.

A latecomer had joined the ladies and was bowing low over Lady Augusta's hand. "A very good evening to you, ma'am. 'Pon my soul, you look as enchanting as ever. How do you keep your youth?"

Lady Augusta had no love for Sir Lambert Lowther. His birth was unexceptionable. He was a fortune-hunter, but often a man needed to find a rich wife and there was no shame in that. Yet there was that about Sir Lambert which repelled her. Stories were whispered about town of women ill-used and abandoned, of questionable behavior in card games, though no one had actually proved him a cheat, and of darker vices practiced with men of low repute. But Lady Augusta had known and respected his parents for many years, and since his father's death she felt she owed his mother increased loyalty. Sir Lambert had approached her during her latest shopping expedition and asked if he might call upon her soon, and she had felt obliged to give her consent. The fact that he chose to do so while a private dinner party was in progress was not conduct to be commended.

Lord Kinver and Mr. Exford made the smallest possible acknowledgment of Sir Lambert's greeting. Kinver's eyes narrowed as Sir Lambert greeted Waring and his friends. If Lowther had any intention of attempting the ruin of Miss

Waring's brother or young Mr. Downham, then the viscount would not hesitate to interfere. After all, the Warings were distantly related, which gave him some measure of right. And if Lowther displayed the remotest sign that he intended harm to Miss Emma Waring, his lordship would seek an excuse to call him out. Any man would, he assured himself, rationalizing his fierce rage at the notion.

Kinver seated himself near Lady Augusta and watched Sir Lambert approach Emma. She smiled up at him and Kinver felt the tension of his muscles. Would she begin yet another flirtation? To judge by Mr. Rowley, she was not overparticular in her choice of admirers, but Miss Waring's nod was cool and she gave the baronet only the tips of her fingers. Then Sir Lambert moved to Lucy, favored her with a deep bow and a kiss that lingered a fraction too long upon her proffered hand, and sat himself at her side and proceeded to talk earnestly to her. Lord Kinver waited for Lucy to rebuff him, or move pointedly away. She did not. She continued to talk serenely to him and Kinver was angry. She was no newcomer to society and must be at least partially aware of Sir Lambert's evil reputation. He rose and walked swiftly across the room and stood in front of Lucy.

The baronet looked up, a smile that held the hint of a sneer upon his rouged lips. His clothes were dark and impeccably cut because any man who seldom troubled to pay his tailor could dress well, but Kinver suspected that his jeweled rings and fobs were of pinchbeck and imitation stones. Sir Lambert had run swiftly through the modest money left by his father, who had fortunately tied up some capital for his widow else she would have difficulty in surviving in reasonable comfort. Kinver would give no credence to the possibility of anyone, least of all a helpless woman, being cherished by Sir Lambert.

With a slight, assumed lisp, Lowther said, "Good God, Kinver, must you stand over us? You appear to menace us, does he not, Miss Venables?" He pulled a violet-scented lacy handkerchief from his sleeve and touched it to his lips.

"Do you feel menaced by me, Miss Venables?" asked the viscount.

Lucy smiled a small, tight smile. "Of course I do not, sir, but I should like it better if you were seated. Sir Lambert was telling me about a problem he has in his succession houses.

The peaches last year were attacked by some disease and I was telling him how my head gardener on my Devon estate dealt with just such a problem. It is so refreshing to meet with a man who reveres country living as I do."

Lord Kinver was aware that Lowther never went near his country home, unless it was to wrest more money from his unfortunate tenants or negotiate the sale of another piece of the land tended conscientiously by his ancestors. He accepted Lucy's invitation to be seated and relentlessly engaged Sir Lambert in a long discussion on the rotation of crops in which the baronet floundered helplessly, but to his lordship's annoyance, Lucy prompted Sir Lambert and explained matters to him whenever he needed help. Kinver began to seethe with fury, almost as much toward Lucy as toward Lowther. He persuaded himself that Lucy was naturally kind and altogether far too trusting. He had best make his intentions toward her known soon. From now on he would escort her everywhere until she and the polite world learned to consider him her accepted suitor.

12

Miss Waring had shown by her cold greeting of the baronet that she knew a hellhound when she met one, and Lord Kinver wondered yet again where the vulgar Mr. Rowley fitted into her life. His lordship judged himself a quick and accurate assessor of character, but Miss Waring had him puzzled. James Exford had no doubts about her. Kinver wondered if he should drop him a warning, but he felt a peculiar reluctance to do or say anything to harm Miss Waring's chances. She needed a wealthy husband and he had no actual proof that she was anything worse than a flirt who, like many another of her sort, would settle respectably to marriage.

"Miss Venables is addressing you, sir." Sir Lambert's tone was altogether too smooth and held more than a hint of derision.

"I beg your pardon, Miss Venables. I was for a moment deep in thought."

"With your gaze fixed, oh, so raptly, on Miss Waring," said Sir Lambert in sighing satisfaction. "One would vow that you found her fascinating, is not that so, Miss Venables? For my part I could not look at any other female in a room that contained your charming self."

"Could you not, sir?" inquired Lucy in an interested way. "Would you have me believe that you find me more engaging than ladies who are younger and prettier than I? Miss Waring particularly so."

Sir Lambert said, "My dear Miss Venables, I would ever prefer to remain at your side. You have such sense, such an air of tranquillity . . ."

Such wealth, fumed Lord Kinver inwardly.

". . . so gentle and delicate a mien. It draws a man like a moth to a flame."

It was well-known that Lowther needed money, though a more prudent man would have lived quite happily on his legacy until the day when he succeeded to the estates of his distant cousin Sir George Croft, whose failure to father an heir had put Sir Lambert in line.

"You are flattering, sir." Lucy's voice was as equable as ever and Kinver wished that she would reprimand this unctuous, painted rake. Miss Waring would have been swift to give him a set-down. So why did she permit the embraces of a mushroom like Rowley? To hell with the girl! She was ruining his peace and he did not even like her.

He forced his voice into normality. "I am sorry I did not hear your question, Miss Venables. Would you mind repeating it?"

"I asked if your grandmama would be coming to town during the Season?"

"I hope so, ma'am. When I visited her, she led me to believe that she might. It depends on—"

"On what, sir?"

"On how she feels," answered the viscount lamely, wondering if he were losing his wits.

He heard a laugh he recognized. Not that irritating trill that he was begining to suspect Miss Waring assumed for some purpose of her own, but the deep-throated, beautiful laugh with which she had surprised him during dinner. He turned to look at her seated in the midst of a group of young men and women that included Gerard, Anthony Downham, that idiot Lord Pembridge, and leaning attentively over the back of her chair, his head close to hers, Mr. Exford. Lord Kinver's heart skipped a beat. Her face was radiant with amusement. He forgot everything around him as his senses flared into passionate response to her beauty, and he had to fight a consuming wish to walk across the room, pull her to her feet and away from all other men, and kiss and caress her until she was breathless and begging for mercy. When her animation faded, she looked tired, he realized, and when she believed no one to be watching her, she stifled a yawn. Was she bored? More likely enervated by her excursions to meet besotted lovers, he told himself savagely.

Lucy, not having been spoken to recently, sat with hands folded in her lap and waited.

Lady Augusta, who had been glaring for some minutes at a man with whom she most certainly did not want Lucy to become embroiled, called, "Sir Lambert, I need your presence to strengthen my argument. I have been telling the young people that three years ago, in 1797, we heard Signora Galli sing at the Theatre Royal, Covent Garden, and that she entranced us although she was in her seventy-fifth year. They do not credit that we of an earlier generation can recall a plethora of genius. No, do not reply from over there. I require you to sit here, by me."

A look of extreme annoyance passed briefly across Sir Lambert's face, both at this abrupt summons and at the way he had been bracketed with Lady Augusta, who must be sixty if she was a day, while at thirty-one he was only three years older than Kinver.

Appreciating Lady Augusta's gambit, Kinver quickly smothered a grin. Lowther, glancing back, saw it and stopped halfway across the Kidderminster carpet covering the center of the polished floorboards and turned and said in his lisping voice, "Do forgive me, Kinver, but I forgot to ask after your mama. I vow I have not seen her since I was quite a boy. I wish that she could grace us with her talents once more."

Lord Kinver's face whitened and a look blazed from his eyes that made Lowther stir uncomfortably.

"I—I esteemed . . . liked your mama," Lowther stammered, recalling belatedly how swift the viscount had been to call him out after hearing of only a vague insult to his mother. He could have destroyed him even in his youth, and a muscle in Lowther's cheek twitched when he reflected how much more deadly Kinver was now with any weapon. His halting attempt at explanation had made the situation worse, though for once he had meant to lessen his offense. He knew, as did Kinver, that her ladyship's talents had been her great beauty, her wit, but above all else, the careless ease with which she had taken any man she craved to her bed. It had been strongly rumored that, just before she had absconded, Sir Lambert's father had been one of her lovers.

Not everyone in the large room had heard Sir Lambert's spite-filled words, and the younger guests would not comprehend, but several pairs of older, knowing eyes were fixed on the viscount, some scandalized at Sir Lambert's disgraceful behavior, a few maliciously pleased. Kinver had made enemies, as had his mother before him. There were whispers, followed by a hush as consciousness of the deadly atmosphere flowed insidiously around.

Lucy appeared oblivious. "Sir Lambert is addressing you, my lord," she informed Kinver. "How is your mama, he asks."

Lord Pembridge blundered in. "Miss Venables is right, Kinver. Man wants to know the state of your mother's health." He subsided with a gasp as a dowager sympathetic to Lord Kinver nipped him savagely between long fingernails.

The viscount swallowed. If the company had been composed solely of men, he would have knocked Lowther to the ground and fought him to the death in the inevitable duel. He had spared him once when he still retained the mercy of youth. His reaction in this gathering was necessarily inhibited. It made Lowther's attack upon his honor all the more despicable. The cowardly thrust had pierced a very weak spot in Kinver's armor and his customary clear reasoning was affected.

His features softened as he replied to Lucy in a strained, but audible voice, "My mama is well, I thank you. I do not think we shall see her in town, but I hope I may take you to visit her soon."

The few guests who were making valiant attempts to begin conversations were instantly silenced. Kinver's words were virtually a public declaration of his intention toward Miss Venables, for no man would suggest that a young lady visit a woman who, for moral reasons, lived a reclusive existence, unless he meant to make her part of his family and needed, if not her approbation, at least her willingness to become acquainted.

Lady Augusta emitted a long sigh of satisfaction, which was remarked by her fellow chaperones. At last her granddaughter would be wed . . . and to such a man. Lord Kinver was handsome in the muscular, austere way that her ladyship most enjoyed; he possessed enormous wealth and an ability to manage it; and he would, she did not doubt, make a wondrous lover, having had much practice, though naturally the latter fact was not one she would expound to Lucy. She beamed a smile at her granddaughter and could have shaken her when she received in return a look of blank incomprehension. No matter; the polite world would be abuzz with the news by tomorrow.

Emma had been looking at the viscount, mesmerized. She could not conceive why a simple question about his mother should have been asked by Sir Lambert in such an obnoxious tone, or why Lord Kinver should appear stricken. She caught the expression in his hazel eyes and it reminded her of a beloved pony of her childhood that had been injured and had to be shot. What had Mama said when she mentioned Lady Kinver? Something about her being an invalid. She recalled how Mama's voice had been stilted and odd and how she had not looked at the girls when she spoke. Emma knew that there were shameful diseases from which unfortunate folk could suffer. Had her ladyship contracted something unmentionable? If so, it made Sir Lambert's question base beyond words.

Then her distress was superseded by an aching wish to go to the viscount, place her hand upon his arm, and somehow enable him to quit the center of the room with dignity. She was exceedingly irritated by her cousin, who still sat mute, looking bemused. The viscount had taken a step toward Lucy, but she continued to regard him with a curious expression. Sir Lambert had drifted to Lady Augusta's side, but even that indomitable lady had been rendered witless by the awful social solecisms that had been committed in her drawing room during her first party of the Season; she had quite forgotten the pretext on which she had summoned him.

Emma looked around and saw the malevolent glee only half-concealed on the faces of some of the company and the pity of others, and wondered which would repel the viscount most. She believed she knew. He would detest pity. There were sibilant echoes of whispered comments, and her eyes went back to the viscount and she knew that he needed time to recover.

She took a deep breath and spoke aloud. "Did anyone happen to read the latest lampoon written about His Royal

Highness the Prince of Wales? It has been printed and I'm told is in all the coffeehouses, and indeed, we heard it declaimed on the day we arrived in London, did we not, Aunt Augusta''

There was another sudden silence as Lady Augusta's guests assimilated the fact that a young female newcomer to society had taken it upon herself to dominate the room with a question related to a subject that all of the gentlemen and most of the ladies believed should not be introduced into a drawing room—certainly one containing young girls. Lady Augusta sat rigid with disbelieving shock. She wished with all her heart that she could box Emma's ears with ringing force, but society decreed that one must never be discomposed.

She managed a laugh that made Emma shiver. "I did hear something when our coach was delayed awhile." She looked around at the faces of her elderly rivals and saw in their eyes, gleaming above the fans that had been unfurled to conceal grins, delight at this further tidbit of gossip to relate. "You must know Miss Waring is a poetess of some renown. She is so *sweetly* innocent and thinks that all verse is just to be looked at as—as—" She floundered. She seldom read anything, and poetry only if it were the subject of general conversation since one must always be adept at keeping up with the *ton*, so she found it well nigh impossible to comment suitably.

Mr. Exford rescued her. "As something to be considered with the sensibility of a connoisseur, is not that so, Miss Waring?"

Emma breathed a grateful sigh. "Of course, sir. I heard only a little of the verses, but they seemed prettily amusing."

Lady Augusta regarded Mr. Exford benevolently. She endeavored to melt the ice in her voice, "You are a poetess, child, but you must learn that London abounds with those who are forever penning scurrilous rhymes and satires. You will disregard them."

Lord Kinver spoke. "I should be most gratified to hear poetry from Miss Waring's pen. I have read the lampoon. It contains a trifle of merit as regards talent, something of verity as to fact, and is amusing, but not memorable. I would so enjoy learning what Miss Waring believes significant enough to be committed to paper."

All Emma's sympathy for him dissolved as his sardonic voice raked her. Every eye in the room was fixed upon her. There was nothing she desired less than to continue to hold the center of attention. She would like to go to her bedchamber, crawl beneath the sheets, and pull them over her head. She looked at Lady Augusta, silently appealing her aunt to command her to remain silent, but her ladyship, thinking of the tongues that would wag incessantly tomorrow about the events of this party, felt that here lay an opportunity for Emma to redeem herself. If the child should prove good at her poetry . . .

Emma rose and would have begun to recite from where she stood, but Lord Kinver intervened. "Come now, Miss Waring, this will not do. You are to stand by the windows at the end of the room, where we can all see your face. Much of the pleasure of a public performance lies in the expression of the face."

Emma disdained to answer. She walked as composedly as possible for a young lady on whom the fascinated gaze of many influential members of the *ton* were riveted to a place in front of the midnight-blue velvet curtains that hung in deep folds to the floorboards. They were a perfect backdrop for her beauty, and Lord Pembridge began to applaud enthusiastically. Gerard joined in loyally, followed by Anthony Downham. Emma knew they meant well, but she could have strangled all three. They were rapidly turning what should be a simple, brief interlude into something unsuitably significant.

She stood for a moment, her mind racing over her verse. Her inclination lay in humor and she had written a number of satirical pieces on current events, but they would not do. There were also several poems with which she was modestly pleased, portraying, she hoped, some of the deeper reaches of human nature. If she quoted one of these, she might be labeled that most denigrating of all things: a bluestocking. So she settled on a short piece she had penned for her younger siblings when they had been shut in the nursery with heavy colds in the head. It contained references to dolls with similar illness, birds and animals missing their little friends, and Nurse with her big spoonfuls of medicaments and healing unguents.

When she had finished, there was polite applause, which

satisfied Lady Augusta. The verses were pretty enough to
please the chaperones, innocuous enough to upset no one,
and simple enough to prove that whatever her niece had
heard in the street she could not possibly have understood.
Only Emma knew what a triumph she had engineered. She
glanced at Kinver to find him regarding her with the tolerant
amusement he would have accorded a kitten tumbling a
ball of yarn, before she dropped a curtsy, respectfully
directed at the elderly ladies and gentlemen who surrounded
her aunt.

She retreated thankfully when Lady Augusta requested Lucy
to sing and play the pianoforte. Lucy walked gracefully to the
instrument and Lord Kinver followed, helped her set up her
music, and waited to turn the pages, which he did adroitly.
Lucy's voice was high and sweet, the words she sang filled
with the joy of loving and uttered without emotion. She
received her plaudits, obliged with an encore, and the party
broke into groups, some to play at cards in the small salon,
some to talk, while others departed to fulfill other engagements. Gerard, Pembridge, and Anthony took immediate advantage of this release. All three came to say good night to
Emma.

Gerard swept her a bow while giving a brotherly grin.
"You set them by the ears tonight, sister dear. You'd best
watch that quick tongue of yours or her ladyship may com-
plain to Papa and you'll be asked to go home."

"More like you'll be in trouble," snapped Emma. "Where
on earth do you find the money to buy so many clothes and
game your time away?"

Gerard shrugged and his young face assumed a look of
cynicism. "Lor', Emma, I'm no Johnny Raw. The rhino's
easy to come by when you know how. Anthony and I are
bang-up and bobbish, thanks to Pembridge here."

"Glad to be of service," murmured Lord Pembridge.

"You should not borrow from Lord Pembridge, Gerard."

"Damme if you ain't a regular Friday-face, and bird-
witted to boot! I'd not dream of asking Ferdy for a loan. He
pointed me to a gull-groper who came across handsome with
the flimsies, that's all."

"Glad to be of service," murmured Pembridge.

During the time it took Emma to translate her brother's cant terms into regular English and she understood that Gerard was patronizing moneylenders, the three gay blades had left.

Mr. Exford was full of praise for her poem. "So prettily sweet, Miss Waring, and just the kind of thing a young woman should write. One day, when you are married with your own nursery, your children will be fortunate indeed to have a mama who can devise such amusements."

Emma slipped back into her role of coquette. She had best stay firmly anchored to it from now on. She unfurled her fan and held it before her face, fluttering both it and her eyelashes. "Sir, you put me to the blush, I vow."

Mr. Exford smiled. "Between you and I, Miss Waring, I am hoping there need not be reserve. We have only just met, but you hold me in the palm of your pretty hand."

"No, no, sir, I protest."

"I do not jest, Miss Waring. Believe me when I tell you that I have never liked any lady half so well as you. I trust that as the Season advances we shall become great friends—even more than friends. Dare I hope?"

Emma was breathless. She had only just made her bow into polite society and had not even behaved well, and here was a handsome, young, wealthy man asking if he might court her.

She lowered her fan and her face grew serious. "Mr. Exford, I cannot—I mean, I do not know you."

"But you do not dislike me?"

"No, sir, of course not. You helped to rescue me nobly this evening. I must like you."

"That will suffice—for now. As for your not knowing me, we can soon remedy that. I shall be at your side whenever the occasion permits. That is, if you have no objection. Have you, Miss Waring?"

"Sir, I can make you no promise. I can only repeat I scarcely know you."

Mr. Exford smiled even more happily. It was meet that a young girl should show proper hesitation. It went further to prove that the lovely Miss Waring had spoken earlier of a lampoon she could not possibly comprehend. "I am content. Shall you be at the duchess's soiree tomorrow night?"

"Lady Augusta has accepted for us."

"I shall not sleep for looking forward to it," he declared, and Emma, in her confusion, gave the trilling laugh that so grated on Lord Kinver, who glared across the room from where he was seated by Lucy.

The hour was getting late by Emma's country standards and she had not had enough sleep, and it was becoming a struggle to keep her eyelids from drooping. Furthermore she knew she must write more tonight and deliver her work to Mr. Rowley early tomorrow. To her intense relief, Lady Augusta raised no objection when she asked if she might retire as she had the headache, though her ladyship's glare informed her that her forward behavior was not forgotten or forgiven.

Emma dismissed Betty as soon as possible, having exerted herself to fib convincingly about her enjoyment of the party, then wrapped a warm shawl around herself, put a little more coal on the fire with the brass tongs, and settled herself to write. Her weariness was forgotten as she dreamed up more tragic circumstances for her heroine to endure, but when she was finished, she was drained of energy. She hid the work in the bottom drawer of the desk, covered it with blank paper, and staggered to bed.

The sounds of doors, raised voices, and carriage wheels over the cobbled roads had told her that the last of the guests were departing, and she only just managed to blow out her candle before she heard the heavy tread of Lady Augusta. Her ladyship opened the door, listened, and proceeded to bed. Emma's brain was a turmoil of impressions, but she was excessively weary and sleep was overtaking her fast. Just before she floated into oblivion, she decided that writing about an imagined high society was very different from living in it. The heroes especially did not behave as they should.

She slept late the next morning, and when Betty called her with tea and a thin slice of bread and butter at noon, she felt refreshed. The maid removed her evening gown to refurbish it and Emma took a deep breath and left the shelter of her room to go downstairs. Lady Augusta was sitting in the morning room wearing a voluminous gown of pink satin, her hair concealed beneath a cap of astonishing proportions, perusing the news in the *The Morning Chronicle*. For the benefit of servants who were placing a light nuncheon on the table, she greeted Emma with forced cordiality.

She rustled the pages of her paper. "Here is a man of seventy years who has wed a girl of sixteen with ten thousand pounds. What a match! Everyone knows that a girl must obey her parents, but I for one would not ask any young lady to mate with such an oldster. It is to be hoped that he will suffer from such excesses of nature and expire soon. It will serve him right, do you not agree, Emma?"

Disregarding Papa's insistence that evil-thinking was evil-doing, Emma replied, "Oh, indeed, ma'am. It scarcely seems natural."

"Here's a piece which says that the government's plan to wrest more money from us by imposing a hair-powder tax has failed. Folk have simply given up powdering. It only goes to show that we have more sense than the government gives us credit for. Do you not agree, Emma?"

Relieved this time to find herself in wholehearted assent with her hostess, Emma said, "I am sure you are right, ma'am."

She wished that the servants would go. Her nerves were being stretched like viola strings as she waited for the inevitable scold.

13

The servants finished bustling about at last and Lady Augusta threw down her paper. "I desire to know, madam, how you dared bring the subject of a scurrilous lampoon into my drawing room?" She did not wait for a reply. "I am prepared to believe that you do not appreciate the full history of His Royal Highness and his—his problems, but you must be aware that verses shouted on the street were scarcely something about which a young lady should speak. If she comprehends any of their content, she should feign ignorance. You must have known that you would draw attention to yourself. Is that what you wanted? Attention? You obtained it, but I assure you, madam, it is not the sort a young woman on the threshold of the Season should seek."

"No, ma'am. I am very sorry."

"That is something, I suppose. It is fortunate that you were able to recite such a pretty poem afterward. We must hope that folk will merely think you foolish. That is perfectly acceptable in young girls. They are not required to be clever."

Lady Augusta had argued herself out of much of her spleen and she smiled almost benevolently on Emma. "Yes, you did recite most entertainingly. Have you written anything else?"

Emma was startled. "Anything else, ma'am?"

"Emma, I vow that sometimes you appear positively witless. Have you penned any more verses?"

Emma murmured that she had, and she busily sorted through her brain, picking out the acceptable from the unrepeatable.

"Good! I shall request you to recite upon every possible occasion, and the *ton* will understand that you are an innocent who spoke entirely without comprehension last night. After you had gone to bed, I did as much as I could among the older guests to redeem you. Indeed, the duchess remarked on your beauty and the clarity of your speech."

"Thank you, Aunt Augusta. It is good of you to go to so much trouble for me."

Lady Augusta basked in this recognition of her magnanimity. Emma asked, "Er, did Lord Kinver stay late?"

"Good God, no, child. He and Exford went to White's to play for higher stakes than I encourage. I have never been one of your gambling ladies. A few guineas lost or won are nothing to speak of. Why do you ask?"

"I—I just wondered. Pray, tell me, Aunt Augusta, why did Sir Lambert sound so—so horrid? And why was Lord Kinver so put out?"

"That is all to do with the past, miss, and no business of yours. Lucy is aware of the facts, and as it is she who will be marrying Kinver . . ."

"Will she *indeed* marry him?"

"Emma, I find your precipitate demands for information most disconcerting. Yes, Lucy is about to fill a high position in the land. Kinver made that clear last night. Lady Kinver never normally sees anyone."

Emma turned her head to look out the window, remarking that the day appeared fine.

"Emma, I saw you in close converse with Mr. Exford. He looks at you in a vastly admiring way. Has he intimated that he may feel a partiality toward you?"

"We have only just met, Aunt."

"What has that to do with anything? A man may not declare his passion for a young woman upon so short an acquaintance, but James Exford has been on the town long enough to know what he wants, and the sooner he makes his feelings plain to you, the better. You will then be positioned to weigh any other possibilities of a closer relationship against his."

"I—Mr. Exford likes me, ma'am."

"Is that so? Likes you? I thought I read more into his expression than mere liking."

"He—he asked me if he might hope?"

"Excellent! Exford is wealthy, since he came so unexpectedly into an inheritance. His manners are engaging and his person pleasing. You could scarcely do better. You have my permission—extended on behalf of your parents, who I know would agree with me—to give him every encouragement in keeping with a young girl's genteel behavior."

"Yes, ma'am. Thank you."

Try as she might, Emma could not infuse her voice, or her feelings, with enthusiasm. She did like Mr. Exford. Undoubtedly he would make a fine husband, but she wanted a man of strength and fire, a man of muscle and bone, a man of quick intelligence and wit, and Mr. Exford was none of these. He was good-looking, entertaining, gentle, and certainly not stupid, but Emma had met only one man who fitted her new pattern, and his behavior to her was arrogant and, on one occasion, intolerably base. How dare he kiss her without permission—and in such a way! Recalling that kiss, Emma smiled and her eyes softened, and Lady Augusta, seeing these manifestations of pleasure, was content that her young charge should already be thinking so happily of Mr. Exford, even if she spoke of him without interest. It was only right and proper in a young girl that she should pretend to such hesitancy. Lady Augusta, who had been so exceedingly put out by Emma's indiscretion last night, felt in charity with her this morning.

Lucy drifted in, wearing a round gown with lace ruffles at the neck and wrists. Emma looked at her with fresh eyes, her mind dwelling on the fact that she was now the definite choice of Lord Kinver, and felt a surge of an unpleasant emotion she disdained to recognize as jealousy. Lucy would make a wonderful viscountess: dignified, calm, able to converse easily about all aspects of society, understanding the running of great estates, self-effacing, wealthy enough to add much consequence to his lordship. In short, she was all that such a man as Kinver could wish for, and Emma strongly suspected that Lucy would conform to order and choose not to see any male indiscretions he would surely commit. Emma could never pretend ignorance of a husband's base pursuits.

"Emma, I have been speaking to you for these several minutes and you have not responded."

Emma flushed. "I beg your pardon, Aunt, I was thinking."

"I know, and it is a habit you must break. I noticed when first we met that you have a tendency to disappear into worlds of your own, and it simply will not *do*. Suppose you should upset someone important. What if you drifted off when being addressed by the Prince of Wales?''

Emma was startled. ''I did not know I would be presented to him, ma'am.''

''Oh, I think there is little doubt that you will, and he will probably seek to flatter you because you are pretty, but I warn you now, do not allow it to go to your head. Gossip would have us believe he is already wed to two women, the princess and . . . Well, it is not a fit subject. I was telling you that the dressmaker has delivered more gowns today and that I should like you to wear the blue-and-white this evening.''

The day was spent quietly. Emma wrote to her parents, and Lady Augusta was able to allot her one of the postal franks that she purchased shamelessly from any member of Parliament who sold them. Mr. Waring would be spared the cost of the letter, and what he did not know would not hurt him. Emma recognized that she was sliding deeper and deeper into pits of deception.

The ladies walked briefly in Hyde Park at the fashionable hour, greeting friends who included Mr. Exford and Lord Kinver, both of whom joined them. They drew envious looks from young ladies and irate ones from guardians who knew of Kinver's public invitation to Lucy to visit his mama. This news, which had enlivened society haunts that day, proved that he had at last been entrapped into a promise to propose matrimony. They could not even have the pleasure of criticizing his choice, and Lady Augusta found it difficult to keep up her pose of indifference when such tremendous triumph was swelling in her bosom.

Lord Kinver greeted Emma politely before turning his attention to Lucy, but Mr. Exford shook her hand and held it a little longer than necessary. Lady Augusta almost burst with her awareness that this too had been noted by her rivals.

Emma was young and healthy enough for Betty's skillful use of a hare's foot and Powder of Pearl of India, and pink Spanish wool (''borrowed'' from Lady Augusta's dressing room), for none of her worries to show on her face. She took a last look in the cheval glass. Her gown of celestial-blue gauze over white tiffany was cut and sewn by the hands of experts. New matching blue satin slippers were decorated by small white rosettes, and the feel of silk upon her legs gave her sensuous pleasure. Lady Augusta sent Wheeler to add the finishing touches to her hair (Betty's indignant murmurings were ignored), which she had arranged into a slightly tumbled disorder: curls clustered on her forehead and hung in ringlets to her shoulders, and one had been cleverly pinned with a white silk rose to fall to her breast. A small sapphire pendant, a gift from her parents, was suspended by a slender gold chain. Her sleeves were short and her white kid gloves almost met them. Betty was vociferous in her adulation and even the dour Wheeler permitted herself a small smile and a compliment.

The Duchess of Frome's house in Upper Grosvenor Street was ablaze with light. The great front doors were thrown open and a line of carriages progressed slowly before the exterior, pausing to allow guests to descend. Crowds of sightseers pushed and shoved and laughed, or cursed as their toes were ground into the unyielding cobbles, and called advice, much of it bawdy, to those entering their Graces' residence. The *haut ton* mostly elected not to hear, but a few young blades returned the banter loudly, and Emma, waiting in the carriage with Lady Augusta and Lucy, was mortified to realize that among them was Gerard. He was, as usual, with Lord Pembridge and Anthony Downham and all three wore exceedingly colorful garb, though Anthony looked somewhat ill-at-ease.

The three men passed into the brilliant hall and soon afterward Emma was being assisted down the carriage steps by a liveried footman. She joined the chattering, gossiping procession making its way across the tiled expanse and up the wide stairway. She was almost overcome by the grandeur of the occasion. There appeared to be almost as many serving men and maids as guests, and the heat from the candles was already melting the maquillage of several ladies and gentlemen. The air was redolent with perfume. Emma recognized rose, lilac, lavender, and sandalwood, though a great number were new to her. Although most of the gowns were of the simpler cut now favored, jewels gave back the light with myriad flashes of multicolored fire.

Emma thought of Sophia, who would so delight in such pleasures, and vowed that she would make a marriage that would ensure a good future for her younger sisters and brothers. The intrusion of doubts engendered by her secret activities and her dismay at Gerard's cavortings were shoved firmly to the back of her mind. Mr. Exford was a prize she could win if she chose. She wished that the idea brought her more joy.

Lucy and Lady Augusta walked by her side, her ladyship in red satin, rubies, and a large white wig supporting a blue turban with three tall red feathers. Lucy wore a primrose-yellow muslin gown of exquisite simplicity, rare yellow opals around her throat, and gold bracelets over her white kid gloves. Her dark hair was dressed in a knot where a small diamond-and-opal pin glittered. Her skin gleamed in pale transparency. She was not beautiful, reflected Emma, but so distinguished, so graceful, so full of tranquil dignity! Emma had not been able to draw any closer to her cousin and wondered if Lord Kinver would break the perfect shell—and how. She took herself to task. Such musings were neither fitting nor any of her business.

They arrived at last at the head of the stairway to be welcomed by their hosts. The duchess leaned forward to brush Lady Augusta's painted cheek with her own. Her eyes roved searchingly over Lucy and Emma.

"Ah, Miss Venables is with us, I see. And Miss Waring, you are most welcome. I wish you joy of your first Season."

Emma sank into a graceful curtsy. "Thank you, Your Grace. You are all kindness."

The duchess beamed, revealing several gaps in her teeth. "What a pretty child you are. Lady Augusta must exert all effort to find you a husband. You must not be so particular as Miss Venables in making your choice."

Lady Augusta smiled without humor. "I am thankful to say that my dear Lucy is so well-endowed—in *all* ways—that she has been able to delay her decision. I think, however, that Your Grace will already have some inkling of the match that is pending for her. And as for my dear Emma, she too has smitten the heart of a very eligible suitor. I fancy it will not be long before I see both of the dear girls wed."

"What felicitous news," replied Her Grace. "One must always be relieved when the dear young people are *finally* settled in life."

As the three ladies passed on into the great salon to mingle, before deciding which of the various amusements they would favor, Lady Augusta muttered, "She is so catty. She has but the one daughter, and she is a dab of a girl, and spotty too. They had to offer an enormous dowry to get her off their hands and she is scarce ever in town, but lives as a country dame rearing babies, cows, and pigs, from all accounts. I know it vexes her mama considerably," she ended happily.

The spacious room was made to appear smaller by a huge throng of people who were producing a deafening noise with their gossip. Friends and rivals greeted one another with exaggerated gratification at this first large event of the Season, as if they had been parted for years instead of weeks. There were enough candles to give an impression of daylight and the heat was intense. Emma felt overwhelmed by the impressions crowding in upon her, though Lucy, used to society, appeared as contained as ever.

The mass of people parted and Mr. Exford and Lord Kinver approached. Each gentleman bowed to the lady of his choice, craving the pleasure of leading her into the country dances, which were to be held in another room.

As it was well-known that Mr. Exford and Lord Kinver usually made straight for the card tables, Lady Augusta glanced swiftly about her to ensure that their improved behavior had been noted. Eyes that had been devouring the incident were turned away and facial expressions rendered bland. She was, therefore, able to exalt in the knowledge that her two charges would swiftly be the subjects of much envious discussion.

The sounds of viols and flutes tuning up led most of the younger people to the dancing. Lucy and Emma took their places in the formation of a long set and Emma began her first dance in London. At first she concentrated on her steps, for although she knew them well she was nervous enough to trip over her own silk-shod feet. She soon realized the similarity of all young folk set on enjoying the moment. Her rather stiff movements relaxed into their usual fluidity; she swung around with various young men and dipped and swayed to the rhythm; and when it was Kinver's turn, he received the full beauty of her smile. For a brief moment Emma forgot the antagonism between them, forgot that he had insulted her, and reveled in the sensation of his strong hand, his muscular arm, as they danced down the center together. His face too was alight with pleasure and she caught a brief glimpse of a very different man, and his commanding masculinity tugged at her mind and body. The dance lasted for half an hour, and by the end of it Emma felt vital and alive as she had not for a long time. As she and Lucy were escorted from the floor, she laughed in sheer enjoyment and Kinver stared at her with narrowed eyes, intrigued by the variations in her behavior.

Mr. Exford grinned and said, "I assume, Miss Waring, that you are fond of dancing. You look prettier than ever."

"Why, thank you, sir." Emma swept him a curtsy. "Do you share my enthusiasm?"

"Up to a point, ma'am. Dancing has its pleasure."

Lord Kinver took Lucy's elbow and led her to a seat, and Mr. Exford followed with Emma and they watched another set form. Someone came to stand before Lucy and Emma looked up from her conversation with Mr. Exford to see Sir Lambert Lowther bowing and soliciting her cousin's company in the dance. It was obvious to Emma that Lord Kinver was outraged, but Lucy smiled and rose and took a place in the set opposite the baronet.

As the music began, Lady Augusta's voice rasped at the three remaining watchers. "Why did you permit her to go?"

The two men sprang to their feet. Emma said, "I did not see you enter, Aunt."

" 'Tis a pity I did not come sooner. *I* would have sent that unpleasant fellow packing."

"What would you have us do?" The viscount was trenchant. "Should I have seized her by her gown and dragged her backward? How was I to know she would consent to dance with such a man? I believed she had more sense."

"Do you expect me to advise you on how to keep a young woman by your side? Damme, Kinver, you are experienced enough . . ." Recalling Emma's presence, she stopped and glared at Lucy, who was tripping down the dance with Sir Lambert.

"I do not like that man at all," she snapped.

"And neither do I, madam! I could scarcely be expected to realize that Miss Lucy would go so readily with him. She has been out long enough to be aware of his doubtful reputation."

Lady Augusta clamped down on her anger instantly as she appreciated the extent of the viscount's fury. It would not do to antagonize him just when he was about to make Lucy the offer of a lifetime. She would have plenty to say to the stupid girl later. This was one dazzling prospect that Lady Augusta had no intention of allowing to slide from her grasp. It was essential to retrieve the situation.

She sank onto the small gilt chair vacated by her granddaughter and fanned herself vigorously. "She accepts Sir Lambert because she has no comprehension of his evil sort. I have guarded her well. When she has her own establishment and her family, she will be entirely happy. She dotes on quiet country pursuits. Such an advantage—in the early days of wedlock, at all events. My dear girl is still inexperienced in the ways of the world. She sees no harm in anyone."

It was Emma's rapidly increasing belief that Lucy possessed very little discrimination and no sensibility at all, and she could not imagine Lord Kinver finding happiness with her. But his future, happy or otherwise, was not her concern. He watched Lucy with eyes that still smoldered with wrath.

Mr. Exford intervened. "Indeed, ma'am, Kinver could not have prevented Miss Venables. She was gone before we realized—"

"You have no need to defend me, thank you, James," said the viscount. Exford shrugged, too used to his friend's moods to allow them to bother him. "Be sure, your ladyship, I shall remove Miss Venables from that rogue as soon as the dance is finished."

"I trust you to do so, Kinver." Lady Augusta managed a passable smile. "The sweet child will need refreshment after two strenuous dances."

Emma attempted to defuse the atmosphere. "How should one refuse, ma'am? It is considered impolite simply to say no." She had the dubious satisfaction of attracting Kinver's sardonic appraisal and knew she had given him yet another opportunity to mock her.

Lady Augusta shrugged. "You are such a babe in society. Tell an unacceptable partner that you have hurt your foot. Send him for refreshment for you and return to your chaperone as soon as he has gone. Tear a small piece of your lace—provided it is not too costly, of course—and insist on retiring to find a sewing maid. Swoon if you must, Emma, but never encourage the wrong man. Too many families have elderly females on their hands who chose the wrong partner at a crucial moment.''

Another figure entered the salon, at the sight of whom Kinver jumped to his feet and hurried to the door. Emma saw a woman a little taller than herself, slender enough to wear a soft, apricot-colored Grecian gown. Her lightly powdered complexion was smooth with only a few wrinkles, which proved that she smiled often. Her snowy hair curled out from beneath a headdress of satin and feathers. Around her neck was a rope of pearls.

"The Dowager Lady Mary Kinver," hissed Lady Augusta, before Kinver brought his grandmother across the room.

Emma rose, curtsied, and found herself the subject of a penetrating look from hazel eyes that resembled her grandson's, though they they were lighter than his.

Lady Kinver asked, "Are you Miss Waring? I think you must be. Kinver described you very well."

Emma was startled. What had he said of her?

"He failed to do you justice," said Lady Kinver. "You are far prettier than I imagined. Do be seated, child, and I shall sit by you. How are you, Lady Augusta?"

"I am well, thank you, ma'am." Lady Augusta's eyes had been taking in every detail of Lady Kinver's apparel. "I see you enjoy wearing the latest styles. I find that I prefer to maintain the modes of our youth. An older woman must needs be cautious. There are some freakish-looking females in society these days."

"I do so agree, dear Lady Augusta, and I delight to note that you have not made such a mistake. I recall that as a girl you were used to be as slender as I, but it would not do for you now to be wearing a gown with a high waist. One needs a waist to do so."

"That is true. However, it is my opinion that no self-respecting elderly lady should worry about an increase in her figure."

Lady Kinver smiled serenely. "Is that so, ma'am? Well, you set us all a fine example."

Lady Augusta altered her tactics. "What brings you from your Hampstead hideaway, dear ma'am? I was fully convinced that you had retired from society. In fact, I heard a rumor that your years weighed so heavily upon you that you could find strength only to walk in your garden—and that with support.''

"One needs to be so cautious where loose tongues are concerned. For my part, I scorn to take heed of any rumor affecting to denigrate you, dear Lady Augusta."

"So sweet! So affecting!" Lady Augusta produced a scented handkerchief and touched it to her eyes, careful not to disturb the blacking with which Wheeler had defined her sparse brows. "I vow I will forever speak up for you."

The two *grandes dames* decided that honors were, for the moment, even and smiled at each other with expressions that would, as Nurse might have said, soured the milk, and nodded. Their feathered headdresses danced above their heads, and Emma was reminded of two horses tossing their manes. It needed only for them to scrape a toe on the floor to make the comparison complete. She had to turn aside to control the mirth that threatened to explode into laughter, and her eye caught Kinver's. She saw that he too was trying not to laugh, and their shared appreciation was altogether too much for them. Their laughter burst and joined in a moment of absolute harmony.

14

Both ladies stared at them. "Have they run mad?" demanded Lady Augusta.

"Who knows?" replied Lady Kinver. "I suggest that we go in search of refreshment. I vow I am already thirsty."

Mr. Exford sprang to his feet. "Pray, allow me . . ."

"Certainly not!" Lady Augusta waved him away. "Your duty is to guard Miss Waring while I am gone."

She glared at Emma and Lord Kinver, whose laughter was subsiding, and she and Lady Kinver left the salon, joined in temporary truce.

Mr. Exford looked at Emma and the viscount good-humoredly. "You might tell me the joke," he complained.

He almost set the pair off again. Emma controlled herself enough to say, "It was just the way the ladies acted. Their feathers . . . their looks . . ."

"I see." Exford smiled, but Emma saw that he did not, and she was disappointed. One of her ideal man's important attributes was a sense of humor to match hers. Lord Kinver's did. In fact, there were a great many things about him that appealed to her. The sooner the viscount proclaimed his intentions toward Lucy, the better. She must forget that tonight she had caught a further glimpse of the viscount's personality and found it captivating.

Lord Kinver and Mr. Exford led Lucy and Emma into another dance, before escorting them into the supper room, facts that were noted by all present. The food was laid out on a long table, but the viscount took advantage of one of the small tables set about the room, and Emma found herself sitting conspicuously with one lady and two gentlemen. By now she knew that their party was giving the *ton* the excuse for a good deal of speculation. There were many glances at them, sometimes turned sharply away or hidden behind a quickly unfurled fan, but quite often she was openly stared at by dowagers and chaperones who had never heard of her and wondered why Mr. Exford, now so exceedingly eligible, should be paying her such distinguishing attention. Questions were asked and answered until everyone understood that Miss Waring was the daughter of a rector with a modest fortune, but that she was the great-granddaughter of the Earl of Abbotsbury and distantly related to both Miss Venables and Lord Kinver, and that her mother was connected to an equally noble line. It was vexing that she could not therefore be criticized on account of her birth, and her financial expectations were unimportant when the recently acquired fortune of Mr. Exford was considered.

There was even more talk of the viscount and Lucy. Those who remembered the scandal of his mother and the tragedy of his dead betrothed had believed that he would never be tempted into the married state, and his reckless mode of living, which had frequently scandalized the more reserved, had added strength to their belief. This had not prevented anyone from presenting eligible girls to him in the hope that one would take his fancy, but it had allowed them to find a perennial excuse for their failure. It was disappointing that Miss Venables was so eminently suitable, thus allowing no room for adverse comment, save the fact that she was not beautiful.

Lord Kinver was aware of the gossip. Normally he would have ignored it, but tonight he was annoyed. He sometimes found it difficult to stop directing his irritation at Lucy. She was unfailingly courteous and gracious, but she offered him no more than she offered others. Of course, a man did not want his future bride to behave in a manner that would draw adverse comment, but she could take an example from Miss Waring, who was openly friendly with Exford.

He found himself watching Miss Waring, and several times she caught his eyes and looked away, once with heightened color. She was extraordinarily lovely. A wonderful armful for any man. The viscount subdued his wayward musings. Did she realize how conspicuous Mr. Exford was making her? He must suppose that she did. No matter how rustic her home, she must have been imbued with all the precepts of polite behavior between a man and woman.

So why did she allow you to kiss her? And not only kiss her, but respond, pressing her sweet-scented body against yours, meeting your lips with hers, betraying a nature that is all too evidently passionate? The floodgates damming memory opened. God, he wanted her! He wanted her as he had never wanted any woman, and she was forever denied him. No man of honor made illicit advances toward a young girl of high breeding. Miss Waring would suit James, who, always amiable and good company, was not an intellectual. Marriage was not all making love; there were many other considerations.

A footman had attended their table and Kinver realized that Miss Waring was offering him a dish containing wafer-thin slices of ham and beef. "You have eaten nothing, my lord. This is delicious. And here is bread and butter. Do take some. Dancing is energetic and one needs sustenance."

"Thank you, Miss Waring. So kind of you to consider my well-being." He cursed himself silently. He had not meant to sound sardonic and hated the way the fun faded from Miss Waring's face.

He took some slices of meat and ate them without tasting them. He also absentmindedly chose two cheesecakes, which he liked, and a dish of boiled custard pudding with cinnamon, which he did not.

Miss Venables worked her way steadily through her supper, informing her companions of the principles of growing the best apples for baking, ways of producing and preserving herbs in winter and which were best for keeping the moth from garments.

Mr. Exford gazed at her in awe. "You know so many things one never gives a thought to, Miss Venables. You positively amaze me."

He glanced at the viscount as he spoke, marveling that such a man was content to settle for a walking encyclopedia for a wife. Lord Kinver caught the look and knew what Exford was thinking and became even more irritated.

"You must do a great deal of studying, Miss Venables," Mr. Exford said.

"Indeed, I do, sir, especially on the subjects of husbandry, gardening, and home economy. I believe that every woman should have a sound knowledge of what she tells her servants to do."

"When you have your own establishment, it will be run with meticulous attention," smiled Emma. "Mama and Nurse were forever castigating me because I paid so little heed to their instructions. My seams were often crooked, and when I tried my hand at baking, Cook threw my cakes to the hens and I believe even they discarded them."

Exford laughed. "A lovely lady should not need to bother about mundane domestic details. She should be content to remain pretty, well-gowned, and amusing."

Emma stared at him. "Do you truly think so, sir? Should she have *no* other accomplishments?"

"Oh, I will allow her to sing and play an instrument, to ride well and drive if she wishes."

"I see."

"You sound surprised, Miss Waring," said Lord Kinver. "I could have sworn that your views matched Exford's precisely."

"But you know little of me, my lord."

Their eyes met and once again there seemed to be a flash of inner awareness. Kinver recovered first. "Only what you have permitted me to know," he said dryly. He was sorry at once as Emma's color rose and she pretended to be examining a dish of fruit.

Mr. Exford frowned slightly. There seemed to be an atmosphere between Miss Waring and Kinver. But the viscount was gazing at Miss Venables, and Miss Waring had selected an apricot and was carefully peeling it. He must be mistaken.

Emma wiped her fingers in a table napkin and said, "Mr. Exford, do you think that a woman should possess a brain and form opinions of her own?" She kept her voice carefully controlled.

Mr. Exford pondered. "I suppose a woman without an active brain would become a dead bore, but she should not allow it to overcome her female nature."

"If her nature is truly feminine, it will always remain so," replied Emma, remembering, as she saw the viscount look sharply at her, to imbue her tone with flippancy.

"Well said." Kinver applauded. "Miss Venables is living proof that it is true."

Lucy looked calmly at him. "Of course I am feminine. I am a woman and have no choice."

"Surely you would not be different," Mr. Exford cried.

"Certainly not, sir. Such a thought would not occur to me. It would be most improper."

"Maybe," said Emma, "but one must admit that men are allowed much more freedom to do what they choose."

"What kind of freedom, ma'am?" Lord Kinver's voice became abruptly harsh.

Emma looked levelly at him, remembered her lessons, and allowed a dainty trill of mirth to ring out. "I scarce know what I meant, sir. Have we finished supper? Pray, let us return to the salon and dance again. I hear the music beginning and I vow my feet are positively itching to move."

Another untruth, thought Emma. She enjoyed dancing, but she would have liked to join the company at the card tables to play whist. This was an amusement not encouraged at parties in young, unwed girls. It seemed like another incentive to get married.

The viscount glared at her as Mr. Exford gave her his arm, then he followed with Lucy. They were in the hall when Lady Augusta appeared, bearing down on them with the undoubted intention of castigating her granddaughter. She stopped, as there was a disturbance at the front door, and the butler and senior footman hurried to it with the duke and duchess in close pursuit.

Kinver said, "His Royal Highness has arrived."

Emma's curiosity was rife as she waited to see the man of whom she had written so satirical a rhyme.

Kinver saw him first. "He grows no thinner. You should introduce him to your reducing diet, Exford."

Mr. Exford grinned. "Be silent, you lunatic! If there's one thing that annoys him above all others it is to be reminded of his girth. Or is it quips about Mrs. Fitzherbert?"

"Now who's risking Prinny's displeasure?"

The company parted and Emma saw the Prince. His second chin was inadequately concealed by his cravat. His garb was conservative in color and style, but his waistcoat and white knee breeches were strained over his girth. He retained much of the handsome appearance over which women had sighed, though his mouth, as curved as a girl's, was weak. But it was the fact of his actual physical presence that gave Emma a jolt. It was one thing to write derisive verses about a man of whom one had only read, but to meet him in his substantial flesh and understand that he would certainly have read her words and been stung by them was entirely different.

The Prince made slow and stately progress through the hall, greeting those he knew and being presented to some he did not. Emma became abruptly aware that he was making for a room where gaming was already in progress and that her party was in direct line. Kinver and Mr. Exford bowed to the Prince, who smiled graciously upon them, his eyes going immediately to Emma.

The viscount presented her, and the Prince held out his hand. She curtsied and the Prince bestowed his sweet smile on her, raised her, and touched her glove with his lips.

"Miss Waring, eh? Where is your home?"

"In—in Gloucestershire, Sir."

"Are you here with your parents?"

"No, sir, with my aunt, Lady Augusta Brancaster. Mama is nursing my brother and sisters, who are ill."

The Prince looked alarmed. "Nothing infectious, I hope."

"Only a childish ailment, Sir."

"And your Papa?"

"He is a parson, Sir, and kept busy by his duties."

"A most noble profession for a gentleman. If Lady Augusta is your aunt, you must be related to the late Earl of Abbotsbury."

Emma's eyes widened in surprise and the Prince laughed delightedly. "You are astonished at my knowledge, Miss Waring, but I am teasing you, a little. I met your parents before they relinquished the pleasures of London. Surely they have mentioned it."

"Of course, Sir, but it amazes me that you recall them. You meet so many."

The Prince smiled again. "You are a welcome addition to society, ma'am. We can do with all the beauty we can get. I am most susceptible to beauty, as anyone will tell you."

He greeted Lucy, whom he already knew, and walked on, leaving Emma speechless and deeply regretful. Prinny might

well be the spendthrift, oversentimental, deceitful seducer
that his opponents claimed, but he had infinite charm and she
was enchanted by it. Nothing would have induced her to
write anything detrimental about him if she had met him
before. Pray God he never discovered the authorship of the
latest ballad that was amusing the *ton*.

She watched the Prince enter the gaming room and saw
that Gerard and his constant companions were there and that
Gerard was looking somber. He was probably losing more
money.

Lord Kinver said quietly in her ear, "You look pensive.
That is your brother playing, is it not? He is showing his
feelings far too clearly. He should never allow others to
realize that he holds a losing hand."

Emma turned and said angrily, "Oh, I daresay you know
all about gaming, sir. It is men like you who encourage boys
of Gerard's age to lose their substance."

The viscount stared at her, and Exford intervened, "Upon
my soul, Miss Waring, I had not thought you had such a
temper, and you do Kinver a gross injustice. In all my years
as his friend I know he has not taken advantage of any young
person at play—or in any other way, for that matter. Once,
when he refused to oblige a boy who wished to hazard far
more than he could afford, Kinver made an excuse to leave
the table. He refused to fight a duel with the silly hothead
who considered he had been insulted. Even when the lad
called him 'coward' before others, Kinver walked away.
That's real courage."

"Have done, Exford," said Lord Kinver in bored tones.
"It is always easier for the young to have someone to blame.
Everyone knows that no man of honor fights a boy."

Emma was chagrined. Should she apologize? She struggled
to find words. She was learning many lessons, and some
were bitter. The events of the past moments, the heat of the
rooms, the late nights, coupled with her frantic efforts to keep
Mr. Palmer quiet, overcame her. To her horror, the room
appeared to darken and there was an ominous rushing sound
in her ears. Emma had never swooned, and was scared as
consciousness slid from her. She was relieved to be caught in
a strong grasp, lifted and carried somewhere, held against
a strongly beating heart. The scent of sandalwood drifted to

her nostrils as she was placed gently on a satin surface, her rescuer still half-supporting her. She could dimly hear voices.

"She has fainted!" That was Lucy.

"Shall I fetch water—or wine?" Mr. Exford spoke.

"Bring both, but open a window first." That was Lord Kinver, and she realized that it was he who had caught her and who must now be kneeling at her side, one arm around her.

Mr. Exford returned with a glass containing a mix of water and wine, which was held to her lips. She sipped and felt herself recovering. She was in a small side room, gulping in drafts of cool air. The viscount gently removed his arm, allowing her head to rest on the cushions of the sofa, and Emma knew that she would have preferred it to remain.

A rustling of skirts and a peremptory demand to know what had occurred heralded Lady Augusta's entrance. "Swooned? I should never have believed her to be the swooning type. Lucy has never swooned, have you, child? Emma, all the world knows that a lady should swoon only when it is socially desirable."

Kinver laughed. "Perhaps the honor of being spoken to at such length by His Royal Highness overcame Miss Waring."

"Yes, he did spend time with her." Lady Augusta looked extremely gratified. "And do you think it caused her to lose consciousness? I shall make it my business to see that it comes to his ears. He will be delighted. That will ensure an invitation to Carlton House for Emma. Do you feel fit enough to continue, child?"

Emma swung her legs to the floor and discovered that she was still dizzy. Lady Augusta tutted. "You must return home. I will find a suitable escort."

She looked meaningfully at Mr. Exford, who immediately offered his services, and Emma was assisted to a carriage and driven back to Hanover Square, her solicitous suitor by her side and a maid sent as chaperone on the opposite seat.

She was greeted by Betty, who had been dozing in an easy chair by the bedroom fire. "You're early, Miss Emma! You look pale! Aren't you well?"

"I swooned," admitted Emma.

Betty was sympathetic. "I was saying only yesterday to Miss Wheeler that you were a bit peaky. You're not used to town hours yet, Miss Emma. I know when I left my village and came here, I could've died of weariness, but it soon passes.''

She removed her mistress's finery, assisted in her toilet, and tucked her into a bed from which she first took the chill of linen sheets with a warming pan. "These spring nights can be deceiving. It's all right in the day, but cool at night. Now you sleep, miss, and I'll see you're not disturbed till morning.''

Betty crept away on tiptoe as if even the sound of her footfall would prove deleterious. Emma waited a while, then sat up and relighted her candle, fetched her paper and pens, and propping herself up with pillows, settled to write. Several times her eyelids drooped and she felt the beginnings of a nagging headache, but she forced herself on. She must finish the episode in time. She did not trust Mr. Palmer. He might even make an excuse to come to the house. She shuddered at the thought and wrote faster.

She put away her work at three o'clock in the morning and was drowsy when she heard the subdued bustle of her hostesses' return.

The threatened headache was thankfully averted by sleep, and Emma was able to join Lady Augusta and Lucy for nuncheon at noon the following day.

Lady Augusta beamed approvingly upon her. "Was your swoon genuine, Emma?''

"I assure you, ma'am . . . the heat . . . the lateness of the hour . . .''

"The distinguishing notice paid you by the Prince,'' put in Lady Augusta.

"It may have affected me, ma'am.''

"To be sure it did, as I told His Royal Highness over cards. I explained that your delicacy of feeling had been quite overset by the honor you felt and that your swoon was so profound I was forced to send you to your bed. He was very moved. You have a conquest there, my dear.''

Emma sent up another silent prayer that the lampoon was never connected with her.

Bardsea entered to announce, "Lady Kinver, ma'am.''

"At this hour?'' Lady Augusta made no effort to lower her voice. "It is scarce the time for a call.''

"Of course it is not,'' agreed Lady Kinver, crossing the

room to greet her hostess, "but we are friends of such long standing that I knew I could trespass upon your good nature. When I learned of Miss Waring's illness, I desired to see for myself if she was recovered. Indeed, you are in fine looks, my dear. I am so pleased that your indisposition was short-lived."

"Do you tell me that you drove all the way from Hampstead simply to ask after Miss Waring! You could have sent a footman."

Lady Kinver sank onto a pretty French armchair, smoothing the folds of her muslin gown, whose pale pink exactly matched the natural color in her cheeks. Her lace cap was small and exquisitely worked, and a matching lace fichu caressed her throat. A dainty white shawl of Norwich silk covered her shoulders, and on her narrow feet she wore pale-blue silk slippers. She was a picture of mature beauty.

"I have driven only from Upper Brook Street, ma'am."

"So! You have opened your house. Is it for the entire Season? What has prompted you to do so? You have not graced society for four years at least."

Lady Kinver smiled. "Now I hope I may have a good reason for being in town."

She looked at neither girl as she spoke, though Lady Augusta's eyes went immediately to Lucy. "You have heard then of your son's attentions to my granddaughter—"

"Grandmama!"

"Have done, child. If Lady Kinver is to be your future grandmama-in-law, she will not mind my plain speaking."

Lady Kinver looked keenly at Lady Augusta. "My son has made his declaration?"

"No," admitted Lady Augusta, "but we live in hourly expectation. He is with us often, you know, and will be escorting us everywhere."

"And what of Miss Waring? Has she such a desirable prospect?"

Lady Augusta said proudly, "I think there is little doubt that before the Season is much older my dear young charge will receive a very good offer. James Exford spends as much time with us as Kinver."

"I see. I will not congratulate you in advance, Miss Waring, but I shall hope that—that you attain your heart's wish."

Emma murmured thanks, but Lucy said, "Grandmama, I wish you would not be so forthright in your statements. Kinver and I have known each other forever and it is quite possible that he attaches himself to us because he wishes other young women to believe he is not available. I should not wonder at it if he never weds. I have heard—"

"Enough," snapped Lady Augusta. "No matter what you have heard! A man must settle sometime, is not that so, Lady Kinver? He may have lived his life a trifle recklessly—what is that in a wealthy, personable young man?—but he knows he owes his duty to his family, as do you, miss. Let me have no more of such foolish talk."

Lady Kinver left an invitation for a dinner party she was giving and departed.

Town was filling rapidly now and Emma's time was increasingly filled with engagements. The coveted invitation to Carlton House had arrived and was propped in a prominent place on the drawing-room mantelshelf where visitors could not fail to notice it. Emma attended routs, breakfast parties, promenades in the Mall and the parks, rode on a pretty pony from Lucy's stables and in Lucy's barouche, and Lord Kinver and Mr. Exford were conspicuous in their attentions. She shopped, though these expeditions were given over mainly to watching her cousin and aunt spend a great deal of money, while she contented herself with a few ribbons and other inexpensive fripperies.

One night she attended Theater Royal Drury Lane for an unforgettable performance of Mr. Kemble as Hamlet, followed by a short farce, which she enjoyed.

The Prince of Wales sat in his box opposite and acknowledged her presence with a bow and a smile. These were duly noted by all the patrons of the theater, the *ton* chuckling and speculating behind fans and hands, the occupants of the pit whistling and making gestures that Emma had no hesitation in deciding were vulgar.

The evening was enlivened by the presence at the Prince's side of Mrs. Fitzherbert, a very pretty and genteel-seeming woman, decided Emma, cringing inwardly again as she recalled the gibes in her verses. To crown the pleasure of high society, the Princess of Wales also occupied her box and the cheers of her supporters vied with the cheers of those who favored the Prince. In the pit insults were hurled along with missiles and several fights broke out, affording the sporting gentlemen in the boxes an opportunity to lay bets.

15

There was to be a brief musical entertainment at the end and in the interval the gentlemen went to procure refreshment.

Lucy said coldly, "Grandmama, the Prince insults us all when he brings that creature to the playhouse with him."

"Come now, Lucy, do not be censorious. If rumor be true, he married her. She is a good woman and believes she is in the right."

"Then all the world must believe the Princess of Wales to be living sinfully," returned Lucy, "and their daughter, the Princess Charlotte, to be a bastard."

Lady Augusta stared hard at her granddaughter. "I would prefer you not to use such a term about the infant princess."

"I believe in plain speaking, ma'am. Either the Prince is married to that woman or he is married to Princess Caroline. He cannot have two wives, not in this land, anyway. I believe in some foreign places a man may have more than one wife. I should dislike that exceedingly."

Lady Augusta rose. "I see the dear duchess is in her box. I shall visit her."

The two girls were left alone and Lucy stared ahead, apparently deep in thought. She spoke so suddenly that Emma started. "I am amazed that Lord Kinver should expect me to meet his mother. No woman of sensibility could do so."

"To refuse would surely be an insult to her."

"What of the insult to me? Such a woman as she is!"

Emma asked tentatively, "Is the viscount's mother ill? I have never heard her story."

Lucy turned cool dark eyes on her. "Have you not? Celia, Lady Kinver, was a wanton. She took lovers and flaunted them shamelessly, shocking even quite debauched members of our sex. She finally decamped with a *groom de chambre*, a servant, leaving her son when he was very young. They say it made him ill. She broke her husband's heart and he died when Kinver was fourteen, whereupon, that dreadful woman had the effrontery to return. Naturally her relatives refused to receive her, as did society, but Lord Kinver, although a stripling, had grown willful during his father's long illness and became quite violent in his insistence on his mother being given a country residence and an income. The family gave way because they feared he would fall ill again, but 'tis my belief he would not have done so. He is as strong as a workhorse."

"What a dreadful thing," breathed Emma.

"I am glad you think so," said Lucy. "It shows very proper sentiment in you."

"I mean that it was dreadful for Kinver, for his boyhood emotions. No wonder he is so—so hard."

"Oh, his mother's depraved actions did not altogether ruin him, Emma. On the contrary. He looked for a woman who would fulfill his dreams of chastity. Lady Sybilla Cole was eighteen, the same age as himself, a very model of perfection in form, face, and virtue. She died soon after their betrothal, and Kinver has lived a rackety life ever since and sported with any woman of low morals who would have him. And plenty have."

Emma was aghast. "How terrible! And he will hear no word against his mother after all the harm she did him. He is admirable."

"Can you think so? It is my opinion that he should have refused ever again to consort with his mother. He should have left it to his relatives, who knew better than he."

"Surely, there is forgiveness."

"Indeed, there is," agreed Lucy. "You do not have to be a parson's daughter to understand that. I have forgiven her—it was not difficult, for she did me no wrong—but I do not have to meet her. Indeed, we are taught to avoid sinners. And now he apparently expects me to become acquainted with her. I cannot comprehend why."

"Because he cares for you. You must make her acquaintance when—"

The conversation was cut short by the return of the gentlemen bearing wine, macaroons, and sponge biscuits. Lucy ate
with her customary composure, but Emma took only the
wine. Lucy's recital of Lord Kinver's anguish and her icy
condemnation of him had shocked her deeply. What sort of
marriage would theirs be? She supposed the viscount would
not press Lucy to meet Lady Celia Kinver. He was so bound
by the rigid divisions he had built between good and evil that
he would most likely end by blaming himself for believing
that his betrothed should demean herself. The full significance of Sir Lambert Lowther's attack was borne in upon
Emma. No wonder Kinver looked so murderous and yet so
wounded. She was glad she had gone to his assistance even
though he had not understood. She wished the viscount thought
better of her.

The weight of her misdeeds lay heavy upon her, and
Lord Kinver gave her a searching look. Her swoon had
undoubtedly been genuine and she still looked indisposed. He
wondered if her lovely face and form contained some illness.
The thought gave him a pang of pity. Young women, as he
knew only too well, could so easily sicken and die. Of
course, Miss Waring could never be considered in the same
breath as Lady Sybilla, who would have suffered torture
before she crept out to meet a secret admirer. Lucy resembled
her. Miss Venables was an upright, serious-minded woman,
the sort a man took to wife. Emma—he savored the name on
his tongue—Emma's beauty was the kind that made a man lie
awake at nights, wishing he could possess it.

She looked up and their eyes met; each was taken off guard
and they seemed to see a reflection of themselves, an inter-
mingling of souls. . . . The viscount turned away abruptly.
What fanciful lunacy! The sooner he made his marriage to
Lucy a reality, the better. He would offer for her within the
week.

A new soprano was introduced to the patrons of the theater, but she might have been a performing ape for all that
Emma heard, for she could not stop dwelling on Lucy's
revelations and see in her mind's eye a boy whose childhood
and youth had been blighted.

Lady Augusta decided that they should return straight to Hanover Square when the entertainment finished. Seated in the carriage, her ladyship glowered at Lucy. "Your wayward behavior has given me a severe attack of indigestion. I shall have to go to my bed and drink peppermint tea."

"It is far more likely to have been caused by the lobster you ate at dinner," remarked Lucy dispassionately. "You know it upsets you, yet you *will* eat it."

"I know my own stomach best, I think!"

"Yes, Grandmama."

The remainder of the drive was silent, but heavy with pregnant meaning, each lady preoccupied with her own musings. Emma felt decidedly flat. Her experience of society was not proving at all what she had expected. It seemed to be a series of unpredictable encounters and uncomfortable dilemmas. She had herself to blame for most of the latter, she admitted. She had begun sending away her stories at the age of sixteen and a half. She recalled her resolve to confess what she had done when her work was rejected. Instead, Mr. Palmer had accepted with praise and demanded more, and Emma had obliged. It had been her delicious secret. She had flowed along with the tide of her triumph and somehow her confession was never made, and as time passed, it had become impossible. If only she had not penned the lampoon on the Prince! It was that more than anything that held her in suspense. She had been unfortunate in choosing Mr. Palmer, who issued many magazines and ladies' pocketbooks and was constantly in need of writers for them and would not easily release one so popular as Delicia. There were many men— and women—in the world of publishing who would have dealt more kindly with her.

She thought about Mr. Exford, who was in love with her. He was of a conventional turn of mind. When—if they married, she wondered if he would permit her to write.

Her mind went back abruptly to the sunny garden where Viscount Kinver had kissed her. At the time she had been so overcome by unfamiliar sensations that she had behaved in a totally unladylike way. No wonder he despised her. To her horror, Emma felt a sob rise in her throat and turned it into a cough.

"You are not catching cold, are you?" snapped Lady Augusta, pleased to have someone on whom to vent her ire.

"No, ma'am, I am never ill."

"Then your swoon *was* assumed."

"No, ma'am, truly I—"

"Ah, we are home at last," sighed Lucy. "I shall be thankful to see my bed. I do not like town hours."

Her grandmother breathed hard, but did not deign to reply, and the three ladies entered the house and retired to their rooms with a minimum of contact, Emma to continue writing as soon as Betty said good night. She was to meet Mr. Rowley on the day after tomorrow and must finish the episode. Lifting a candle to her mirror, she sighed as she thought of her increasing need to hide the shadows under her eyes with *pomade à baton*.

The following day the ladies went shopping, and Lucy and Lady Augusta purchased a variety of expensive items. Emma used a little of her precious money on new gloves, two more pairs of evening pumps, and silk stockings, wishing that some of the gentlemen would take dancing lessons and tread less on their partners' toes. Her guineas were fast vanishing and it made her furious to know that if Mr. Palmer would behave in an honorable manner, she could forget minor financial worries.

In a circulating library to which Lady Augusta subscribed, Emma was delighted to see shelves filled with three-volume novels, most of which, it appeared, were written by A Lady, though some bore names.

Lady Augusta chose a book of fashion plates before joining a group of ladies seated in easy chairs partaking of coffee.

Emma would like to have borrowed an armful of books, but knew that she must not. She was tired enough without sitting up the remainder of the night reading. Lucy, whose customary reading consisted of heavy tomes filled with dissertations on gardening and land management, interspersed by books of sermons, found the bound copies of a magazine that contained articles on the rearing of young calves before joining her grandmother for coffee.

There were few men around, and as Emma was lovingly turning the pages of Mr. Defoe's *Robinson Crusoe*, recalling with a reminiscent smile the hours of pleasure it had given her, she was startled by a voice behind her.

"That is probably not to your taste, Miss Waring. May I suggest this."

Emma replaced Mr. Defoe, took the book offered by the viscount, and read its inscription. *Old English Baron*, by Clara Reeve. She had read it twice and thoroughly enjoyed it. It was a very good tale.

She resented Lord Kinver's patronizing attitude and handed it back "No, thank you, my lord."

"But I distinctly recall your telling me that you enjoy novels."

Emma remembered all too clearly what had followed that discussion. There were times when she could have sworn that Kinver's lips had left an indelible impression on hers.

With an effort she managed a simpering smile. "I vow my life is too full of pleasures at present to allow me time for reading."

"Naturally, Miss Waring, you would regard pleasure-seeking as being more rewarding than reading. And tonight is to be yet another evening of gaiety. I daresay you have not yet visited Ranelagh."

"No, sir. I look forward to it tremendously."

"Have you been to Vauxhall? No? Well, Ranelagh will suit you better, I think. It is more genteel now than Vauxhall, which is favored by merchants and the like."

"Heavens!" Emma was wide-eyed. "It would not do at all for your lordship to rub shoulders with common vendors."

Kinver looked keenly at her. There was a tone in her voice that approached sarcasm, but she was smiling at him, her brilliant blue-gray eyes sparkling and guileless.

"I did not mean that it mattered for myself, madam, but you would not—"

There was no mistaking the exact moment at which he recalled the obviously vulgar Mr. Rowley and her clandestine meeting with him. His eyes flickered and a tinge of red touched his cheeks.

Lady Augusta inadvertently came to their rescue. She had amused her companions by failing several times to attract the attention of Lucy without appearing obvious, but the foolish girl was immersed in her book. Her ladyship relinquished subtlety, rose, issued a peremptory command to her grand-daughter, and stalked across the room, Lucy bringing up the rear.

Lord Kinver heard the brisk rustle of her ladyship's taffeta skirts. He grinned. "In her gown of blue and white she reminds me of a galleon in full sail, while Miss Venables is a smaller craft attempting to keep pace."

Emma quickly put up her hand to hide a smile as Lady Augusta reached them. "Ah, Kinver, you are here."

"I am, indeed, ma'am."

"And here is Lucy."

Lord Kinver bowed. "That too is evident, ma'am."

Lady Augusta's brows drew together and she stared at him from beneath them, endeavoring to ascertain if he was mock-ing her. She decided he would not dare.

Kinver bowed to Lucy, smiled courteously, and held out his black-sleeved arm. Lucy placed her fingertips upon it and together they promenaded the large room, while Lady Augusta returned to her seat to enjoy the envy of her peers. Emma's pleasure suddenly died and she took Lucy's vacated seat and waited to leave.

She dressed for Ranelagh in an ivory slip with a white muslin overdress. Her gloves, slippers and stockings were white, her hair was pulled back in Grecian style, and around her head she wore a bandeau of twisted white-and-blue silk with a blue feather. Her necklace of pearls and a pair of pearl eardrops completed her outfit, and she went downstairs pre-pared to enjoy her visit to a place of which she had heard so much praise.

The others were ready, Lucy in a gown of pale gold with a spangled overdress and jewelry of gold filigree with yellow diamonds, and Lady Augusta magnificent in purple crepe with lilac embroidery, a yellow velvet mantle, and a purple silk turban with a tall feather. She seemed to be sprouting amethysts wherever one looked, and Emma felt like a humble garden flower dropped among gorgeous hothouse blooms.

A footman placed her burgundy velvet cloak over her shoulders and a gold velvet one over Lucy's and they drove to the steps where they were to take a boat on the Thames to Ranelagh. Lord Kinver and Mr. Exford were waiting to assist them. Both gentlemen were garbed suitably for the expedition, in buckskin breeches and dark coats, Mr. Exford's of midnight blue and Lord Kinver's a red deep enough to appear black in the half-light.

Escorted past a fountain that played into a large hexagonal pond in formal gardens, Emma drew a breath of pleasure. "This is so lovely," she exclaimed, quite forgetting to sound fashionably unimpressed.

Kinver exclaimed, "Why, Miss Waring, you amaze me! I should have thought that any young lady reared within reach of the delights of Bath and Bristol would be accustomed to public pleasure parks."

"Yes, indeed, sir, of course," she answered, mendaciously, adding a trilling laugh, "but—but nothing can be preferred to London. No one could think so."

"I could," announced Lucy. "I would say that almost anywhere is preferable to London. Anywhere out of a town, that is."

"She is such a sweet, simple girl at heart," said Lady Augusta, her teeth showing yellow and white where the false were interspersed with her own, "but she enjoys the town, do you not? Lucy, my dear, tell Lord Kinver that you enjoy town pursuits."

"I would prefer Miss Venables to be honest," said Kinver mildly. "It is no shame to prefer country to town."

"No, indeed," agreed Mr. Exford, doing his utmost to sound sincere.

He reeled slightly at the basilisk glare he received full on when Lady Augusta turned to him. She altered it speedily to a benevolent beam when she spoke to Lord Kinver. "Why, see over there, my lord, I do believe that is Miss Waring's brother. Yes, and he is with young Mr. Downham and Lord Pembridge. I wish that you gentlemen would go over and invite them to join our supper party. They are such lively young men."

Emma had already noticed Gerard and his friends, strolling among the ornamental trees, bandying words with any company that included pretty girls. She was sure, even from a distance, that he had been drinking. The viscount acknowledged Lady Augusta's command with a bow.

"Ah," said Mr. Exford, "are you going, Kinver? Then I need not—"

"Indeed, you must accompany me." Kinver's voice was soft, but implacable, and Mr. Exford blinked, glanced at her ladyship, whose face was growing redder than her rouge, and hastily moved off with his friend.

"Lord Kinver is tactful as well as possessing all the qualities desirable in a gentleman," said Lady Augusta, her voice icy with rage, "and you, Madam Lucy, are giving him no encouragement at all in his courtship."

"I never said I wished to be courted by him."

"That is neither here nor there. He is clearly coming up to the mark and you should endeavor to please him in every way. God knows, he is surely the best chance you will ever have. Nothing matters so long as he marries you. Afterward—in the due course of time—you can live your life and he his, but until you are securely wed, you should do all in your power to secure him."

"Does not Kinver like the countryside, Grandmama?"

Fearing that her aunt might explode into apoplexy, Emma intervened, "I think, Lucy, that your grandmama merely wishes you to listen to Lord Kinver's likes and dislikes and agree with him. It is what Mama and Nurse have always taught me."

Lady Augusta looked at Emma with gratitude. "That is what I and her nurses and her governess and all her teachers of deportment and dancing and many other accomplishments have forever been telling her. Gentlemen do not care to have their opinions thwarted."

"They are not all the same." Lucy looked surprisingly mutinous.

"Maybe not," hissed Lady Augusta, seeing the men approaching, "but Kinver is used always to having his way, and you cannot afford to forget it. Good evening, gentlemen" —her voice became honey-smooth—"so pleasant to meet like this in so pleasant a spot. It is all really very, er—"

"Pleasant?" supplied the viscount, and once more Emma had to turn away to conceal a smile.

The three young men were surprised at being invited to join Lady Augusta's party. Most great hostesses avoided them in public. This did not weigh upon their spirits. They were having a rollicking time and hoped it would never end, though Gerard was suffering more than occasional digs of apprehension at the financial tangle he was weaving, having begun to comprehend that his two companions were backed by substantial means. Lord Pembridge's fortune allowed him an enormous income, Anthony's doting papa would pay his debts with an indulgent grin, but his father . . . Here he always turned his musings away from unpleasant fact and played even harder at being the well-breeched man on the town.

They moderated their behavior in the presence of Lord Kinver, whom they admired greatly—Pembridge for his perfect address, Anthony for his prowess at sport, and Gerard for everything, including his excellent tailor. Glancing at his companions and down at his own satin knee breeches, large tassels on his hessians, waistcoat striped in green and pink, and pale-blue cloth coat, Gerard suddenly felt overdressed.

Kinver comprehended the way young Waring's mind was working. It amused him. The boy was playing an idiot game, but he was ingenuous and likable. He glanced at Miss Waring and saw that she was on pins, presumably fearing that her brother would annoy his unexpected hostess. Miss Waring looked more jaded and anxious each time they met, and he wished he understood her better. He had not missed her quick smile just now. She had an excellent sense of humor. His lordship was suddenly recalled to himself by realizing that Lady Augusta had said something to him and was awaiting a reply. He begged her ladyship's pardon and asked her to repeat her question.

"God save us if you are not lost in a daydream," exclaimed Lady Augusta. "In my youth we always paid strict attention to our elders and did not permit our thoughts to go a-wandering."

Lucy said dispassionately, "Wheeler told me that when you was in love with Grandpapa, you wove dreams all day and were locked in your own world."

Lady Augusta's eyes flashed fire and Emma said hastily, "My aunt was asking if you wished to walk and then eat, or eat and then walk, my lord."

"I am prepared to follow whatever you desire, ma'am," the viscount said.

"Then we shall eat!"

They made their way into the Rotunda, where an orchestra played. Gerard winced. "Do we have to listen to that caterwauling all night? If there's one thing I don't care for above another, it's wailing violins."

Lady Augusta's voice was frosted. "The orchestra is one of the particular attractions of Ranelagh, Mr. Waring, and I hope that the musicians do not tire all night."

Gerard subsided, his face pink, and Emma heard him mutter to his friends, "We should have gone to Vauxhall. I said we should have. One can have sport there concealed among the shrubs and walks."

Emma was fascinated by the size and decor of the amphitheater. Two tiers of boxes ran around the building, the music came from a tiered stage, and a great centerpiece, supported by pillars and classical statues, held a roaring fire, which was welcome on a spring evening in so vast a place. Ladies and gentlemen strolled around the circumference, greeting friends, cutting enemies, gossiping, laughing, and staring at the parties in the boxes, where food was being served. In one, people were mincing chickens while a lady cooked them at the table. A variety of odors drifted to her nostrils. Her mind was lulled by the sweetness of the music, and the talk and laughter combined and winged their way to the great dome above until she felt she was floating in pleasure, her troubles for the moment forgotten.

Lord Kinver found he was unable to prevent himself from watching the expressions of delight chase across Emma's face.

16

Lucy touched Lord Kinver's arm. "Grandmama's booth is here, sir. She wishes you to escort me to a seat."

The viscount looked down at his intended bride. Her perfect complexion held its usual pallor, her glossy hair was expertly dressed, her figure good, her dark eyes calm. A man could not ask for a more serene and refined lady for his wife. He escorted her to a seat in the booth, followed by Exford and Miss Waring. They were a little crushed by the extra numbers, and his lordship found himself pressed inexorably between Miss Venables and Miss Waring. There could be few men who would not ache to slip an arm around the slender waist of so lovely a creature as Miss Waring, or desire to take her lips with his or to feel her soft curves touching his body. He felt hot, and angry with himself.

Waiters brought food, but Lord Kinver ate without pleasure, talked with effort, and drank more than he normally would in the presence of ladies. He could not fail to notice when Emma's body suddenly tautened beside him. Her face was stricken with apprehension, and when Kinver followed the direction of her eyes, he saw Mr. Rowley, standing so close that his coat almost touched their table.

Lady Augusta glared at the intruder. "You stare, sir! I do not believe we know you."

Mr. Rowley's voice was smooth. "I am acquainted with Miss Waring. She and I are friends."

Lady Augusta threw an astonished look at Emma. "How can that be? Did you know this person before you arrived in London?"

Emma shook her head in mute anguish.

"You cannot have met him since. You have been well chaperoned and I would know."

Emma said, a quaver in her tone, "I encountered Mr. Rowley in—in the library, Aunt Augusta. He was kind enough to recommend a book. It was a novel by Miss Clara Reeve."

Kinver was astonished. Without a moment's hesitation Miss Waring had put Mr. Rowley in his role. Her face was flushed and she appeared close to tears. The viscount was filled with frustrated rage. She could probably produce tears whenever she wished; very likely she could swoon at will also. She was despicable.

Emma gulped for air in the heated atmosphere of the booth and Mr. Rowley said, "You look warm, Miss Waring. If I was you, I would walk a little. It's cooler beneath the dome. I'll be pleased to escort you."

Emma thought his tone menacing. She rose, which caused others to rise so that she could edge her way out. Her progress, her fingers on the arm of Mr. Rowley, was watched by her companions. Lucy looked amazed, Lady Augusta angry, and Mr. Exford thoughtful. His dear girl could not realize what an undesirable this Mr. Rowley was.

"Who the devil is he?" demanded Lady Augusta of them all.

Lord Kinver found himself coming to Emma's rescue. "It is as she says, your ladyship. I was present when they met. I am sure that your charge is too innocent . . . too unaccustomed to society to know how to depress the pretensions of such a mushroom."

Lady Augusta was appeased. "Yes, it must be so. I shall have a talk with her. That is the trouble when a girl is reared in a country rectory."

Gerard, who knew his sister to be far too clever to be taken in by the likes of Rowley, had been staring after her in astonishment.

"I shall go after her and bring her back," he declared, springing to his feet and upsetting a glass of wine.

"Now see what you have done," Lady Augusta shrieked. The evening was proving nightmarish. "Sit down, sir. Will you make your sister an object of curiosity by creating a disturbance? Mr. Exford, pray call a waiter and ask for a fresh cloth."

Gerard subsided, muttering dire threats regarding Mr. Rowley.

"Man's a commoner," pointed out Lord Pembridge. "Anyone can see it. Not your sister, Waring. Sweet girl. Should be saved from him."

"Be silent, Pembridge!" His lordship obeyed Lady Augusta's increasingly hysterical voice of command.

Emma knew that she was exposing herself to censure as she walked beside Mr. Rowley. He was a clergyman, his garments quiet, his manners not gross. Far from it. They were too polished. He behaved like a man who had needed to spend many hours in learning the lessons of polite society and was overcareful lest he slide back into whatever mire he had sprung from.

"How could you accost me in this way?" she asked in low, angry tones.

"Accost you, Miss Waring? I did no such thing. I invited you. You could have refused."

"Then what would you have done?"

"Ah, that's something we shall never know. The truth is, I was glad to see you tonight because Mr. Palmer said I was to tell you that he desires your presence in his shop at your earliest opportunity. Now I need not wait until tomorrow and you can make your arrangements to come to the shop instead of meeting me in Holles Street."

"I cannot. It is too difficult."

"Well, you're the best judge, Miss Waring, but Mr. Palmer has a business matter he wants to get cleared as soon as he can, and needs your help."

"I know nothing of business!"

"You just come along and he'll explain. Shall I say you'll be there?"

"No! Yes! I do not know! I must try, I suppose."

"Good evening, Miss Waring."

Mr. Rowley halted and Emma saw that Sir Lambert Lowther was blocking their way, bowing and smiling. She almost closed her eyes in utter dejection as she responded to a greeting from yet another man she detested. Both men looked interestedly at each other and Emma was forced to introduce them. They greeted each other coolly. The baronet was used to calculating the reactions of women and he knew that Miss

Waring was anxious and afraid. The situation intrigued him. He took a place on the other side of her and the two men escorted her back to Lady Augusta's box, where Sir Lambert was received with cold politeness.

Emma's pleasure was spoiled once more and she lay awake that night, reflecting on how her first deception had built into a morass that threatened to engulf her.

She was up early, and Betty, her excitement at the prospect of a further amorous adventure showing in her shining eyes, smuggled her out through the small door and obtained a hackney coach for the ride to Paternoster Row.

The press was being prepared and the air was redolent with the smell of ink. Today it afforded Emma no pleasure.

Mr. Palmer greeted her with huge affability. "Such good news, Miss Waring."

Emma tried to conceal her dislike. "Surely nothing is so urgent about my affairs that you could not have sent a message."

"Now, that's where you're wrong, my dear." Emma resented the familiar term, but held her tongue. She could not afford to antagonize this man. "Your writings have taken the attention of a rich person who desires to become your patron."

"What? It is not possible."

"I do assure you, ma'am." Mr. Palmer had noted Emma's annoyance of his familiar approach and moderated it. He needed her cooperation. "I have had a visit from someone— the person prefers to remain anonymous at present—who would like to see your stories in two- or three-volume works. This person has developed a great admiration for you. A wonderful chance for you, Miss Waring. You'll be famous."

"Good God, sir! That is the last thing I want."

Mr. Palmer's eyes narrowed. The bird would need more coaxing toward plucking than he had realized. "My . . . Ma'am . . . if you wish, you may publish under your pseudonym, or simply use 'By a Lady.' It is done often."

"The whole thing is out of the question. I made it clear that I do not intend to continue our association once I have completed my present work. It is making life impossible for me."

"You needn't see me at all. The books are to be published by another man," said Mr. Palmer in his most ingratiating tones, not feeling it necessary to mention that the rich patron's representative had flatly refused to deal solely with him. He had declined to reveal the writer's identity unless he was given shares in the venture, and some had been reluctantly granted.

"How can I make you understand, Mr. Palmer? Of course I am gratified that someone would like to become my patron. It is flattering, but"—she took a deep breath—"my future husband would not care for his wife to incur publicity."

Mr. Palmer had not taken his eyes from her face. "Supposing," he said softly, "just supposing I gave you my word of honor as a gentleman that no news of your other activity—as a poet one might say—would ever leak out . . . Would you oblige me—and of course, your hopeful patron—if I promised?"

Emma's temper flared. "I gave you no license to publish those verses. You had no right, no right at all, and now you use them to threaten me. You are no gentleman!"

Mr. Palmer stood up so abruptly that his chair pushed over a pile of dusty manuscripts that had been balanced on the floor. "No gentleman, eh? You think you can insult me."

"Impossible, sir. You would appear to be beyond insult," drawled a voice from the door, whose opening had been drowned by the clatter of the printing press.

Emma and Mr. Palmer turned together, and she almost shrank back in her chair when she saw who was there.

Lord Kinver strolled to the desk, kicking the door shut behind him. He brushed a speck of dust from his caped coat before turning to Emma. "I think you are in need of assistance, ma'am."

Emma expected Mr. Palmer to shout for someone to throw the viscount out. He might be a gentleman of high degree, but he had no right to burst in on a man's private affairs. Mr. Palmer did no such thing.

"Now, sir, there's no need to get into a taking. Miss Waring and me were just having a little talk about—"

Kinver ignored him. "Miss Waring, is this man threatening you?"

"Yes, no, please, my lord, you cannot help. Pray do not anger him."

Lord Kinver looked a moment longer into Emma's troubled

face, fighting down an intense longing to fold her in his arms and soothe her worries away.

Mr. Palmer cleared his throat nervously. "My lord, I had no wish to upset Miss Waring. You see, it's this way . . ." He paused, licking his lips.

"Yes?" encouraged the viscount, his eyes flinty.

Mr. Palmer said hurriedly, "You are acting on behalf of someone who admires Delicia so much that they want to become her patron. Miss Waring says she don't want a patron. She wants to stop writing. Says her future husband won't like it—"

"Hold hard! Are you saying that Miss Waring is Delicia?"

"*You* are acting on behalf of someone who wishes to become my patron?" aked Emma.

Her voice was lost as Mr. Palmer said with induced heartiness, "That she is, sir. It's not a bit of use denying it, ma'am."

"I was not going to," said Emma, weary and resigned.

Again the viscount's impulse to console her almost got the better of him. Emma! The name lingered sweetly in his mouth. She was beautiful; she shared his sense of humor, his appreciation of the ridiculous; and now he knew her to be clever too. His grandmother's decision to offer her patronage to Delicia had led to his reading several of her stories. They were vigorous and passionate with acutely observed characters. She used Gothic backgrounds and overdramatized situations to suit a market that clamored for them, but he was soon convinced that Lady Kinver was right in her belief that the unknown writer could make a name with more profound, yet still popular books. His grandmother was also of the opinion that Delicia's sparkling dialogue was well-suited to the stage, where it was possible to earn a fortune from writing, and should the author prove to be in need of money, she was prepared to act as patron there too. With his newly recognized admiration for Miss Waring, Kinver was in no doubt that even the unspeakable Mr. Rowley could be explained.

He needed all his self-control to speak with any semblance of normality. "Emma—I beg your pardon, Miss Waring, you have succeeded in surprising me. *You* are Delicia!" He felt he sounded inane, but it was peculiarly difficult to marshal his wits.

"You thought me a brainless female, I collect."

"You permitted me—no, you encouraged me, to think so."

She stared at him without an answer.

"How long have you been writing your stories?"

"For almost two years, sir."

"But you are still young. You must have been in the schoolroom."

"I was never in a schoolroom, my lord, except one conducted by my father for his pupils. I learned some lessons . . . a few, just a few." She was being sorely tried as she clung doggedly to the tatters of the admonitions drilled into her by Mama and Nurse. But the viscount knew of Mr. Waring's erudition and was in no doubt that Emma's quick mind had learned more than "just a few" lessons. Her imagination was prodigious. He was aware also of the kind of instruction that would have been drilled into her by other females, and for the first time he began to comprehend her inconsistencies.

"I have read some of Delicia's tales."

"You, sir! But you are a man!"

"That has never been open to doubt, ma'am, but even a man may read."

Emma frowned at him, and he thought how enchanting she looked when she was irate. "I thought my stories were read only by ladies."

Mr. Palmer felt it was time he took a turn. "Indeed, no, Miss Waring. I have letters from gentlemen praising you."

He had redirected attention to himself, and Lord Kinver gave him a glance that closed his mouth.

"Have you been working for this person ever since you reached London?"

Emma nodded. The situation had gone beyond her.

"No wonder you have been looking fatigued."

"I am surprised you noticed!"

The viscount could never say the words that came pouring into his mind, where revelations of a startling nature were bursting. *Of course I have noticed. There is nothing about you which I do not see. My God, what a fool I am. I have been searching for most of my life for a woman of perceptive mind, a warm and loving creature. And she has been under* my gaze—and lovely too—and ready for courting, and I've ruined everything by my dull-witted, idiotic, *lunatic* refusal to recognize truths that have been hammering at me. This rogue, Palmer, mentioned a future husband. Is there an understanding between Emma and James? And I am committed to Lucy.

The viscount kept his face and expression bland with difficulty. "I also heard something about poetry."

"It is nothing, sir, I do assure you," began Mr. Palmer.

"That—that *damnable* lampoon!" Emma was revolted by all the deceit. It was a relief to tell someone, even though it would further lower her in his view, and she was stupid enough to care about that. "The one on the Prince of Wales that everyone seems to find so hilariously funny—except possibly His Royal Highness, and lately myself—I wrote it. I sent it to this—this *man* for a private jest, and he saw fit to give it into the grasp of a nasty little cleric. You have met him, the dreadful Mr. Rowley, and between them they put it on the streets in ballad form. I have been forced to do more work so that my awful secret will be kept and Mr. Palmer will not even pay me the monies he has owed me for an age. If I am discovered, I shall be ruined and"—her self-control broke and she fought to control angry tears—"and my sister Sophia will never have a Season and my family will be disgraced and my dear parents wounded . . ."

She sniffed and searched for a handkerchief in her reticule. She found a large one being tucked into her hand by the viscount, who had to exert all his will not to stem her tears with kisses.

Mr. Palmer said in an unsteady voice, "I never would hurt Miss Waring. Why, I look upon her as—as fondly as I would a daughter."

"The Lord help your daughters," replied Kinver. "I would like some clarity on the subject of the lampoon. Miss Waring did not give her permission for it to be made public?" Mr. Palmer shook his head. He was sweating a little. "And yet you saw fit to do so. Has the secrecy of its authorship anything to do with the way you were bullying this lady?"

"Not bullying, sir, I swear. I was a bit flustered. I've already signed an agreement for her future work, as your lordship knows."

"But everyone, save you, of course, believed that you had the author's full consent. The others are people of honor who would not have arranged anything against a lady's wishes."

"Nevertheless, my lord, the matter is arranged. All legal and right and tight. It cannot be got out of."

The viscount said in a voice so laced with contempt that it penetrated even the rogue publisher's skin. "The agreement must be canceled if Miss Waring wishes. You may even be compensated for loss of business."

"But, Lord Kinver, I cannot pay Mr. Palmer, and neither can my family. Papa has had many expenses: Gerard, my Season . . ."

"The money can quite easily be found, Miss Waring," said the viscount gently.

"If you mean that you . . . Sir, I could not accept money from you."

"Nor would I take it," Mr. Palmer assured them. His voice was affable as he saw a way to revenge himself for slights offered him by the haughty viscount. He had a foot in a larger and richer publishing house, and he did not mean to withdraw. No embarrassing questions could be raised because that would bring publicity, something that terrified this little ladybird. And judging by the way his fine lordship was eyeing her, he would not want her to be hurt. Mr. Palmer could have rubbed his hands at the unexpected way the interview was going.

17

The viscount waited for Emma to regain command over her emotions.

"You mentioned money, Miss Waring. Does this—does Palmer owe you money?"

"Yes, sir, and he refuses to give it to me."

"Nay, ma'am, I did not refuse, not exactly refuse. The money is here in a drawer. I got it from the bank especially for you."

Neither Emma nor Lord Kinver believed him, though the gold was real enough. Kinver watched as Mr. Palmer quickly counted out her guineas and put them into a small leather pouch. The viscount took it, tipped the money on the table, and counted with greater care.

"I protest, my lord! If you think I mean to cheat Miss Waring, you do me wrong."

The viscount looked briefly at the bookseller, but it was a look that made him bite his tongue. So fine, these people thought they were. If he could get revenge on them for the slights they put upon him, he would. He breathed hard as Kinver finished.

"It is all there, Miss Waring."

"You do me injustice to doubt it."

Kinver and Emma took no notice of Mr. Palmer's protest. Emma looked at the pouch, but did not touch it. The viscount dropped it in her lap. "It is yours by right. You have earned it and I daresay much more money has been taken than you will ever see."

A snort of indignation broke from Palmer as Emma put the pouch into her reticule. Circumstances had made the gold seem tainted, but it *was* hers. She would find a way to give it to Lady Augusta, who she was sure was spending more than the allotted money on her. She would need to say it had come from Papa and then invent the manner of its arrival and the reason why he had not sent it directly. More deception. She felt desolate at the idea.

Lord Kinver had doubts about the legality of a contract signed by strangers on behalf of a minor, but any attempt to discredit Palmer might goad him into publicizing the writer of the lampoon. He held out his hand to Emma, who took it and rose and was escorted to the street. She had no argument this time when Lord Kinver offered the use of his carriage. Betty sat opposite. With the maid's eyes and ears alert, Kinver and Emma kept to desultory remarks of a commonplace nature, disappointing Betty, who had hoped for something more loverlike.

The viscount's mind was in turmoil. He had desired Emma since their first meeting, and he still ached to possess her exquisite body, but now he wanted to understand more of her thoughts, her aspirations, her interests, her mind. It was fortunate that he was not facing her and could turn toward the scenes outside the window, for he felt sure his eyes must reveal his intense interest. Emma had deliberately allowed him to think her a society butterfly, but he could not blame her for that. It was part of her upbringing and her retreat into flirtation had been a defense against him, just as his cynical approach was his defense against further hurt. He cursed himself for a coward. By running from emotion he had lost a girl he might have loved with all the ardor of his impassioned nature. Her dependence on him, her trust in his judgment today had invoked responses deeper than he knew he possessed.

Emma sat in her corner, her mind also churning. He was wonderful! He had come to her rescue without hesitation, and so decisively. Later she must ask him the name of her proposed patron. Later, when she had herself more under control. She ventured a peep at the viscount and saw that he had risked looking at her, betraying a yearning that almost made her gasp. He desired her. It was in his eyes and she longed to move to him and be taken into his arms and kissed and caressed. Her breathing quickened and his eyes fell to the revealing rise and fall of her breast. The air seemed to echo with unspoken dreams while Betty, planted in the middle of her seat, watched unwaveringly.

"Will you be in Hyde Park later?" asked Kinver abruptly.

"I daresay we shall, my lord."

"Then I shall look forward to our meeting."

Betty's eyes grew rounder. Mr. Exford would probably be there too. By all accounts, Miss Emma was as good as promised to him, and Lord Kinver had been Miss Venables' escort since the Season had begun. The behavior of the gentry surprised her. Back home in her village if a man poached another's preserves, he would soon get a bloody nose and a chuck into the duck pond, if not worse. She wondered if Mr. Exford and Lord Kinver would fight a duel over Miss Emma. How exciting that would be.

The viscount's carriage was halted just before Hanover Square, and Betty shepherded her mistress to her room. Emma longed to be able to pause and think about her next moves as she locked her money in her jewel box. Guilty gold! She was lapsing into melodrama.

She composed herself enough to reach the morning parlor for nuncheon just before Lady Augusta and Lucy and afterward they went for fittings for the girls' presentation gowns. Emma stared at her reflection, feeling faintly ridiculous in white muslin draped over the unfashionable obligatory hoops.

The day was fine and for their afternoon perambulation the ladies dressed in pretty clothes and light shoes. Emma wore a gown of pale yellow and a straw bonnet with yellow daisies, and draped her Norwich silk shawl over her shoulders. Lucy's cashmere shawl with red and black designs toned with the Greek motif around the hem of her pink muslin gown. Lady Augusta was splendid in green brocade that opened at the front to reveal a red-flowered petticoat; she wore a red velvet mantle and a hat that would keep off the sun. A footman was waiting in the hall with two pretty parasols for the young ladies.

Lady Augusta remarked the brilliance of Emma's eyes. "Are you hoping to see Mr. Exford?"

"Why, yes, I am sure he will be there, ma'am."

Her ladyship congratulated herself. Emma was going to marry Mr. Exford and her chaperone would receive all the commendation from the Warings that such a good match deserved. But irritation was scratching at her as day succeeded day and Kinver did not make his offer for Lucy. It might be politic to give him a tiny jolt. Lucy should not always be where he thought to find her. She ordered the coachman to drive to the Mall.

"But, Aunt," Emma was surprised into protesting, "I thought we would go to the park. I made sure you said—"

"What I did or did not say is neither here nor there, miss. I am set upon the Mall. Have you seen it? No, you have not! Surely you wish to taste the delights of a new setting?"

Lucy accepted the change of direction without a single sign and Lady Augusta could have slapped her. Lucy would never succeed in bringing Kinver to the mark if she remained so placid. She must act for her. It was time to encourage him to make a firm move. When he did so—and no gentleman of honor could fail after making a lady so conspicuous—Mr. Exford would be affected by the general rejoicing and propose matrimony to Emma. Lady Augusta gave a small sigh at such promised contentment and thanked God that her daughter had not been blessed with more offspring. How happily she would settle into the company of men and women of her own age and spend her days gossiping and her evenings playing cards—and gossiping.

Emma discovered that walking in the Mall was similar to walking in Hyde Park. The fashionable throng greeted one another, chattered and twittered like a gathering of brilliantly plumaged birds, and ripped apart reputations with less consideration than they ripped outworn lace from a gown.

There was one significant difference: Lord Kinver and Mr. Exford were not present. Lady Augusta, having been so positive about the change of plan, now simulated satisfaction.

This became momentarily genuine when they saw a friend from her girlhood who, she whispered to Lucy and Emma, had once outshone all her contemporaries in beauty and form. Now her face was pitted by the ravages of overmuch painting and her figure had run to corpulence, a great deal of which was revealed by her modern attire.

"You see," muttered Lady Augusta through her fixed grin. "Did I not tell you how some ladies who should know better deck themselves like young belles?" She turned her grin to a welcoming smile as she exchanged compliments.

Lady Kinver was strolling also, accompanied by two gentlemen of her own generation who vied with each other in their attentions. They fell into step beside Lady Augusta, who wandered with them a small way ahead and did not see that the young ladies were joined by Sir Lambert Lowther. He had been to Hyde Park and, not finding Lucy present, had hastened to the Mall and was now paying her fulsome attention. Emma said nothing. Sir Lambert was odious and she was amazed by Lucy's ready acceptance of his escort. Her unvarying behavior must stem from having been reared from birth in an aristocratic manner. She would make a splendid viscountess. Emma drew a painful breath at the idea. Since Lord Kinver had rescued her from Mr. Palmer, he had dwelled in her mind with even greater tenacity. His sympathy and practical help had made a profound impression.

When she heard his voice, she imagined for a moment that she had conjured him out of her imagination, but he was real enough. And so was Mr. Exford, who joined her on her other side.

"We missed you in the park," said Kinver. "We could not endure such disappointment, so came as fast as we could to the Mall." His eyes were fixed on Sir Lambert with an expression that made Emma shiver.

"Thank heavens we did," exclaimed Exford in mock-heroic tones, "else we must needs have waited until an evening engagement to find you."

Emma laughed her deep, beautiful laugh and Lady Augusta stopped in her tracks and turned around. When she saw Lucy giving Sir Lambert her full attention, while Emma was engaging the notice of both Mr. Exford *and* Lord Kinver, she would have ground her teeth had she not been afraid that the false ones might come loose.

She spoke with spurious animation. "Why, Lady Kinver, here are your grandson and Exford. So you found us. We decided to try a change of scene."

"So I discovered," said Sir Lambert, "and I flatter myself that I was first to arrive here, is not that so, Miss Venables?"

Lucy inclined her head graciously. "Grandmama, Sir Lambert has been telling me such an interesting thing. It appears that during a lambing season one of his ewes gave birth to three live lambs and his shepherd was able to deceive another sheep to give suckle.''

"How—how diverting . . ." breathed Lady Augusta. "Now, my dear Lucy, you must come and pay your respects to Lady Kinver. I know she is longing to talk to you."

Lady Kinver acknowledged Lucy's advance with a smile, while her eyes flickered to Emma. She was giving her grandson a look that interested her. If the girl was not in love with Kinver, she would eat her newest hat. The viscount followed Lucy to his grandmother, whose hand and soft cheek he kissed. Mr. Exford began to talk to Emma, and Lady Augusta firmly engaged Sir Lambert in conversation.

Sir Lambert was fully aware of her dislike and that of the overproud Miss Waring. Kinver's hostility he had endured for years, ever since the day he had spoken disparagingly of Celia, Lady Kinver, his mother, and had been trounced in a humiliating duel. Sir Lambert's increasing poverty made him hate the wealthy viscount more. Now, thanks to Mr. Rowley, he could take revenge for all the slights of years.

He had followed Mr. Rowley from Ranelagh and into an ale house nearby, where he had greeted him for the second time that night as if by coincidence. Over many glasses of gin he had brought the cleric to the point where it had been easy to extract the information that Miss Emma Waring had actually penned the lampoon that it was said had enraged the Prince. A word dropped at the right time would disgrace Miss Waring. His Royal Highness himself had connected Miss Waring's bloodline with that of the viscount, and she was a guest in the London home of Miss Venables, so she and Lady Augusta would be included in the general scandal. Sir Lambert was sure he understood Lucy Venables. He knew she disliked town pursuits and she appeared to welcome his company and enjoy his conversation, which he was careful to keep within her limited enthusiasms. He intended to be on hand when the family fell into disrepute, and he would engage her affections by showing her a way to escape disapprobation. Once married to her, he would enjoy her large fortune.

He had kept secret the letter he had received a week ago because it was essential that no one should learn of his sudden overwhelming need for a rich bride. He would have preferred to live unhampered and receive his all owance from

Sir George's estate, which he was in line to inherit, at which time his creditors knew that his bills could be honored.

Now his damned cousin-by-marriage, who had so happily (in Sir Lambert's opinion) previously dropped all her offspring from a reluctant womb a few weeks after conception, had actually carried a child to eight months and her accoucheur assured her and her ecstatic husband that the baby was healthy and certain to be born alive. The estate was not entailed and would go to the child. And, Sir George had written, now that dear Lady Croft had carried one child, she might even bear others. She had begun strangely late in life to prove fruitful, but her physician assured them she could continue.

Sir Lambert broke into a cold sweat at the thought of his creditors gaining only a hint of the approaching birth. He would be blocked at both ends. Finished! Ruined! He might yet see the inside of a debtors' jail. Sir George had never cared for him and despised his mode of life. He would be disgusted and horrified at the total of his debts and certainly refuse to be associated with them, especially now that he looked forward to filling his empty nursery.

Sir Lambert, accustomed to dissimulation, was perfectly well able to conduct a conversation with Lady Augusta while the larger part of his devious mind engaged itself with plans for the downfall of the people he strolled with on a fine spring afternoon in the Mall. They had dropped a little behind the others. Mr. Exford was with Miss Waring, whom it was said he would marry. He too would be implicated. Sir Lambert felt the justice of this. Exford also had dueled with him and beaten him, and that only over a common wench ripe and ready for deflowering. And there was Lady Kinver, who remained serenely impervious to censure and visited her erring daughter-in-law, yet treated him as if he were dirt beneath her dainty feet; and Kinver, whom he hated above any. By God he would see them all disgraced and his triumph would be sweet.

Sir Lambert walked contentedly with Lady Augusta until the brilliant company in the Mall dispersed to make ready for their next meeting, which would be tonight at Viscount Kinver's ball in Grosvenor Square at which the Prince of Wales was expected. Tonight, Sir Lambert vowed, would be the perfect opportunity for which he hungered.

Emma chose one of her prettiest evening gowns for the ball: a cerulean blue chemise of the very latest mode, trimmed with delicate rose-pink frills around her throat. Rose-pink bands of satin ribbon were entwined in her hair by Wheeler, who dressed it in the Greek coiffure that so became her. A slender gold chain held a sapphire pendant around her neck and matching eardrops fell from her dainty ears. Her white silk stockings and shoes were new, as were her white kid gloves. Betty stared entranced. Miss Waring looked so beautiful! Surely one of her admirers would soon offer for her.

The ladies traveled to Grosvenor Square in Lucy's imposing town carriage. Lady Augusta for once was quietly garbed, wearing an ocher-yellow overdress opened at the waist to reveal a cinnamon-colored gown. She had contented herself with plain amber adornments and her wig was an unremarkable brown, though she had been unable to resist trimming it with several large emerald-green feathers that touched the carriage roof at every jolt.

Lucy was in a white gown with gold trimmings. The ribbons threaded through her glossy dark hair were gold and so was her jewelry. She looks like a bride, thought Emma. She glanced at her cousin several times on the short journey, but Lucy stared from the window into the darkening streets, as pale and composed as always. Emma wondered if Lady Augusta was harboring secrets. She fancied she detected an air of simmering anticipation, and when her aunt caught her eye, she smiled expansively, which added to Emma's suspicion.

Kinver's mansion was illuminated like a beacon and the crowd of sightseers was raucous as the carriages pulled up one by one at the canopied and carpeted steps leading to the open double doors. Emma was assisted down by Lucy's groom, smart in his livery, apparently impervious to the vulgar horde that called advice to him and made pertinent comments on the size of his calves.

The large, square hall with a marble mosaic floor was bisected by a line of chattering, laughing men and women. Emma advanced with the others up the wide stairway. She was received first by Lady Anne Harvey and then by the viscount. His garb was sober; black velvet coat and satin knee breeches, white stockings and black shoes. His dark hair was brushed into slight disorder, as fashion decreed. The customary gold watch chain lay across his white waistcoat, but his ring was of thick gold and carried a dark stone stamped with his family crest. Did he always wear it when he was host, or was there some deeper significance, such as a contemplated proposal of marriage? Emma made her curtsy with downcast eyes, but as she rose, she looked straight into his and read an expression that made her heart race.

"I must speak with you later, Emma," he murmured.

Her happiness at his using her given name was ridiculously out of proportion. He had used it once before—in Mr. Palmer's shop. It made her feel pleasantly close to him. He was able to say nothing more as Lady Augusta bore down on him with Lucy. Emma stopped to wait and looked back as Kinver raised Lucy from her curtsy. He was smiling at her and Emma felt a stab of jealousy that frightened her. Lady Augusta beamed upon the pair and Emma's spirit grew heavy with the weight of social pressure that would ensure that Kinver and Lucy came together in an irreproachable match.

It took effort to simulate the animation expected of a young lady at her first society ball. Mr. Exford arrived soon after and solicited her company for a number of dances. Enough to prove to the indefatigable watchers that he favored Miss Waring, yet not sufficient to make a vulgar show.

Emma danced a minuet with him and took her place in a country dance, followed by a gavotte. She usually enjoyed the physical expression of rhythm, but tonight everything was an effort.

18

Emma and Mr. Exford elected to miss the next country dance and, with Lady Augusta's beaming approval, strolled in other rooms thrown open for the pleasure of the guests.

Emma tried her best to converse, but eventually her companion asked, "Is something troubling you? You seem distracted and have just sighed for the third time."

She looked up into his face and the gentle sympathy in his eyes smote her conscience. "I do beg your pardon! Do I truly keep sighing?"

"Are you worried about your brother? Young men often behave in a wild manner. You must not take it to heart. Tonight he is acting with decorum. No doubt he will soon return to Oxford and make his family proud of him."

Emma used the offered excuse. In truth she had paid little heed to Gerard beyond feeling thankful that he was not rioting in Kinver's house, but now she realized that a part of her mind had registered the fact that he looked harassed. She wondered if another disaster was about to befall the family. She realized that Mr. Exford had taken her hand. Her heart thudded and she did not remove it. It was the duty of a young lady to marry to oblige her family! Mr. Exford was rich, handsome, and eminently suitable—and available.

He glanced around. No one else was present in the room and he ventured an arm about Miss Waring's slender waist. She did not stop him and he bent his head and softly kissed her scented cheek. He was ecstatic. He thought of the day when he could hold her in his arms and she would be entirely his. He went hot, a flush suffused his face, and his mouth became dry. He vowed to speak to Lady Augusta tonight. To

have Emma Waring for his wife was the most important
prospect of his life. In fact, he would speak now. Not with an
outright declaration. That would not be proper, and Mr.
Exford's behavior was always socially impeccable, but a few
words to discover the lie of the land.

He still held her hand and was about to speak when someone entered. He dropped Emma's hand and looked around in
irritation that became more extreme when he saw that the
interruption came from Sir Lambert.

The baronet was seething with disappointment so intense
that he needed solitude to compose himself. His quick eyes
saw Exford drop Emma's hand, and had he not been so
enraged, he would have found it amusing. He had got into the
ball by engineering himself a place at dinner in a party whose
host and hostess had received an open invitation, and he had
not missed the flicker of contempt in Lord Kinver's eyes. Sir
Lambert had disregarded the slight, hugging to himself the
thought that the final triumph would be his. Then the news
had got around that the Prince of Wales was indisposed and
could not attend. People were having fun speculating if Prinny
had discovered a woman who welcomed his embraces and
had remained secluded with her. In spite of his continuing
devotion to Mrs. Fitzherbert, he was not one to allow an
opportunity to slip. The Prince had rendered his scheme void,
but nothing was going to prevent his eventual exposure of
Miss Waring as the authoress of the degrading verses. He had
looked forward keenly to seeing Kinver and his whole tribe
receive a royal snub in their family home, and it would have
relieved his feelings to say something unpleasant to this
woman who was to be the instrument of his revenge, but that
would be unwise. Nothing must detract from the first shock
of his revelation. Besides, he recalled Exford's fighting
expertise. He wondered if a marriage proposal had yet been
made and accepted. He hoped so.

Mr. Exford returned Sir Lambert's bow with a curt nod
before he led Emma out of the room, as if, thought Sir
Lambert, she was too pure to be contaminated by the likes of
him. Well, James Exford—and all society—would learn different. His invitation to Carlton House lay at home on his
mantelshelf, and at the memory his anger died and a smile
spread across his narrow, painted face. It would be far better

to reveal his secret in Prinny's own residence. He would have the intense satisfaction of watching the entire bunch of them ejected. Sir Lambert's equilibrium was restored.

Lady Augusta had given permission for Mr. Exford to lead Lucy into a country dance and it was perfectly seemly for Emma's cousin, Kinver, to stroll with her a little. The viscount had asked approval to request Lucy's hand in marriage and he would do so this evening. They could announce it, mused her ladyship, just before the supper interval, which would offer a good opportunity for the news to be discussed and for congratulations to be given. It would make everything absolutely certain at last. Her granddaughter's lack of enthusiasm for anything that did not include country matters was puzzling. There must be some earthy farming landowner in their ancestry. Well, it mattered nothing. Once Lucy had produced an heir, she and her husband could live together or apart as it suited them. Lady Augusta had a twinge of regret when she considered her own happy marriage, but consoled herself by reflecting that Lucy was not at all like her. The girl seemed to have been born without the ability to care much for people, preferring the company of her animals. If Lucy had her way, every home she owned would be infested by dogs, cats, and God knew what other pet creatures.

Lord Kinver looked down at the satin-banded head of Emma as he escorted her from the ballroom, and he had to restrain an impulse to touch the smooth red-gold hair or curl a finger into some of the tendrils that had escaped during the leaps of the country dance. Feeling his eyes upon her, she looked up and quickly averted her gaze, keeping her head turned from him so that he could not be certain if she blushed. He led her through the large public rooms where folk chattered and flirted, past the card rooms, and finally into his library. Emma enjoyed the scent of leather, the sight of books resting beside chairs, the realization that the volumes were enjoyed and not simply for show. A large desk held scattered papers.

"How Papa would love this," she exclaimed. "He has a book room, of course, but it is small compared with yours. He must use it to instruct his pupils. No other room is available."

A branch of candles had been lit and a log fire smoldered

in a stone fireplace. There were some of the modern easy chairs set about and a comfortable couch near the fire.

"I—I admire your choice of furnishings, my lord."

The viscount closed the door and Emma said nervously, "Please let us return to the public rooms before I am made a subject of gossip."

"Sit down, Emma."

For an irresistible moment she stared at him. He might be garbed in velvet and satin, but his muscular build and lithe walk proved he did not live life softly. She raised her eyes to his face, bony, lined, austere.

"I did not give you permission to use my name."

"My dear girl, pray come down from the boughs and be seated. I assure you I have no designs on your virtue."

As the words passed his lips, Kinver knew he was speaking less than the truth. She was inexpressibly lovely in her blue-and-rose ensemble, her face lit by the glow of candles and fire. He wanted to enfold her in his arms and kiss her; he wanted to . . .

He pulled his mind to order. He could never have her, and he had best accept it. James, his friend of many years, showed clear signs of being enamored of her. The polite world awaited an announcement concerning himself and Lucy and must wait no longer, or it would begin to treat Lucy with derision. He had singled her out and, as an honorable man, had no choice but to speak to Lady Augusta, who was now secure in her victory. Lord Kinver believed that Emma found him attractive, but it was Exford whom she had chosen as husband. He had picked Lucy for himself. The prospect brought him no particular joy, but he had never expected much from marriage. So few unions seemed anything more than convenient arrangements, and after the tortured years of his mother's philanderings and the death of Lady Sybilla . . . Yet lately her memory was fading. It kept getting lost in a pair of blue-gray eyes that were at this moment staring at him, while a white-shod foot tapped impatiently.

"Did you bring me here to gaze at me, my lord? You could as well do that in the ballroom."

The viscount bowed. "Forgive me. I was deep in thought. I wished to let you know that I returned to see the unpleasant Mr. Palmer."

Emma clasped her hands. "What now? What has he done?"

"Calm yourself, Emma. I pointed out to him that you would not be delivering another serial story to him."

"But he has advertised it. I promised—"

"A promise extracted from you under threat. He can make some excuse to his readers. There are plenty more writers who can fill his pages."

Emma flushed. "You speak as if my work was of no value. Of course, I realize that my stories have been trivial. It was expected of me, but I—"

"But you would like to write something deeper, with more sensibility."

Emma sighed. "You *do* understand."

"I read between the lines of your gothic romances and I detected a keen brain at work. As did my grandmama, the Dowager Lady Kinver."

"She admires my work? Does she truly? Oh, that makes me proud. I like her."

The viscount's harsh face softened in his sweet smile. "Good! It is she who is your would-be patron. Will you accept her patronage and settle to writing a three-volume novel of your own choosing?"

Emma's world suddenly exploded into joy. "Oh, I will, I most assuredly will!" She paused. "Though I cannot conceive how my parents will view it. They would wonder how Lady Kinver discovered me, and that would mean confessing my past activities. Papa would be so hurt and Mama so shocked."

"It is considered perfectly respectable for a lady to write novels these days."

"Yes, so I have discovered, but you do not know my parents. They are strict, and I have deceived them grossly for a long time."

"You have more than a clever mind, Emma, you have courage too. Tell them what has happened. Ask their forgiveness and their permission to write. You may be surprised by their reaction."

Emma doubted it. She rose. "We must go back. I'll do as you suggest. I have found it increasingly difficult to act underhandedly anyway."

She was convinced that she would be forbidden to write

another word of fiction, and that would interfere with the
odious Palmer's plans. He would revenge himself by making
the authorship of the lampoon known. Would the conventional James Exford be prepared to ride out a social storm
with her? What man of any distinction would? She would
return home without a husband and therefore with no opportunity to assist her needy brothers and sisters and Sophia
would *never* have her longed-for Season. She had made an
utter shambles of everything. A sob rasped over her throat
and Kinver walked swiftly to her.

"Don't cry, Emma, please don't!"

His arms went around her, and as he felt a convulsion
shake her, his control deserted him. "Emma . . ."

He touched her hair with his long fingers, finding it to be
as silken as he had envisaged, his hand traveled to the nape of
her neck.

She realized with shame that she was being caressed by
Lucy's future husband, and her head jerked up. It brought her
enchanting mouth within his reach, and his lips descended
upon hers in a kiss that deepened with her helpless response.
For a moment they were close enough to detect each other's
heartbeats before they broke away and stood apart, staring in
total dismay.

"I'm sorry, Emma. I never meant it to happen. I'm truly
sorry. You are so beautiful, so enchanting. Your face, your
form . . ."

Emma put her hands to her burning cheeks. "I should
never have entered this room with you. No wonder Mama
was insistent that girls should always be chaperoned. I daresay your lordship has had many such encounters. In fact, we
both know of one."

Kinver stepped back. A tinge of red touched his cheek-
bones; he strove to regain his senses. He could not deny that
his body yearned for the lovely Emma, but he had ample
proof of what a deceiver physical passion could be. His
mother's escapades had all but ruined his boyhood and hastened his father's death. He had made love to more women
than he could remember, and it meant nothing. He admired
Emma's keen brain and her beauty, but these were no basis
for marriage, which was a contract to be undertaken by two

people of equal status, a step to be considered with care and a cool head, never with a body aching with desire.

He said formally, "I must ask your forgiveness, Emma . . . Miss Waring. You are so very lovely you turn a man's head, make him forget his duty."

Emma's hands fell to her sides and her face paled. "I am as much to blame. I should not have stayed alone in a private room with you."

The viscount muttered a curse. "I brought you here only to tell you that you need not fear Palmer. I dislike the idea of his profiting from his shares in your future work, but it can't be helped."

"I am grateful to you, more than grateful, but you could have told me this without bringing me here."

"I saw how emotional you became in his office. I wanted you to be safe from prying eyes."

"I see that your intent was good. Everything is my own stupid fault anyway."

The viscount conquered a further impulse to hold her and soothe away her fears. He must put a safe barrier between them. "It is time I made public my honorable intentions toward Lucy. I shall do so tonight."

Emma stood very straight. "That makes our embrace all the more dishonorable. Once you and Lucy are husband and wife, you *may* settle down. Some men do."

Kinver was stung into indignation. "Many years ago I vowed that if I married I would not stray. I have seen too much of the misery it can cause."

"Then, sir, you will amaze your friends."

The viscount bowed, his face cold. "You have a poor opinion of me."

"I had no opinion at all until you thrust yourself at me on our first meeting."

"And what of you, madam? I noticed no reticence in your response."

The silence that fell was filled with seething emotion. In an effort to assuage their wounds, each had wanted to hurt the other and each had succeeded, and the unhealed wounds grew more painful.

Lord Kinver opened the library door and took a quick glance around. "Come, Emma, there is no one about."

"I deplore this clandestine way of behaving."

"I do not see why. You appear to have had plenty of practice."

"What?"

"In the matter of your writing. I do not accuse you of promiscuity."

"How exceedingly magnanimous of you. Now perhaps you will return me to Lady Augusta."

They were nearing the ballroom when Gerard walked out of one of the card rooms. "Emma! Just the person I've been wanting to see. Can you spare me a moment?" He bowed respectfully to Kinver. "If your lordship does not object."

Emma watched Kinver's retreating back with burning eyes.

"Emma, pay attention. I have to talk to you." Gerard pulled her into an alcove, where she sank onto a brocade covered couch. "Have you any money?"

Emma stared at him. "Yes, some."

"Thank God. Can you let me have twenty pounds?"

"Well, yes, I can, but . . ."

Gerard picked up her tiny pink satin reticule and rummaged in it. "There's nothing here but a handkerchief, a small powder box, and some perfume."

"What did you expect? A bank vault? I don't bring money to a ball."

"Damme, you made me think I was safe."

"Gerard, what have you done? Why do you need money so urgently?"

"You act as if it was a vast sum."

"It is almost all I was given by Mama for pin money."

"Almost *all*? Then how can you help me? You must have spent something since your arrival."

"I have, but . . . I do have some other money."

Gerard looked sharply at her. "You've been playing too? You've won? I wish you'd tell me the secret. I damn near always lose."

"Am I to take it that you need twenty pounds for a gambling debt?"

He nodded and Emma said, "I understand that a promissory note is acceptable."

Gerard slumped beside her and his head went down into his hands. "The fellow who's won is chary of accepting a note.

Truth is, he has others of mine that I can't yet pay, and he demands money now. He has just insinuated in front of everyone that I shall never pay all my debts. I got some very curious looks, I can tell you. And, Emma, they're right. I can't pay. I don't know what Papa will do when I apply to him again. Last time he was so angry. He just doesn't understand.''

"None of us understands, Gerard. If you had an ounce of sense, you would appreciate that your family is in financial low water because of you. I am here now only through Lady Augusta's charity.''

"All right, don't rub my nose in it. Oh, sorry, Emma. I'm so worried I scarce know what I'm saying. If I can find a way to pay off my creditors, I swear I'll return to Oxford and never gamble again. Not until I can afford it anyway.''

"Do you really swear to that?''

Gerard looked at her with hope shining in his eyes. They were much alike in appearance, though her mouth was well-formed and firm, while his showed traces of weakness. "Can you see a way? I'm badly dipped!''

"How much do you owe?''

"I can't be exact, not without counting the sum—and I have scarce glanced at my tailor's bills, or my hatter's, or the bootmaker's, or—''

"You surely have some notion.''

"I reckon it must run to—to well over a thousand.''

"A thousand!''

"Hush, Emma. Keep your voice down.''

Emma thought of her parents. Gerard's debts would not signify if his sister had a rich husband. The right kind of man would see it as his duty to settle debts incurred by his wife's brother. Mr. Exford was just such a man. She genuinely liked him and would be a good wife to him. An announcement of their betrothal would stave off all Gerard's creditors. "You can stop worrying, Gerard. To whom do you owe this twenty pounds?''

"Sir Lambert Lowther. You've met him. I owe him much more.''

"You *must* find a way to make him take one more note, Gerard. Trust me.''

Gerard gave his twin a swift embrace and planted a kiss on

her face. "You're a good 'un, Emma. Always was." He left and returned to the card room with a spring in his step that was lacking in Emma's. His suddenly jaunty air would imbue confidence in his gaming companions, and Sir Lambert would be regarded with disfavor if he continued to refuse a promissory note.

Lord Kinver, who had waited, escorted Emma silently back to her aunt.

19

The country dance had just ended and the ballroom, in spite of its great size, was hugely overheated by the hundreds of flaring candles and the exertions of the dancers.

Lady Augusta sat fanning herself languidly. "I believe that Kinver will now wish to walk awhile with Lucy."

The smile she directed at her granddaughter and the viscount was one of arrogant command, and they left the ballroom.

Emma pictured them in the library. The ensuing scene would be vastly different from the one just enacted. She seated herself by her chaperone, her whole being in turmoil. The heat, the noise of hundreds of chattering voices laced with shrill laughter, the wail of the instruments being tuned for the next dance, the mingled odors of scent and overhot bodies, the reaction from her interview with Lord Kinver, began to take a toll, and she knew she must have a breath of fresh air.

She touched Lady Augusta's arm. "Please, ma'am, may I allow Mr. Exford to escort me to one of the balconies? I am suffering from—from the heat."

Her ladyship was delighted. She had not expected such a sophisticated approach from her little country niece. When she returned, no doubt there would be two announcements to make. Kinver had seemed agitated. Well, in spite of all his amorous adventures, he had not proposed marriage more than once before and fortunately—for Lucy that was, of course—his betrothed had succumbed to illness and gone to a higher place, thus leaving this great catch for her worthy granddaughter.

Mr. Exford held Emma's elbow in a proprietary manner as he steered her to a balcony overlooking the garden behind the house. He closed the door behind them and the sound of music became muted. Lights from windows tinged the tree-tops with gold and made gold-green light and shade in the garden. Emma took great gulps of cool air and her head began to clear.

Mr. Exford gave her time to recover before speaking. He would always be considerate, thought Emma. He would co-coon her in his protection. With his aid she could give Sophia and her other sisters their chance and Gerard's debts could be settled. He might even allow her to continue her writing, though she had a worrying doubt about that. He was far more conventional than his friend Kinver, who was being accepted by Lucy at this very moment. A shudder ran through her.

Her companion exclaimed, "You are shivering! I am thoughtless. I should have had your wrap brought."

Emma assured him that she was not cold, and Mr. Exford said, "Was your shiver one of excitement?"

Emma murmured incoherently, but it seemed to satisfy him. He took her hands in his. "They are cold, Emma, your hands are cold." He held them close to his chest and released them there, putting his arms around her. "I can warm them, dear Emma, just as I can warm you, if you will give me the right. You are not indifferent to me. Can I hope, dare I hope, that you care for me?"

"I like you exceeding well, Mr. Exford."

"James, if you please, Emma. Emma! I've said your name to myself so often. It is wonderful to say it aloud to you. Emma, I know I have Lady Augusta's approval and I think your parents will not object to me."

"They will esteem you very much," said Emma truthfully.

"Does your sentiment go further than mere liking? Could you love me? Emma, will you marry me?"

So it had come. The proposal for which she had angled. She felt despondent over her duplicity, and much deeper, a terrible sense of loss. She drew a deep breath. "You do me honor, Mr. Exford. I am very happy to accept your offer."

"James! My name is James. Let me hear you say it, Emma. Answer me again."

Emma said in firmer tones, "I am happy to accept your offer, James."

He lifted her chin with fingers that were not quite steady.

His lips were gentle, reverential as he kissed his promised bride. And unbidden came memory. Of other kisses, demanding, passion-filled, irresistible.

"Can we tell Lady Augusta at once, Emma? May the announcement be made public tonight?"

"There is no reason why it should not, James. Lady Augusta is my guardian."

"I am the happiest man in London, in the whole world!"

"And I am happy too," lied Emma as she walked through the door from the balcony, back into the ballroom, where her expectant aunt waited for her.

Her ladyship looked keenly at the couple and was satisfied. Mr. Exford had the air of a man whose suit had been successful. Emma looked decorous, as befitted a young lady of quality. Lady Augusta found it difficult to retain an air of calm as she waited for the other pair of lovers to return so that she could give directions for the double announcement.

She patted a vacant bench by her side. "Well, my child, I believe I must offer you my felicitations."

"Yes, indeed, ma'am," said James. "Emma has made me the happiest of men."

"This is a wonderful night for us all," beamed her ladyship. "At any moment my dearest Lucy will return with Kinver. I shall have the announcements made before supper. Oh, what envious looks there will be."

She sat up very straight and Emma saw that Lord Kinver was approaching. Without Lucy. The dowager's eyes narrowed, then her anxiety died as she took in his demeanor. Lord Kinver's face held a half-smile; his step was buoyant.

Lady Augusta greeted him. "My boy! You have made an old woman happy. Where is Lucy? Has she gone to the ladies' retiring room? No doubt she is overcome."

The band played a loud chord and the orchestra leader informed the grateful throng that supper was set out in the dining room downstairs.

Lady Augusta moved swiftly. Having brought Kinver up to the mark, she must make the betrothal public.

"Madam!" The viscount put out a restraining hand, but she swept past and hurried to the orchestra platform. Lord Kinver followed, pushing his way through the mass of guests in a way that several dowagers pronounced rude, especially in his own house.

Her ladyship had reached the orchestra and another, louder chord was struck, halting the guests.

She spoke. "My dear friends, my dear, dear friends, I have something of moment to tell you. This evening my family has been blessed by—"

The viscount reached her side at last and she looked down from her place on the platform. "Do not be tugging at my arm in so vulgar a manner, Kinver," she hissed. "What ever has got into you? Surely this is the best place from which to announce your betrothal."

The viscount stepped up to join her and said a few quiet words. The guests, who had been whispering, fell silent. Lady Augusta appeared to be swelling as her face reddened beneath her maquillage, reminding the more irreverent of a turkey cock. She swayed and Kinver took her arm. She shook it off angrily. Speculation began to run among the guests like a small fire that might break into a great conflagration. But Lady Augusta's wits had deserted her only for a moment, and her long training saved her.

"As I said, my dear friends"—the guests noted gleefully that Kinver once more tried to speak and was ignored—"I am enchanted to be able to tell you that Mr. James Exford, whom you will all know, has just become betrothed to my beloved niece, Miss Emma Waring. Many of you have not yet had the pleasure of her acquaintance, but I am persuaded that you will wish to drink a toast to their happiness."

The news surprised many. Polite society murmured their insincere pleasure on learning that the now-wealthy Mr. Exford had been snatched from their marriageable females by some minx newly out, but all eyes remained on Lady Augusta and Kinver, awaiting the expected announcement of Lucy Venables' triumph.

Lord Kinver placed an arm beneath Lady Augusta's elbow and assisted her from the platform, and they walked among the simpering, congratulating guests. Lady Augusta's teeth showed in a smile that failed to reach her eyes, and Kinver's affability had been unaccountably destroyed.

The *ton* was ecstatic. Those who had seen the viscount and Lucy leave the ballroom together enlarged the knowledge of those who had seen him return alone, yet appearing satisfied. And no one had missed the intriguing scene enacted on the orchestra platform. It was all very mysterious and much better than the playhouse. They were disappointed when Lady Augusta and Kinver entered the supper room a little later and joined Miss Waring and James Exford with every outward appearance of pleasure, but nothing could spoil completely the delightful prospect of regaling the unfortunates who had not received invitations with the account of tonight's intriguing events.

Viscount Kinver entertained his guests with punctilious courtesy until almost three o'clock in the morning, at which time carriages were called for and everyone departed proclaiming the ball a wondrous success. He and Lady Augusta had not spoken since a short, angry confrontation in the library before they joined the guests for supper. Lucy was not in the retiring room. She had gone home, sending the carriage back for her grandmother. The viscount had done his duty and Lucy had rejected him. To her ladyship's question on the subject of his apparent satisfaction he had replied that he did not care to permit anyone to witness his humiliation. This had satisfied Lady Augusta, as he had known it would. He could scarcely tell her the truth, which was that when Lucy had refused him he had felt as if the gates of heaven were opening. He had, he hoped, managed to appear suitably chagrined, but it was almost impossible when her words had released great torrents of dammed-up emotion. He was free of obligation. Free to pursue the promptings of his heart. Free to allow himself to recognize that what he felt for Emma was far stronger than esteem and admiration. He loved her. The difference between his feeling for Lady Sybilla and Emma was as a tiny stream compared with an ocean. He could scarcely drag up enough social awareness to express his disappointment in suitable terms to Lucy, who remained serene. He wondered if she sensed his reaction. He wondered if she experienced any emotion at all. Apparently she did. She was not prepared to meet her grandmother in the ballroom and give her the dreadful tidings.

"I shall return home immediately, my lord. It will be better so."

Lord Kinver had no argument to refute this and sent a

footman to call discreetly for her carriage. He had handed her into it himself. He had hurried back to the ballroom and sustained a profound shock as he stood beside Lady Augusta and heard her announce Emma's betrothal to James. He had not thought his friend so deep enough in love yet that he was ready to propose marriage. He meant to court Emma openly, assuring himself that the best man would win her. How could he have been so mistaken? He would have to watch James wed Emma and see their happiness stretching down the years. The ball became a ghastly ordeal, but he moved among his guests, smiling and talking, unwilling to approach James and Emma after offering his felicitations.

Lady Augusta stayed doggedly to the end. James escorted her home, sitting close to his betrothed and smiling in what her ladyship thought was a fatuous way. She swept through the front door, calling to Emma to follow instantly, and James was left outside.

Lady Augusta breathed hard as she climbed the stairs fast. She hammered with her clenched fist on Lucy's bedchamber door, which opened at once, revealing Lucy, her face paler than usual. Her grandmother entered, banging the door behind her.

Emma went slowly to her own room, where Betty was waiting, and the two girls heard her ladyship's voice rising in fury and penetrating even the thick doors and walls.

Emma dismissed Betty and paced her room. There was a brief silence and abruptly her own bedchamber door was thrown open. Lady Augusta stood there, her wig tilted and her feathered headdress awry, and Emma saw with sympathy that tears were turning her blackened lashes and painted face into a morass of color.

"My dear aunt . . ."

"Yes, *you* may call me dear. You are a good and obedient girl. Come with me, Emma, to your cousin. I think she has lost her wits."

She swept along the corridor and Emma followed her into Lucy's room. Lucy wore a lawn nightgown and a white wool shawl. On her feet were dainty silken slippers. She had not been to bed. Her face was tinged with a little color, though that might be because she was seated near a bright fire.

Lady Augusta flung out her hand in a gesture worthy of

Mr. Kemble, an actor she much admired, and pointed to her granddaughter. "There you see," she informed Emma, "a snake I have nourished in my bosom, an ungrateful viper, a girl lacking apparently all sense of duty and obedience to those who have her best interests at heart, a wicked—"

"I refused Kinver," explained Lucy.

Lady Augusta screamed hoarsely. "How calmly she says it! As if it mattered nothing! Folk will twist everything around and insist that Kinver never came up to scratch. You will be left on the shelf. I hope you will enjoy it there. I . . ."

Lady Augusta's voice continued, but Emma's attention wandered as the full implication of Lucy's words struck her. She was not to marry Kinver. He had looked happy when he returned to the ballroom. He had been *glad*! He must simply have been performing what he saw as his duty. The knowledge of his freedom opened her eyes to her own deep feelings, and she knew she loved Kinver and always would, all down the years she was wed to James.

"For the love of God, don't go moon-eyed on me now," shrieked Lady Augusta, and Emma realized she was being addressed.

"I am sorry, ma'am. What?"

"Well, I daresay a newly engaged girl is to be permitted a little happy dreaming. I am enlisting your aid, Emma. This wicked, ungrateful viper in my bosom—"

"You repeat yourself, Grandmama," said Lucy.

Lady Augusta raised her arm and Emma thought for a horrified moment that she would strike Lucy, before she turned and swept to the door. "Talk to her, Emma. Try to find out why." She departed, rigid with fury.

Lucy looked at Emma. "Won't you sit down, cousin."

Emma sat. "Lucy, I—Lucy, it is not for me to question you."

"Grandmama has ordered it. One must obey her ladyship."

"You do not."

"No."

"Do you wish to confide in me? I hate to pry."

"You are not prying, Emma, and yes, I will confide in you, though I do not think my news will do anything to relieve Grandmama's rage. I am going to marry Mr. Phineas Treen."

"Papa's curate!"

"That surprises you."

"Yes, no, yes. Oh, Lucy, are you sure? Yes, You must be. When did he propose? Why did you not tell Lady Augusta? She has been setting her hopes on Kinver."

"I did not tell her because there is nothing to tell. Mr. Treen does not yet himself know of my intention."

Emma's mouth dropped open. She recovered herself. "He does not know?" The words came out in a whisper.

Lucy's door opened and Lady Augusta reentered. Wheeler hovered in the background with wet flannels, a towel, and a very anxious expression. Lady Augusta closed the door in her dresser's face. Her ladyship had removed her wig, and her own sparse gray hair above a face without makeup, revealing the wrinkles she usually hid, made her look older and vulnerable.

Lucy rose and begged her grandmother to take her chair near the fire. "You are shivering, Grandmama," she remarked as she drew up a stool for herself. "The nights are still cold."

"I am not cold," said Lady Augusta, seating herself. "I am shocked. Yes, shock is making me ill. Yet I have had moments to ponder, Lucy. Possibly you refused Kinver out of a sense of maidenly modesty. I will explain and he will approach you again. He is a man of the world. He will understand. In fact"—Lady Augusta became briefly indignant—"I wonder at his taking a first refusal so finally."

Lucy sighed in resignation. "He might not have done so had I not informed him that my affections are already engaged."

Lady Augusta stared incredulously. "It is not possible! By whom? What other man of substance do you know so well?"

Emma, feeling cowardly but rising nevertheless, murmured that she was intruding. Both ladies waved her back to her seat and she sank down.

"He is not a man of substance, though that will be rectified when we are married, but he is of unexceptionable birth. He is Mr. Treen."

Lady Augusta looked blank. "Who?"

"Emma knows him and so do you." Her ladyship glared at Emma. She had no business remembering men unrecalled by herself.

Lucy said, "You have met Mr. Phineas Treen several times, Grandmama. He is Mr. Waring's curate."

"Mr. Waring's *curate*?"

"That is so, Grandmama."

"It isn't possible! Tell me you are funning. I must be asleep. I am in the grip of a nightmare. I recall him now. Mr. Waring's curate! Two yards of pump water whose sermons are overlong and prosy, whose conversation is ditch-water dull. *He* has had the temerity to approach *you*, a woman with all the graces that a careful rearing can bestow, with all the advantages that an immense fortune—"

"I do not regard Mr. Treen as you do, Grandmama. I find his sermons full of sincerity and truth. I wish only they had been longer. I admire his healthy looks, and his conversation is fascinating to me. He knows a great deal about animal husbandry and crops and—"

"All of which would be so *useful* in polite society."

"No, of course they would not, but we shall not reside in London."

"Not reside in . . . Well, upon my soul! How did you come into my family? You must be a changeling. Take warning, my girl, once you wed this curate, you will find he is only wanting your fortune to cut a dash in town. I have seen it happen to other girls. You will be abandoned in the country, breeding children incessantly while he remains in the capital city enjoying the favors of other women."

"That would be impossible, Grandmama."

Lady Augusta's jaw slackened. "What?"

"It would be impossible for me to breed if I stayed always in the country and Mr. Treen in town."

Emma had not believed that her aunt could be any angrier. She was mistaken. Lady Augusta's fury rose to new heights. "How dare you! What kind of farmyard talk is that?"

"It is no worse than your own."

Her ladyship's eyes bulged. "I am permitted. A woman of my years can be freer with her tongue. Is that the sort of remark your curate makes?"

Lucy's delicate dark brows rose. "Certainly not. Our conversation has been most discreet. There has not been a word said that anyone could not have heard."

"Not even his proposal, his *clandestine* marriage proposal.

What an ill-mannered man you favor, madam! He did not even have the courtesy to approach me first.''

"There is no reason why he should . . .''

"No reason! There is every reason!''

" . . . because,'' continued Lucy calmly, "he has not yet proposed.''

Lady Augusta's screech of rage made Emma jump. "You fiendish girl! You have put me through all this torment for nothing. You have refused the offer of one of the richest men in England and all for a delusion!''

"Not so, Grandmama. Mr. Treen and I have exchanged glances of unmistakable meaning and I have several times allowed my hand to linger in his. I have given him all the encouragement a gentlewoman may give a gentleman, but he is so humble, so unassuming, he would never dare to proffer himself to me as a husband.''

"Thank God!'' breathed Lady Augusta. "I will see Kinver and explain that you were so overcome that you hinted at another attachment and he will renew—''

"You will do no such thing. I did much more than hint. I am going to visit my Warmley estate as soon as we have fulfilled our engagement at Carlton House. One cannot slight His Royal Highness, however careless he is in his own behavior.'' Lucy looked at her grandmother, who began to choke on words. She continued, "I shall make it absolutely clear to Posty—''

"Posty?''

"That is my pet private name for him. His middle name is Posthumous because he was born after his father's death. I always think of him as Posty. I hope he may like it.''

"I have no doubt he will like anything that hands him a fortune of the size of yours.''

"As I was saying, I shall make it clear to him that he may make his proposal, which I shall accept at once, and we can be married within the month. He may continue a career in the church if he wishes, but I think he would prefer the life of a landed gentleman.''

Lady Augusta spoke low and bitter. "No doubt he will. No doubt he will readily relinquish his curacy once he has hooked a prime fish like you. No doubt he will enjoy your wealth to the full.''

"Is there any reason why he should not?"

Lady Augusta opened and closed her mouth twice. She could not deny that many a respectable man lived in luxury through the fortune of his wife. There could be no disgrace in it.

"I shall leave my money to someone else. You shall not have it."

"That is your affair, ma'am. We have distant relatives who will be glad of it. I have plenty enough money of my own."

"You think yourself so clever, madam." Lady Augusta's first frenzy had burned itself out, leaving ashes of cold anger. "I will prove to you that you are deceiving yourself. I will offer him a fortune if he will not pursue you. I will make it large enough to enrich him."

Lucy's voice took on a quality that amazed Emma. "If you dare to do so, you will never see me again. Mr. Treen will refuse such tainted money because he loves me. I love him. I am going to marry him. I do not wish to break with you, Grandmama, but you are warned."

Emma felt miserably uncomfortable. She would have given anything to escape. She had made two tentative moves and had been waved back by both Lucy and Lady Augusta, each of whom believed she had Emma's support. Now she was held by the suddenly charged atmosphere.

Lady Augusta's shoulders sagged. "I could not enjoy life estranged from you, Lucy."

"Nor I from you, Grandmama."

"Mr. Treen is the brother of the present viscount . . ."

"An honorable son of an honorable father . . ."

"His birth equals yours, his education was good, but I find him tedious . . ."

"You need not be in his company unless you choose."

"If you will not have Kinver . . ."

"I will not."

Silence fell. A coal shifted and flared.

"That nasty toad Sir Lambert Lowther has been encroaching upon you of late."

Lucy smiled. "You must know I could never entertain the suit of such a man."

"Lucy, why did you come to London for the Season at all when you meant to have Mr. Treen?"

"It was easier than arguing. I prefer to live peacefully whenever it is possible."

There was a long silence. "You will be married, then. I have always wanted that for you. And you will be happy?"

"I am as sure as one can be of anything in an uncertain world, Grandmama."

Emma rose and walked quietly to the door, opened it, and escaped at last, returning thankfully to her room. How astonishing to discover that behind Lucy's bland exterior lay such resolve.

She sat on the silk brocade bedcover, turned down for her by Betty, and considered the wreck she had made of her own life. She was engaged to an excellent gentleman. Mama had assured her that love grew with time. But could it when she was aflame with the knowledge that she loved another man?

20

In the days after the ball the three ladies followed the customary pursuits of people of fashion. They strolled under trees burgeoning with the yellow-green leaves of spring in the park or the Mall, visited friends and received visits, and shopped.

Emma was constantly surprised by the number and variety of objects that were considered indispensable by her wealthy relatives. Even Lucy, who intended to spend her life in country pursuits, continued to purchase anything large or small that took her fancy, and she now added elegant snuffboxes and gentlemen's fobs, as gifts for her curate.

Lady Augusta fussed over Emma, whose conduct was worthy of a young lady, offering her much advice on bride gowns and underwear, the idea of which Emma found unwelcome. She had no wish to imagine herself in intimate proximity with James when she was unable to dampen down the fires raging through her at the memory of Lord Kinver's embraces. Lady Augusta was not displeased by her niece's reluctant attitude; it showed a proper sentiment.

James was assiduous in his attentions and the engaged couple were smiled upon by the *ton*, who had accepted defeat on behalf of their marriageable females where Mr. Exford was concerned. But they were intrigued by the failure of Miss Venables' rumored attachment to be made public, and Lady Augusta fumed inwardly at the number of times their entry into a room was a signal for conversation to cease momentarily, only to resume with false vigor.

Trunks had already been fetched from the attics and packing was well under way. Her ladyship seethed with discontent

at the prospect of leaving London and missing a large part of
the Season, but even she felt unequal to watching polite
society's first reaction to the news that the wealthy, unap-
proachable Miss Venables was to marry a penniless curate,
however well-born. And Emma could not be left unchaper-
oned. Another dilemma!

Lord Kinver still accompanied them quite often. He had
himself under absolute control and smiled and jested and took
the dance floor equally with his two cousins and with hopeful
young ladies; and he joined James in escorting Lady Augusta
and her charges to the reception at Carlton House. Lucy wore
white gauze over a white gown, enhanced by costly lace and
tiny pearls. Her hair was simply dressed with pearls and lace
flowers. Her face radiated inner happiness and she appeared
almost beautiful. Emma had lost her enthusiasm for the round
of pleasure. She allowed Betty to assist her into a turquoise
gown with a spangled white gauze overdress. A turquoise
pendant hung on a silver chain around her throat, her ears
were adorned by matching drop earrings, and there were
silver ribbons in her hair. White kid pumps and gloves completed the ensemble. Lucy's maid arrived bearing a white
shawl with spangles that her mistress believed would go well
with Miss Waring's outfit. Emma sent back thanks, her throat
suddenly tight with emotion. Such a stupid thing to make her
want to weep.

Lord Kinver's carriage, containing himself and James, followed that of the ladies and they joined the slow procession
in Pall Mall moving along the front of the coupled Ionic
columns, in through the gates and behind the new classical
Corinthian columns, to the main door of Carlton House. Lady
Augusta and her charges waited for their escorts inside the
enormous hall with its porphyry, granite-green, bronze, and
yellow decor. In spite of her worries, Emma had to exercise
self-control not to gape at the splendors of Carlton House as
conceived by Henry Holland and embellished by the Prince,
who had ordered the plentiful use of gold paint.

"If you think this is ornate, wait until you learn His
Highness' intentions for his Pavilion at Brighton."

Emma turned quickly and smiled up at Lord Kinver, whose
responsive smile made her heart thud. James took her elbow
to steer her past a group of gossiping dowagers, at whom

Lady Augusta glanced with envy. Kinver's eyes darkened at his friend's familiar gesture and he went to walk beside Lucy and her grandmother.

"It is so warm," murmured Emma.

"The Prince keeps his residences like hothouses," said James. "Ladies are always swooning with the heat and gentlemen have been known to do so. Do not worry, dear heart, I shall catch you if you fall."

Emma smiled dutifully at her future bridegroom, who gazed at her beauty and wished they were alone. Her ladyship led her party through the crimson drawing room and into the yellow Chinese room.

"It is to be hoped that if Prinny ever succumbs to jaundice, he will remain out of here or one would have difficulty in finding him," said Kinver.

Emma forgot her society simper, and her deep-throated laugh caused several heads to turn. Kinver was infected by it and laughed too. Lucy looked blankly at them, James was apprehensive lest his friend be overheard, while Lady Augusta dug him in the ribs with her fan and frowned at Emma.

The Prince came among his guests at nine o'clock, accompanied by several friends. His girth was inadequately imprisoned in corsets that occasionally creaked, his high white cravat permitted the appearance of only one chin, his hair was curled elaborately in an unorderly style. He talked constantly. Once when the crowds parted, Emma caught sight of Sir Lambert, who saw her at the same moment. She was startled by a gleam in his eyes that seemed directed at her with acute malevolence, before he was hidden from her again. She was thankful that Gerard and his friends had not received invitations, so she need not worry about their conduct. She had seen her brother twice since his request for money and his jaunty demeanor declared how much his consequence had improved since the news of his sister's betrothal to a wealthy man was filtered through society.

Refreshments were served at midnight and Emma, who was affected by the overheated rooms, could manage only a sweet cake and a glass of wine. Their party decided to seek a less-crowded place where they might sit awhile. The circular room, with its high, painted, domed ceiling, from which hung a crystal cascade chandelier, contained only a few people—all of the highest *ton*, Lady Augusta hissed in an aside to Emma. There were other chandeliers with candles, but it was a little cooler and certainly more peaceful, and Emma sank onto a blue couch with gilded legs that, though handsome, was not designed for comfort. She was developing a niggling headache and the cake sat uneasily on her stomach and she wished they could go home. Of course, no one could leave until the Prince retired, and he was unpredictable. Sir Lambert Lowther arrived, peered around, and immediately withdrew.

Shortly afterward the guests heard the unmistakable tones of the Prince as he approached along the wide corridor outside.

"You say you are sure, absolutely positive?"

Someone replied in tones too low to be caught, then the Prince entered and everyone in the room rose. His Highness's eyes were glacial as they swept the assembled company and the atmosphere became uneasy. The gentlemen with him were all portly, and it was a moment before Emma saw Sir Lambert Lowther, who was beckoned from behind.

"You say that it was written by someone here in this very room, by one of my guests?"

Emma felt as if her insides were being squeezed by a giant fist as Sir Lambert's lizardlike gaze rested on her. "I was told directly by a clerical gentleman, Sir. He was vastly shocked—as indeed I was myself."

"Quite so," said the Prince testily. "I require less opinion and more fact."

Sir Lambert bowed low. "I beg Your Royal Highness's pardon. The culprit is indeed here. The one who penned the disgraceful lampoon even now being bruited abroad, shouted in the streets, sniggered at in—"

The Prince frowned at the baronet, who stopped speaking and flung out his hand in a flamboyant gesture toward Emma.

"The author of the lampoon . . ." He paused for dramatic emphasis.

The room became still and hushed, then Kinver rose to his feet and bowed to the Prince. Never had his bow been more graceful, never had his voice sounded so full of ennui as he drawled, "Forgive me, Sir, but I cannot permit this to continue. I refuse to stand accused. I prefer confession. I fear that in an excess of regrettable muse I wrote the lampoon that appears to be the subject of Sir Lambert's, er, excitement.''

"You!" The Prince's voice held incredulity. "You, Viscount Kinver? I would never have thought it possible." His face grew red with rage and his eyes bulged. "I know you are a wit, but I had believed you a gentleman loyal to your Prince. Have you nothing to say? No defense? No, there can be no defense! Even in your cups—and I have seen you—your tongue is discreet."

Sir Lambert attempted to speak and was ordered to be silent. He tried again and the Prince commanded him to leave. Sir Lambert hesitated and two liveried footmen who had been standing motionless at each side of the door came suddenly to life and advanced on the baronet, who declined to be manhandled and left.

Lord Kinver bowed again and Emma, standing by Lady Augusta's side, felt as if the giant fist had moved to her throat. She would suffocate. She knew she would. But she must speak, she *must*. She opened her mouth and no sound came. To her horror she felt nausea rising. She struggled for breath and Lady Augusta glanced at her, looked more closely.

"She is going into a spasm. Bring my reticule, Lucy. There is hartshorn in it. Pray, excuse her, Sir."

"She is of course excused. I should not wonder if all you ladies do not need reviving. Such perfidy from one I trusted. Such—such—" Words failed the Prince and he turned and walked away.

Emma fought the nausea that threatened to engulf her. Through the haze she could hear the voices of witnesses of the scene that must secretly have enchanted them, exclaiming loudly in their horror and disgust at Lord Kinver's betrayal of his Prince. When the disgraceful truth was bruited abroad, they could say, "We were there!"

A footman brought a message to Lord Kinver, who read it and said lightly, "It seems that His Highness would like our party to leave."

Emma, her stomach heaving, was assisted from Carlton House by James and Lord Kinver, followed by Lady Augusta and Lucy. A number of people contrived to be in the hall, and Emma saw that some scarcely troubled to veil their gloating relish.

Lady Augusta dismissed the gentlemen when she stepped into her carriage. "I shall expect you to call tomorrow, James, and I must suppose you will visit also, Kinver. You may wish to explain this incredible lapse in your conduct, though what elucidation can wipe away the horror . . . what you can ever say that will lessen the infamy!"

Kinver said, "Should you not cut my acquaintance immediately?" His voice held a hint of grim humor.

For once Lady Augusta was bereft of words, and the carriage rolled off. Just before it moved, Emma raised her eyes and looked at Kinver. He smiled and his eyes sent a message of such compassion and understanding that she began to shake.

Lady Augusta's voice returned. "Well! Never did I believe that I should have to endure such a scene! Disgrace! That's what stares us in the face."

Lucy spoke languidly, "It won't be all gloom, Grandmama. After all, Kinver wrote the lampoon and it is he who will be ostracized. Besides, you will probably be welcomed to the entertainments given by their Majesties, for it is a fact that they favor anyone whom their son does not."

"Their Majesties' court is of such unspeakable dullness I would much prefer to be in the country. It is no use to blink the fact. From this night forward I shall be a social outcast."

"No, oh, no," gasped Emma, and had to breathe deeply in an effort at control.

"I say yes," grated her ladyship. "The Prince has influence in the houses I desire to enter. I shall lose all my friends—at least until this is forgotten, and the Prince has a long memory for slights. As for your Season, Emma, you had as well return home."

"If people disdain us, they cannot be counted true friends, Grandmama," pointed out Lucy.

"I swear I should have had you beaten as a child," breathed Lady Augusta. "What do I care if they are counted true or not? My friends are my contemporaries, ladies and gentlemen whom I knew in my youth and rely upon in a way you cannot conceive."

Emma's feelings of guilt became even more untenable. She barely reached the safety of her room before she was overcome by nausea. Betty held a bowl and wet towel for her,

and when her mistress lay back exhausted in a chair near the
fire, she bathed her forehead.

"You've been doin' too much. Still not used to town
ways, Miss Emma. It'll all get better."

Emma shook her head weakly and Betty assisted her to
bed, where she lay a long time unsleeping. Exhaustion claimed
her and she drifted into uneasy dreams, and when she awoke,
the threatening headache had become severe. Lady Augusta
came to her and dosed her with a potion, talking more gently
than Emma would have believed possible, murmuring that
she was not surprised. Lucy, she said, appeared unaffected.
Lucy had never possessed much sensibility, but as she intended to spend her life rusticating, her ladyship supposed it
did not signify. As she left, she turned and said, "I can only
thank God that she refused Kinver! I know he's been a
hellhound, but I had assumed he was socially impeccable.
One never can tell. Mr. Treen . . ." Lady Augusta breathed
hard through her nostrils. "Mr. Treen is respectable, if nothing else."

Emma watched her aunt depart and knew utter despair. The
soothing potion took effect and she slept. She awoke several
hours later and felt better. Betty brought her tea and she was
sipping it when her bedchamber door opened and Lady Augusta looked in and announced that she had surprise visitors.

A slender figure in white darted across the room and
planted a resounding kiss on Emma's cheek, almost upsetting
the tea.

"Sophia! What are you doing here? How . . .?"

A movement by the door made her look past Sophia.
"Papa!"

To her dismay and chagrin she burst into tears, and Sophia
hovered by the bed, wringing her hands. "Her ladyship has
told us what happened, Emma. It is so dreadful for you in
your first Season. Mama warned us what a perfectly horrid
man Lord Kinver is. How you must wish you had never met
him."

Emma put her tea on the bedside table and slid out of bed
and ran to her father, who enveloped her in a hug and patted
her soothingly.

"Oh, I am so glad you are here, Papa."

Sophia brought a warm shawl, and Emma and Mr. Waring

sat by the fire. A nod from her father sent Sophia tiptoeing to the door as if Emma were an invalid. "I'll see you later, dear sister. We shall have such a cosy talk."

"Cosy" was the last word Emma would have picked for the talk she knew she must have with her father. "I need your advice," she said.

"I have met Mr. Exford," explained Papa. Emma was surprised, having, for the moment, forgotten her betrothed's existence. "You need no guidance from me on that score. I like him exceeding well and I am sure Mama will also. You have chosen wisely, Emma."

"Thank you, Papa. Mr. Exford—James—was going to visit you, but now that you are here . . . Lady Augusta said she had your authority to act."

"And she has used it reliably."

Emma looked searchingly at her father. He looked less than well. "Was your journey trying, Papa?"

"I have been somewhat indisposed for a week or two. Nothing to distress yourself about, but you know how Mama fusses. The physician attending the children told me I should rest more."

Emma was concerned. She had seldom known her father ill. "Traveling to London is scarcely resting!"

"No, indeed. But it was my intention, persuaded by your mother and Nurse, who believes we are all children, to have a small vacation, which meant that I had already engaged an old friend to care for the parish and was free to come. Sophia is deputized by Mama to watch over me. Emma, your mother and I have been concerned for some great while, as you know, by your brother's reckless behavior. I have had a letter from a baronet, asking me to settle Gerard's gaming debts." Mr. Waring took a letter from his pocket and placed a small pair of spectacles on his nose. "He says he has promissory notes and they amount to over two hundred pounds. Of course, if they are genuine, I shall pay the man, but he also hints—more than hints—that Gerard is gaining a poor reputation for himself in town by his continual failure to pay what the writer entitles 'debts of honor,' though I consider gaming losses debts of *dishonor*. It is almost a threatening letter, couched in quite extreme terms."

"Is the writer Sir Lambert Lowther?"

"Why, yes. Do you know him?"

Emma nodded. "He is an excessively unpleasant man."

Mr. Waring removed his spectacles, slipped them into a leather pouch, and rubbed his eyes. "Emma," he said gently, "I have also had a letter from Lady Augusta applying for more funds on your behalf. Mama and I know that a London Season can be costly, but we did hope that the money we laid aside for you—"

"Oh, Papa, no! I reminded my aunt that I must stay within limits. I have not been extravagant. I still have some of the pin money Mama gave me. Papa, I would not have caused you and Mama this anxiety for worlds."

The rector nodded. "That is what I told Mama, but the fact remains that her ladyship confidently expects me to pay her seventy-five guineas for your presentation dress."

"Seventy-five guineas!" repeated Emma. "It is a plain white gown over hoops! How can it have cost so much? I would far prefer to have done without a presentation."

Mr. Waring looked happier. "I told Mama there would be an explanation. You are such a good girl, and of course, you must be presented, as Mama was in her day."

"It does not signify now, Papa. After last night . . ."

"James is of the opinion that you need not be implicated. And I have brought a few trifling odds and ends to sell. All the debts will be settled."

Emma looked miserably at her father. He knew nothing of Gerard's other debts, and now she must tell him her own bad news and hurt him more.

21

"Papa, Sir Lambert Lowther has injured us more than you know. I must speak before more injustice is done."

Mr. Waring looked searchingly at his distressed daughter. Emma continued, "You have heard of Viscount Kinver's confession to the Prince. Papa, I was never more shocked in my life."

"I am not surprised. Such an insult!"

Emma swallowed a lump in her throat. "The shock made me ill. I was terrified I would disgorge my food in His Highness's presence. Every time I tried to speak, I felt worse."

"None of this is remarkable, Emma, but what—"

"The chief reason for my agitation was the fact that Lord Kinver . . ."

"Yes?" prompted a puzzled Mr. Waring.

"Lord Kinver claimed to be the author of the lampoon that has infuriated the Prince, but, Papa, *I* wrote it!"

Mr. Waring stared at his daughter. "You! How can that be? You? It is not credible! Why should his lordship take the blame?"

"Because he is a noble gentleman. I am betrothed to his friend."

Mr. Waring was astonished. "A friend, indeed."

"I shall explain everything and I can only pray that you still love me when I have finished."

Emma told her story succinctly, but leaving nothing out, revealing how her deception had begun, how she had allowed folk to believe that Mr. Treen assisted her with the conundrums, how she had taken her early walks to catch the carrier with the post and to give him more work. And having started, she told him about the odious Mr. Palmer and how Lord Kinver had come to her aid, and about the Dowager Lady Kinver, who wished to become her patron, and that she was not sure if there was a legal contract in existence that she feared might be binding. She finished, and there was what seemed to her an interminable silence.

"Papa, I implore you, say something."

Mr. Waring said, "Emma, I will not pretend that I am not deeply shocked. You would not expect less. But what has me in a profound puzzle is why you believed you had to begin such a dreadful web of deception."

Emma looked up then and her face flooded with color. "Because I want to write so very much. I was afraid you would think me frivolous, unladylike—even ungodly—and forbid me to continue. It means so much to me, you see."

Mr. Waring passed a hand over his eyes. "But I have never objected to you and Sophia reading the tales in magazines."

"That is not the same as writing them! And I have been hearing from Mama and Nurse forever that no lady who wishes to gain distinction in the *haut ton* can allow herself to be thought a—a bluestocking."

"Oh, Emma! If you had but been more open with us. Mama has always advised you in the way she believes proper. She was taught from childhood that a woman's place is in the home, ruling her servants with justice, tending her family. Her mama told her that all women *must* have husbands if they are to be considered as having achieved anything of note. The words 'meek,' 'clinging,' 'helpless,' 'dependent,' are only a few that were drilled into her. It has been a matter of wonder to me that she could even read. She was led to think—and partially by the great Dr. Johnson, whom you revere—that all marriages would be the better for having been arranged."

"Oh, Papa, was your marriage arranged?"

Mr. Waring smiled. "We fell in love, as they say, and there were no objections. I do not know what Mama would have done if her parents had insisted on her accepting a most unpleasant earl who wanted her. She was a very dutiful daughter who accepted that to be an old maid is the worst fate to befall a woman. And Mama saw bluestocking women who wore breeches and rode astride horses, who aped men in offensive behavior and language while affecting to despise them. She meant everything for the best, as she always does. Nurse merely repeats what Mama says. And how could you think that I would allow you to read what I could not permit you to write? Mama reads magazine tales when she retires to bed. She says they soothe her mind, though I would think that some of the gothic horrors would have kept her wakeful.''

Mr. Waring held out his arms and Emma knelt by his side and they embraced. "What name do you use, my child?"

Emma told him and he exclaimed, "Delicia! One of the best! My dear daughter, I shall be proud of you."

For a few moments Emma basked in the relief of knowing that she was understood and forgiven. "What am I to do, Papa? I have told you I never meant the stupid lampoon to be made public. Mr. Palmer is horrible! And Mr. Rowley is worse. He says he is a clergyman, though I can scarce believe it."

"I can," said Mr. Waring, sounding grim. "He is not the only one to degrade my calling. Emma, my dear, have you an idea of what you want to do to set matters to rights?"

"I wish to inform the Prince of Wales that I am to blame for the lampoon."

"That will finally destroy your hopes of remaining in society."

"I know, Papa, but it is my own fault. I am distressed more for Mama and Sophia and . . . others."

Mr. Waring sighed. He raised her from her knees. "Sit here, near me. I think I might get you an audience with His Royal Highness. Mama and he share the same birthdate, which means that Mama was at her prettiest when the Prince was still the gorgeous Florizel. He admired her exceedingly. I will send a messenger to him."

Emma said disconsolately, "I must tell James first. And there is Lady Augusta . . ." Emma's voice faded as she pictured her ladyship's reaction to the revelation.

"I will tell her, Emma, and you must dress and come downstairs. James awaits you there. I shall write to the Prince immediately."

A different maid came to assist Emma.

"Where is Betty? Is she ill?"

"No, miss. She's been banished to the laundry. It seems

she's been going errands she shouldn't, though no one knows the rights of it except Miss Wheeler, and she keeps her lips buttoned, as the saying goes.''

Emma's remorse grew deeper. Betty was being punished for helping her. She recalled her repugnance for the laundry and could have wept. She had injured everyone she cared about.

The maid helped her into a sober gown of chestnut-brown silk with a decorous neckline and long sleeves. She added a small chain of amber beads and banded her hair with brown ribbons. She presented a somber picture, one that was not destined to be seen by Lady Augusta, who, Lucy explained, had retired to her bedchamber with recurring spasms after hearing Mr. Waring's news.

"So unlike her," mused Lucy. "She despises ladies who get hysterical. I am thankful that I do not, though I am astonished by your clandestine behavior. You will lose all credibility in the world. Mr. James Exford awaits you in the library," she finished.

A voice from the open doorway spun Emma around. "Miss Waring, I must express my surprise at what we have just learned from your respected papa. Never would I have believed such a thing possible for a young lady of your delicate upbringing."

"Those are my exact sentiments, Mr. Treen," remarked Lucy.

Emma looked coldly at her papa's curate. "Why are you here? Surely you should be at home looking after Papa's interests."

"I confessed to him my attachment to Miss Venables and explained that I was sure she returned my esteem, and so he permitted me to accompany him to ascertain if dear Miss Venables was truly as encouraging as I had hoped."

"And I was," said Lucy. "Dearest Posty has proposed marriage and I have accepted."

"And dear Lady Augusta has raised no objection." Mr. Treen sighed lovingly at Lucy.

"Grandmama was all graciousness until your papa told us of your dreadful lapse. I do not recall ever having seen her so overset."

Emma managed to congratulate the happy pair before she

went to the library. James was waiting, restlessly picking up books and putting them down. He looked anxious. "What has occurred, Emma, dear heart? There has been such a commotion. I was requested to wait alone here because Mr. Waring had something of a private nature to impart to Lady Augusta, and it must have been sorely distressing, for her ladyship shrieked and I heard her maids and footmen assisting her upstairs and she sounded to be in a most perturbed state."

Emma explained as precisely and as gently as she could, and it was impossible not to see that her betrothed looked more and more horrified.

Mr. Exford tried to speak, cleared his throat, and managed to croak, "And you say your papa is asking for an audience with the Prince so that you may confess? Are you sure that is wise?"

"Would you have me leave Lord Kinver in disgrace?"

A flush stained James' face. "Of course he must be absolved. Is there no other way? No, I suppose not."

He looked inexpressibly dejected and Emma said, "James, I think when you asked me to marry you believed I was a very different kind of woman."

"I care for you!"

"Enough to share social ostracism with me?"

James swallowed hard. "I must take you as you are! Oh, Emma, I do so wish you had not done this. And as for your writing, I cannot like it—"

"I deceived you, James, as I did everyone else."

His mouth opened and closed several times, but he could think of nothing to say. He could not deny that he was scandalized by Emma's revelations. He was not a bookish man and the notion of having a wife whose intelligence exceeded his own made him apprehensive. As for the ghastly tangle she was in . . . His vision of a high-society life was fading, yet to abandon her now would be the act of a coward.

He took her hand and raised it to his lips. "You are my betrothed, Emma."

Emma looked down at his bent head and a wave of affection flooded over her, even as she acknowledged that she could never love him as she did the viscount. She was cheating him, but not in any way the *ton* would recognize. She was performing the duty of a young lady and marrying to oblige her family. She thought of Gerard's debts and her parents' need to sell their treasures. James moved his lips to her face in a chaste caress and she pushed aside the memory of Kinver's strong arms and warm, searching mouth.

Mr. Waring coughed before he opened the door. James stepped forward and bowed, "Sir, Emma has told me. I am desolate for her. She is being so very courageous. I esteem her for it. She has my support."

"I knew I was not mistaken in you. My daughter will have a fine husband. I feel sure she will agree to be guided in future by you. Emma, my dear, I trust you are feeling brave. My messenger has just returned from Carlton House. His Royal Highness has a short period of free time and will see us."

"Now? Oh, Papa!"

"The sooner it's over, the better," said James heartily, his heart sinking lower as he realized how soon he was to be banished from society. Emma did not know how vindictive the Prince could be. He would sear her with his scorn. Mr. Exford departed in great need of a restorative.

Emma and her father emerged into the hall to find Lady Augusta, her lace cap awry and her body slack in her loosened stays. She was attended by her maid and Wheeler, who gave Emma an icy look as she assisted her mistress to totter into a small parlor, followed by Mr. Waring and Emma, who were summoned with an imperious gesture. Wheeler dismissed the maid, but remained to give succor to her stricken mistress.

Lady Augusta sank onto a sofa and leaned back. "They tell me . . . I have heard, though I could scarce believe it, that *you* wrote that scurrilous lampoon and that you are actually going to confess to the Prince of Wales. Are you insane?"

"Forgive me, your ladyship, I have no choice. Kinver—"

"Kinver has played the part of a true gentleman and taken the blame. For God's sake, leave it at that!"

"Aunt, I cannot! Tell her, Papa."

Mr. Waring spoke gravely. "Emma cannot allow Lord Kinver to suffer for her. I have brought her up—"

"You, sir, have brought her up to be a viper in the bosom of her relatives. First, Lucy, and now *her*. Well, I thank heaven that Lucy did not accept Kinver's offer."

"Aunt Augusta, I can only say that I am deeply sorry, but I must tell the Prince."

"Nonsense!" Her ladyship sat up surprisingly straight, her voice unexpectedly vibrant. "Kinver is used to censure one way or another, and it does not signify to him where he is! He can go back to—to—the West Indies, or Greece, or—or Hades for all I care, and for all he cares. Have you no thought for me? And what about James Exford? Answer me that."

"James does not like what I have done, but he has promised his support."

Her ladyship's voice rose. "He is mad! You are *all* mad! *Demented*, as I shall shortly become, I shouldn't wonder."

A tap on the door heralded the entrance of Lucy followed by Mr. Treen. "Grandmama, Posty and I could hear you from the breakfast room."

"Are you surprised? I am beset by ungrateful, stupid, lunatic people. I feel positively ill."

"Dear Grandmama-to-be, do not be overset. I am here to assist you."

Lady Augusta glared at Mr. Treen. "I suppose I must take comfort from that. You and Lucy will rusticate forever and I shall be forced to join you. I suppose I must embrace huntin' and fishin' and the like."

"You will be most welcome," said Mr. Treen. "I will recommend suitable books and we can look forward to instructive discourses on worthy matters."

Lady Augusta leaned back and closed her eyes. Her face took on a look of pain as it worked and her lips moved soundlessly. Emma and Mr. Waring crept away.

Carlton House was very different from Emma's last visit. She and Mr. Waring were asked to wait, and the hall, looking even more vast now that it was empty except for stationary liveried footmen, seemed a lonely place. They were conducted to where the Prince sat waiting for them. The private parlor was decorated in blue, green, and gold, and the Prince, with a fine appreciation of appearances, wore a long gold brocade morning gown embroidered with blue flowers and green leaves. Beneath it Emma caught a glimpse of Hessian boots. Presumably His Royal Highness was almost ready to begin his daily pursuits. He was seated in an upholstered chair large enough to accommodate his bulk. He smiled as they entered, and Emma shuddered at the knowledge of how quickly his affability was about to dissolve.

"Mr. Waring! And Miss Waring! You were presented to me the other night. I amazed you, did I not, by recalling your ancestry? You could not know that your mama was once a valued friend. I was amused to present you with a puzzle. How is dear Mrs. Waring?"

"Well, thank you, Sir," said Emma's father.

Emma curtsied and smiled with difficulty. Her heart was thundering in her ears and her mouth felt half-frozen with nervousness.

The Prince graciously waved a bejeweled hand toward a carved, gilded wood settee, upholstered in gold-and-blue-striped silk, situated about six feet away. Mr. Waring and his daughter sat, and Emma folded her hands on her lap in an effort to prevent their shaking.

The Prince said encouragingly, "May I know your business with me? I have much to do. It was only our former acquaintance that persuaded me to see you at such short notice."

"My daughter has something to tell you, Sir. She cannot remain silent and allow another to suffer in her place."

The Prince looked surprised. He reached for a bonbon, which he put into his mouth and chewed. The sight of his moving jaws made Emma feel even more ill-at-ease.

"Sir . . ." she croaked. She began again, "Sir, there is a lampoon circulating the streets and coffeehouses—"

The Prince scowled. "There is indeed. One of many I have had to endure. In this case I have discovered the author, but of course you are aware of it. You were rendered ill by shock. A lady of such sensibility." He produced a lace-trimmed handkerchief from a pocket and touched his mouth delicately. "Do you know, Miss Waring, that such verses could be construed as treason? I think you do not. One day I may make an example. But what has such disgraceful contempt for the dignity of my station to do with you? Lord Kinver has admitted his guilt. He will, of course, remove himself from society."

"Sir, Lord Kinver is not guilty. He did not write the lampoon."

"Eh? Eh? What's that you say? Then, why did he confess? Answer me that!"

Emma gulped as the Prince's color rose. "Because he is a noble gentleman who was protecting the reputation of a lady. Sir, I can only ask your pardon. I—wrote it."

22

The Prince half-rose from his chair, fell back, swallowed the remains of his bonbon, and stared at Emma. "I do not understand. You! But why—why did Kinver . . .? Let me caution you: if you are here to plead for him, it is in vain."

Mr. Waring looked at his distressed daughter. Quietly he told her story to the Prince, who listened with a variety of expressions flitting over his plump face. Chief among them was anger. When the rector's voice stopped, there was a profound silence, broken only by the Prince's somewhat hoarse breath as it whistled in and out of his large frame.

He finally spoke. "In all my days I have not heard so shameful an admission. For a well-bred young woman to write such a thing! So scurrilous, so insulting, not only to me but to a lady who—who is honorable. If you but knew her, could but see her . . ."

"I have seen her, Sir, for the first time the other night at the playhouse, and was struck by her beauty, her gentility, her sweet demeanor."

The Prince stared at Emma hard. "At the playhouse? And was my—the Princess of Wales also there? Did you see her? If so, you cannot fail to understand my wretchedness. You must share my opinion."

Emma felt unequal to denigrating the Prince's royal wife. She licked her lips. "Indeed, I did see both ladies, Sir. I have been consumed by contrition. I had no intent to permit publication of the dreadful verses. They were the prank of a very stupid schoolgirl and I was exploited by men without honor. Oh, Sir, I know I must return home in disgrace, but if I could but have your forgiveness . . ."

Emma's voice faltered, and to her horror tears rolled down her cheeks.

"Madam! No tears, if you please. Pray do not weep. I cannot like women to weep. Miss Waring, I forbid it."

Emma gulped and controlled herself. The Prince sat tapping his fingernails on the wooden arm of his chair—tap! tap! tap!—until Emma's nerve almost broke.

"I am moved by your confession, Miss Waring. I cannot condone what you did, but I admire you for your honor."

"Thank you, Sir."

"But why did Kinver say he had written the lampoon?"

"To save me, Sir."

"The act of a knight of old." The Prince smiled and for the first time Emma felt hope. "Is he in love with you?"

The question pierced an exposed nerve and Emma almost snapped back an answer. "I know not, Sir," she murmured, lowering her eyes.

Again the Prince was charmed. "Do you love him?"

"I cannot confess to esteem unless a gentleman has given me a reason, Sir."

"Damme, I believe you love the fellow, and he you, or why should you both be tumbling over yourselves with these confessions? I am always affected by true love. My own path has been fraught with pain." The Prince gave a sigh and frowned, his eyes opaque.

Emma took another deep breath. "Your Royal Highness, I must be completely honest with you. Mr. Exford has asked me to wed him."

"Upon my soul! And what does he think of all this?"

"He was exceedingly shocked at my behavior, Sir, but he is supporting me in my need."

Emma reflected briefly that the whole conversation was sounding more and more like one of her stories. She quelled the irreverent thought.

"You have many good gentlemen to ease your life, Miss Emma."

Emma's heart leapt. He had used her name.

"And your papa said that you write novels. You must be a very talented young lady. I daresay you know that I delight in all forms of art and am patron to many people, some of whom are pleased to dedicate a work to me."

"I have been asked if I would write a three-volume novel, Sir, and I would deem it a very great honor if Your Royal Highness would permit me to dedicate it to you."

The Prince stared at her. "Have you a patron?"

"The Dowager Lady Kinver, Sir."

"A sweet creature, if overslender. And you would dedicate your book to me?"

"If Your Royal Highness permits."

"What would you say?"

Emma thought swiftly, recalling other dedications she had seen: " 'Sir, permitted to lay at Your Royal Highness's feet this humble tribute of great respect, I can only regret my inability to render it as deserving of Your Royal Highness's acceptance as, gifted with the power to do so, my inclination would suggest.' That is how I would begin, sir. Of course, there would be much more, elucidating my realization of your most cultured and enlightened appreciation of the creative arts."

The Prince looked gratified. "That sounds highly acceptable."

Emma suddenly thought of Kinver and the expression of humorous derision his face would display at such subservience. How he would appreciate it! She dared not glance at her father, whose astonishment might cause her to blush. She watched the Prince anxiously.

He frowned. "You have been very bad, you know."

"Oh, I do know, Sir."

"I should punish you."

Emma allowed her head to droop low and the Prince heaved his bulk from his chair and moved to her. Mr. Waring and his daughter rose, and Emma curtsied low. The Prince took her hand and raised her.

"There now! I am constantly reviled by cruel folk who have no true comprehension of my nature. I am persuaded you will be an ambassadress for me now. You are young and I daresay you emulated the wickedness of your elders. You could have been scarce more than a mischievous child when you wrote the lampoon." He sighed again. "It will run its course, like the others. But you will not forget your forgiving Prince, will you, Miss Emma? And you will dedicate your book to me. You give me your word on that. I have your word. And no more naughty rhymes."

Emma found herself outside Carlton House scarcely understanding how she had got there. Mr. Waring assisted his dazed daughter into the waiting carriage.

"Papa, he forgave me! I cannot believe it. He was so angry with Kinver. Lady Augusta makes him seem like a monster, yet he forgave me."

"The Prince has always been a creature of moods, Emma. He can be unbelievably generous one time and the next destroy another's hopes with no true provocation. You are fortunate to have found him in a receptive frame of mind."

Emma sat for a few moments savoring her relief. Then memory came racing back. "Papa, Lord Kinver must be told."

"Of course, he will be."

"He must know at once, Papa. Oh, pray, take me to his house. He will surely be there. There is scarce anywhere he can visit now. Let me be the one to break the good news."

Mr. Waring looked wonderingly at his daughter. Her face was rosy and her eyes brilliant. He changed instructions to the driver.

"Emma, I admired your 'performance' before the Prince of Wales. If your inclination were not toward authorship, you could have been a play actor."

"*Papa!*" Emma's face became even more rosy. Her fright and worry had been genuine, but she had used them to their full extent. She would do much more for Kinver. The memory of his hazel eyes laughing into hers, his strong arms encircling her, his mouth half-tender, half-savage, took her whole body in a grip of need. She stared from the window unable to speak. They drew up in Grosvenor Square.

The butler who answered the door informed them that his lordship was not at home.

"Is that a genuine message or a social one?" inquired Mr. Waring. "Our business with Lord Kinver is urgent."

The butler bowed. "I assure you, sir, that Viscount Waring is not here. He departed a short while ago. He has left town."

"Where is he?" demanded Emma.

The butler raised his brows. He was not accustomed to

being so vehemently addressed on the doorstep by a young lady of quality. There had been other kinds of women insolently demanding entrance. Too many in his opinion. He had frequently wished his master would settle down. And now he had behaved in a very uncharacteristic manner and offended royalty, which necessitated his rampaging off to foreign parts again.

"Viscount Kinver has departed to take a ship to Greece, sir. He has not informed me of all his future plans, though I understand them to include his West Indies estates."

There was no shortage of callers to inform the Dowager Lady Mary Kinver of the awful fate of her grandson. Lady Kinver was astonished and somewhat skeptical. She had no illusions about him. From the time of the second terrible blow dealt him in his youth he had hardened into a hellion who had first followed, then led, the exploits that kept the *haut ton* in pleasurable expectation of yet another whispered *on-dit*. She had hoped in vain for a girl who would possess enough beauty to attract him, intelligence to enslave him, spirit to tame him and keep him amused, and the breeding to ensure marriage. She was sure she had found the right one in Emma Waring. She had been enchanted to learn that she was Delicia, whom she so much admired and to whom she had offered her patronage. Kinver wrote too, and it seemed a perfect match. Now her idiot grandson had permitted this prize to escape, and the child had accepted James Exford. Someone had told her an odd and unbelievable tale of Lucy throwing herself away on a prosy, penniless curate. There were mysteries here, but she was unconvinced that Kinver would pen a lampoon on the Prince of Wales and permit it to become public knowledge.

Lady Kinver called for her town carriage and ordered it to Grosvenor Square. As she arrived at her grandson's house, she saw Miss Waring and a gentleman in converse with Hardy, Kinver's butler, who, when his master's grandmother arrived, was thrown so far out of his customary calm as to hurry out to greet her.

Lady Kinver's footman opened the carriage door, let down the steps, and watched with some indignation while the butler performed his allotted task and helped his mistress to the pavement. She was interested to note that Emma flushed a deep scarlet when she saw her.

Mr. Waring bowed. "A great pleasure to meet you again, ma'am."

Lady Kinver recognized him. She had liked him in his youth. He and his wife were well-born and eminently acceptable. More than ever she wished that Kinver could be allied to such a family.

She turned to Hardy. "Is my grandson at home?"

"No, your ladyship. I was just telling the Reverend Mr. Waring and Miss Waring that my master has gone to take ship for Greece. He left you a written message. Very put out Mr. Kidwelly was—that's Lord Kinver's valet, Miss Waring, sir—because he said it's not as if they'll be able to travel direct to France like you could until these French wars started going on for years and years, and when they arrive on dry land, it'll be miles across country and foreign inns. Mr. Kidwelly said he came close to resigning his position."

"Would that he had done so if it meant that we would not need to stand here all day listening to his drivel," said Lady Kinver.

"Oh, I beg you to excuse it, your ladyship. Please enter."

He bowed low and the small party was conducted to a pretty blue-papered parlor on the ground floor, where a wood fire glowed.

Hardy said, "Mr. Kidwelly thought, we all thought, hoped, that his lordship was home to stay at least for a while."

Lady Kinver seated herself upright on a small tapestry-covered stool and Emma sank into an easy chair. She had gone pale and her hands shook slightly. Lady Kinver interrupted the butler's doleful flow to order wine, and Hardy hurried out.

"Now, Miss Waring, perhaps you can inform me of exactly what is going on. I have heard such rumors . . . something to do with a lampoon."

"Not rumors, ma'am," explained Emma. "Lord Kinver has behaved so finely, so nobly, like the gallant gentleman he is . . ."

Her voice became croaky and Lady Kinver raised her brows over hazel eyes so like her grandson's that Emma was even more overset. "Indeed! I have been informed that he has behaved like a fool."

Again Mr. Waring rescued his daughter and began explaining, leaving out nothing, but minimizing his daughter's deceit as much as he could, a fact that pleased Lady Kinver, who believed strongly in family loyalty.

"So you see," broke in Emma at last, "I could not possibly permit Kinver to take the blame for me. And now he has gone! And we came to tell him that he could stay in London. And Cousin Lucy has engaged herself to Mr. Treen, Papa's curate, and Kinver has lost all chance of changing her mind, which he might have done since the betrothal is not yet public knowledge."

"So it's true!" Lady Kinver refrained from adding aloud fervent thanks to God. "I hear I am to offer my felicitations to you, Miss Waring."

"To me, ma'am?"

"On your betrothal to Mr. Exford."

"Oh, that! Yes, thank you, your ladyship."

Lady Kinver was satisfied. She promised to write to her grandson and inform him of the latest events, and the Warings were shown out. A footman brought her grandson's message and Lady Kinver learned that his lordship apologized deeply for his untoward behavior to his Prince, and that he was relieving his friends from embarrassment and taking the post-office packet later today at Harwich for Holland; he remained her most loving grandson. Lady Kinver hurried from the room and, ignoring Hardy's outraged expostulations, opened the front door before a footman could reach it, and climbed into her carriage with an instruction to get to Upper Brook Street fast.

Within minutes of her arrival the house was in uproar, with orders sent for the post chaise and a bag to be packed with necessities for a journey. Half an hour later, dressed in a traveling gown of violet cashmere with long sleeves, a black cloak, and a small bonnet of black velvet with silk violets around the crown, she was seated in her post chaise beside her dignified and disapproving maid, Miss Turner, behind four bay horses ridden by two postilions and accompanied by two outriders. The upper members of the servants' hall were of the opinion that her ladyship had run mad and would make herself ill.

The postilions, both middle-aged "boys," were startled when their mistress's voice ordered them to "spring 'em," and understood that Lady Kinver wished to reach Harwich without an overnight stop, although it was all of seventy-one miles away.

"Good thing I thought to pack brandy and hartshorn," muttered Miss Turner.

"You are more likely than I to need them," replied Lady Kinver.

In this she was proved wrong. She found the journey more than tiresome. The spring rains had melted the winter ice, which had wreaked its usual damage on the road. Roadmen were filling potholes with large stones, leaving them for passing coaches to break into smaller sizes. The chaise rocked and bounced, and Miss Turner begged her mistress to allow them to go slower.

Lady Kinver was acting on an impulse fired by instinct. She could not rid herself of the notion that Emma and her grandson cared for each other and that if only they would admit it, they would live happily ever after, as in all the good stories. She loved Kinver more than any being on earth and would do anything to see him really content. So she pushed aside all the complications that had arisen and concentrated on surviving this unpleasant journey as best she could.

At first an outrider asked at every posting inn if Lord Kinver had been seen. Sometimes he was remembered as stopping only for a change of horses, though never for refreshment, and sometimes no one recalled him. They could not be certain which inns he had used, and after another disappointment at the Swan at Witham, she decided to ask no more but to complete the second half of the journey with all speed.

Darkness and a fitfully clouded moon eventually forced the postilions to check their mad pace and she arrived in Harwich to be told that the post-office packet had sailed half an hour since.

23

The disappointment after the rigors of the journey was too much, and Turner was alarmed to see that her mistress's delicately rose-tinted cheeks turned white and that she shook. The maid, assisted by the outriders, conveyed her ladyship into the White Hart Inn, where private rooms were engaged and Lady Kinver put firmly to bed.

Lady Kinver even permitted Turner to give her brandy in milk. She refused to see a physician. "I'm certain to get some gruesome apothecary who will bleed me as like as not with a dirty knife and I'll end up in worse case. I need only rest. And peace," she added as Turner tried to speak again.

When Lady Kinver's bed curtains were drawn, she felt the full tide of her disappointment wash over her. She had made her bid for her grandson's happiness and failed. And Emma Waring would wed James Exford and that would be the end of her hopes. Weariness and the brandy took effect and she dozed. She was awakened by a commotion in the inn yard beneath her bedchamber window. Horses had just turned in; there was the usual slithering of hooves on cobblestones, the rattle of harness, and calls of ostlers, but there was something else, something that caused Lady Kinver to sit bolt upright in bed and jerk aside the curtain, her weakness forgotten.

Shouting angrily and accusing the packet of having left early, which Lady Kinver knew was not true, was a voice she could not mistake. Impossible as it seemed, since he had left London before her, Kinver had only this minute arrived.

She threw back the covers and got up, calling for Turner, who was lying on a truckle bed by the wall. The maid had just fallen asleep and sat up, blinking her eyes.

"My lady! What are you doing out of bed? It is almost midnight and you need rest."

"He is here!"

Turner stood in her long white cotton nightgown staring at her mistress, whose reason she was sure was weakening. "Who's here? What are you about, madam?"

"Stop gabbling, woman, and assist me," ordered Lady Kinver as she grabbed at a chemise.

Turner cast her eyes to heaven and helped her mistress to dress, all the time adjured to make more haste. Lady Kinver waited only for her snowy plait to be bound around her head before she hurried downstairs, followed by her grimly devoted maid.

They met the landlord carrying a tray on which reposed a bottle of wine, a glass, and a large portion of raised savory pie. He stopped, scandalized, as he understood that he was in the presence of a lady, in his nightshirt, beneath which stuck his bare legs and a pair of scuffed slippers. Lady Kinver was able to precede him into the dining room, which was empty except for her grandson, who sprawled in a chair, booted legs stretched toward a newly made-up fire.

"About time," he muttered. "Does it take all night to bring a bite of cold food? Damn you for a dolt and damn the weather and damn the roads and—"

"By all means, Kinver," agreed her ladyship.

The viscount sprang to his feet. "Grandmama! What . . . ? Why are you here? How . . .?"

"I came in a post chaise drawn by four horses, and how I arrived before you is beyond my comprehension, since I must suppose you drove yourself and your exploits on the road are well-known and I daresay you brought six horses."

Kinver's color rose. "Pray, sit down, Grandmama."

She dismissed Turner and chose an ancient, but comfortable-looking, reclining bergère. The landlord, who had hastened to pull on a pair of breeches and a shirt, placed sustenance on a small table before his lordship.

Kinver drank a glass of canary, pronounced it passable, and bit into a large slice of pie. "Now, my dear Lady Kinver, what are you doing here?"

"Now, my dear Lord Kinver, why are you leaving England?"

"You know! Nothing escapes you even when you are incarcerated in the country. And I must suppose you to have read the letter I left."

"You confessed publicly to insulting the Prince of Wales."

"Then you have your answer."

"What you do not know, my boy, is that Miss Waring has been to His Highness and told him the truth."

Again Kinver sprang up, overturning the small table, which disseminated its load in a mixture of pie and wine at his feet. "Emma has done *what*?"

"Emma, is it? Are you on such terms? She is betrothed to your friend James Exford." The dowager had noted with satisfaction her grandson's reaction.

"That I know!"

The landlord knocked and looked in, tutted over the accident, and hastened back to the kitchen.

"Is that why you claimed to be the writer of the lampoon?"

"What other reason could there be?"

"What indeed?"

His lordship glared at his grandmother, who shook her head. "It's not a bit of use being cross with me. You could scarcely expect me to stand aside and allow you to leave the country when there is no need."

"There is need."

"No longer. Emma has confessed."

"She should not have done it. The poor, brave d—girl! Now she is ruined."

"Indeed, she is not. The Prince forgave her. I was exceedingly surprised to learn it and can only suppose that the well-fleshed lady whose virtue he has been besieging for these past weeks has yielded and put him in good heart. If so, we owe her thanks."

Kinver grinned unwillingly. "Even so, I believe I had better travel once more."

The landlord entered with a tray containing more wine and a game pie and mopped up the mess. When he had bowed out, Kinver drank some wine, but ignored the food.

Lady Kinver watched his brooding face with calm eyes behind which her mind was racing.

"Will you not stay to watch your friend wed Emma? The

occasion will be a joyous one. I am sure he will want you there.''

His lordship's hand tightened on his glass. "They do not need me.''

"What of your courtship of Lucy Venables?''

"That is done for. She is betrothed to a curate. Youngest son of a viscount. Good breeding. No money.''

"Lady Augusta will be so put out when she learns that you are once more returned to the ranks of the eligible and could have contested this curate's suit." The dowager mused contentedly for a moment on her rival's chagrin. "Ah, I begin to comprehend. You are heartbroken because Lucy would not have you. You cannot bear to watch her wed another and picture her in his arms; to see her happy and contented as a wife and mother—''

"Stop it!''

"There is no need to shout. I have said nothing untoward. You loved Lucy and lost.''

"I did not.''

Lady Kinver waited hopefully, but the viscount bit his lip savagely in silence. This was proving a most difficult interview. Clearly he would not confess to a partiality for Emma while she was to marry Exford.

"How did James take the news of Emma's possible disgrace?''

"As any gentleman would. He vowed to stand by her.''

"I was sure he would. I am delighted." Lady Kinver was interested to note that her grandson's face expressed the opposite. She half-wished she had told him otherwise. No doubt he would have raced back to London to rescue Emma.

"You have not yet explained how you were delayed, Kinver.''

The viscount gave her a speaking look. "At Kelvedon almost all the horses were out. After a delay they found me six. Of all the ill-matched, wind-sucking, jibbing, spavined creatures! I hope I may never meet their like again! They were devilish hard to manage, and a wheel struck a rut and broke. I had to lead the horses to Colchester.''

"What about your valet?''

The viscount raised his brows. "Kidwelly? What has he to do with anything?''

"Could he not have led the animals? Could you not have ridden one and caught the packet? I'm glad you did not, but I simply wonder at it."

"Kidwelly," replied his lordship, "is afraid of horses. And he refused to leave my gear, which he treats as if it were life's most important factor."

"Which, in his case, it is, else why would you keep him?"

The viscount chose to ignore this remark. "I discovered a farmer and charged him with the return of the horses. He lent me a carriage and harnessed the two best of the sorry lot." Again the viscount paused. "The carriage had been, I collect, used forever by the older members of the farmer's family to attend church. It creaked and groaned a good deal. Suffice to say I fetched Kidwelly at a snail's pace, drove to Colchester, and hired a better rig."

"Kidwelly must be exceedingly put out. Your butler told us that he dislikes foreign travel too."

"If it were not for his way with shirts and boots . . . Whom do you mean by 'us?' "

"I arrived at your house and met Emma and Mr. Waring. He is still such a charming man with a fine, open manner, and his wife, so pretty and gentle, as I recall—" She caught her grandson's fulminating gaze and hastened on. "Which is how I learned what Emma has done."

"How did she look? Was she happy?"

Lady Kinver pondered. "Not especially so. I congratulated her on her betrothal. She appeared to have forgotten it."

"A small lapse caused by her trying experience." The viscount stared gloomily into the fire.

Lady Kinver was even more positive that he was in love with Emma. She longed to see them married, though it would prove difficult to contrive. Her first task must be to get them together.

"What are your plans, Kinver?"

"Plans? To travel. I am undecided."

"In that case you may as well return to London."

"No!" He was vehement; his eyes were tormented.

Lady Kinver did the only thing possible in the circumstances. She confirmed that she was in no peril of damaging her person, and swooned.

Lord Kinver leapt to his feet, yelling for help, and Turner, who clearly had been lingering outside, rushed in.

"I knew how it would be," she lamented, placing smelling salts to her mistress's nose.

It became increasingly difficult for Lady Kinver to remain apparently insensible as the sharp ammoniac fumes assailed her.

"What do you mean, you knew how it would be?" demanded Kinver. "Has she been ill?"

"She would come chasing down after you, my lord, and did the journey all in a few hours at breakneck speed and was white and sick when we arrived and needed brandy in milk."

In his concern the viscount managed to conceal his disapproval of such a ruin of brandy. He called for the landlord and asked for tea to be brought. Mine host, deploring the eccentricities of the aristocracy, who demanded tea in the middle of the night, went kitchenward.

Lady Kinver had taken the opportunity to open one eye to assess her grandson's manner. Deciding that he still looked ill-tempered, she hissed, "Take the demmed stuff away!"

Turner, who had not missed the opened eye, comprehended immediately that her beloved mistress was employing a well-known female device for enlisting the sympathies of a male, and obligingly put her thumb over the mouth of the phial. Lady Kinver remained motionless a moment or so longer, coughed, choked a little, and sat up. Holding a hand to her disarranged plait, she asked feebly, "Where am I? What has occurred?"

Turner's voice was gravely solicitous. "There, there, my dear, *dear* lady, do not be afraid. You did but swoon and are now recovered. Turner is with you and will never leave you no matter *who* oversets you."

"Don't overdo it, woman. Kinver ain't a simpleton," muttered the dowager as her grandson returned to her side.

"Are you feeling better, Grandmama?"

Lady Kinver waved a flaccid hand and replied in languishing tones, "As well as I can expect after so harrowing a time. I wish . . . But it is of no use, you have set your mind. Go, if you must! Turner will care for me."

"That I will," murmured Turner, giving the viscount a reproachful look.

Lord Kinver stared down at his elderly relative with a measure of suspicion. "Grandmama, if there is anything I can do, you know I will. Even to remaining in England long enough to escort you back to London—as soon as you are well enough to travel, that is."

"That will be tomorrow," said the dowager promptly.

"If she is strong enough," interposed Turner.

"Always supposing that," agreed Kinver.

"I shall be quite well by the morning and we shall reach London by nightfall so long as we begin our journey early."

"That you will not do," said the viscount, who had perceived that his grandmother really did appear less than well, and Lady Kinver, recognizing that she had pushed him as far as he would go, did not argue.

Emma and Mr. Waring returned to Lucy's house. Mr. Waring gazed out at the teeming, noisy, often noxious streets and said how thankful he was to reside in the sweet country air. "Has Mr. Exford a country estate, Emma, where you may rusticate sometimes to repair the ravages of town life?"

"I—I do not know, Papa. He has not been long possessed of his fortune. I suppose he owns property. I have not asked him."

Mr. Waring gave his daughter a searching look. She sounded lethargic, exceedingly weary, and very different from the lively daughter he remembered. "What troubles you, Emma?"

"N—nothing which signifies, Papa." She could not confess to her father, not to any soul on earth, that her whole being was crying out for a man who had left England, believing her to be in love with his friend—for a man she might not meet again for years, by which time she would be a matron with, probably, a full nursery of children resembling Mr. Exford.

She gave a strangled gasp at the idea and Mr. Waring took her hand. "Emma, my dear, something *does* ail you."

"I hope, Papa, that I have not created more trouble. I have promised His Highness to dedicate my first novel to him, and I do not know yet if James wants me to continue to write at all. He seems uneasy about it."

"Yet he asked you to marry him."

"That was before he knew," said Emma in a small voice.

"Do you mean to say you did not discuss it with him before accepting his proposal? You cannot expect to be happy if you are not open with him. Is there anything else you have not told me? *Anything!*"

Emma shook her head. Her mind raced on. Only the small matter that I love Lord Kinver to distraction and I do not know how I can bear to be married to another man.

Lady Augusta awaited them in the principal drawing room, seated upon an imposing high-backed winged chair, as if the elegant grandeur of her surroundings would assist her to receive bad news. She was dressed in dark-red silk and wore rubies around her throat and in her hair piled atop her head. She felt like a storm-tossed ship, veering from despair to hope and back again. Just as she had been congratulating herself on Lucy's escape from involvement with Kinver and learned that he was, quite properly, leaving the country, she had learned that Emma, whom she had so graciously chaperoned for her come-out, was about to tell the Prince the incredible truth instead of allowing a gentleman to take blame for her as any sensible woman would. It was one of the better uses to which gentlemen could be put. She looked, thought Emma, as if she were going to execution by beheading. She had a fleeting wish that Kinver could have enjoyed the sight with her, before she was assailed by contrition and told her ladyship quickly what had happened.

"My dearest Emma! Not disgraced! Not to be ostracized! Forgiven! How magnanimous! How generous! How noble! How right royal! His Highness is to be revered for his compassion. And he will accept a dedication from you in your first novel. What an honor!"

"What is that?" James entered in time to hear most of her ladyship's ecstatic words. "You were well-received, Emma. I am considerably relieved. I will confess to you now that I dreaded the idea of having to leave the *haut ton*. But what is this about writing a novel? You have not consulted me. I assumed that you would relinquish your dabbling in literature and undertake more wifely pursuits. As your husband, I must have my say in this."

"You are not yet her husband," pointed out Lady Augusta, then qualified her retort. Mr. Exford needed to be humored. "Emma cannot afford to overset the Prince of Wales again."

"Emma must obey Mr. Exford. She is betrothed to him as I am to dearest Lucy, and that is as binding to a person of honor as is marriage." Mr. Treen and Lucy had followed James to learn Emma's fate. "I also am relieved to know that you are not to suffer the pangs of disgrace and banishment from society, but I am obliged to agree with Mr. Exford, or Cousin James, as I must learn to address him, that a *literary* wife is most undesirable. My own dear Lucy would not dream of setting pen to paper except to write an occasional letter. Writing a novel could label you a bluestocking, and that would reflect on us all. Not that dearest Lucy and I will be intimately concerned, as we mean to live our lives in pastoral peace, but it seems that Mr. Exford—Cousin James-to-be—was not fully conversant with your literary proclivities and—"

Lady Augusta spoke coldly. "I believe you have made your views clear, Mr. Treen."

"Pray call me Phineas, or even Posty, as my dearest Lucy does, dear Grandmama-to-be."

An expression that would have caused Lady Kinver ineffable pleasure passed briefly across Lady Augusta's countenance.

Mr. Waring said pacifically, "I think that Emma and James should be permitted to discuss their future in privacy. Meanwhile, may I suggest a loyal toast to the Prince, whose conduct has proved so magnanimous."

Wine was brought and drunk, a maid was dispatched for a shawl, and Emma and James strolled in the garden. They were silent for a while and Emma affected to admire the scanty spring flowers that struggled for existence in the sooty air.

"Delightful flowers. Quite delightful," agreed James in an abstracted way.

Emma asked abruptly, "Will you forbid me to write?"

"If I did, would you obey?"

She avoided a direct answer. "My forgiveness by the Prince was attendant, I believe, on my dedicating a book to him. I cannot go back on my word."

"N—no, that is so. You have got yourself in a sad tangle,

Emma. It appears that I must permit you to write at least one book, but after that . . .''

"After that?" prompted Emma, trying to keep her desperate anxiety from her tone.

"We shall see. How long will it take to write?"

"I cannot say exactly."

"Three months? Six? Have you any idea?"

"Certainly nearer six months than three. Possibly longer."

"Ah!"

"What do you mean by 'ah,' James?"

"By the time you have finished, I am hopeful that you will be occupied with a different kind of production. I am looking at property with good nursery quarters."

Emma turned her head and bit her tongue. James took this for bashful approval.

Sophia approached them along the paved way. "Aunt Augusta begs you to join her for a nuncheon and says we are to pay as many calls today as are feasible. She is going to tell everyone that you are to write a novel and about the Prince's graciousness in permitting you to dedicate it to him."

James asked, "What of the lampoon? Someone is bound to raise the subject."

Sophia smiled at him. "My aunt says that as Lord Kinver has decided to travel again and will be as oblivious of censure as he is impervious to it, we shall ignore all reference to it. She says that though there may be rumors, as His Highness will probably have mentioned the matter to his close associates, they will not signify, as few will know the absolute truth. And by the time it is established, there will be a more edifying scandal for them to enjoy." Sophia paused. "Aunt Augusta is so arbitrary in her behavior she quite terrifies me at times. Are you not fearful of her, Emma?"

"Not now," said Emma, her voice almost suspended by emotion at the idea of continuing to permit Kinver to take the blame for her reckless action.

Before she could express her view, Sophia said, "I must say it seems unfair that the viscount should shoulder such a burden, yet I could not endure to see you suffer, dearest Emma. And if you confess openly, his sacrifice will have been in vain."

"What excellent sentiments, Miss Sophia! A sensibility to

both honor and the happiness of your sister. She is to be commended, is she not, Emma?"

"It goes much against my will to allow another to stand in my place," said Emma.

"We know that, Emma," cried Sophia. "No one would doubt your honor. You were resolute in your determination to confess to the Prince whatever the consequences. I wonder if I would have been so brave. And you are clever too, is she not, Mr. Exford?"

"James, if you please, Miss Sophia. You resemble your sister in looks. Are you bookish?"

"I fear not. I have to confess to being rather a dunce."

James was not devious enough to be able to conceal his approval at this acceptable reply. He held out an arm for each of the ladies. "What a joy it will be to have you for my sister, Miss Sophia. Are there any other clever girls in your family?"

"No, sir. Emma is the only one."

Emma caught her betrothed's faint sigh.

Nuncheon was taken. Emma's spirits were cast down. James kept glancing appraisingly from Emma to Sophia; even Lady Augusta was thoughtful, planning her strategy for her calls. There would have been almost complete silence were it not for Mr. Treen, who maintained a generous flow of information regarding his views on the rearing of game birds. Lucy agreed with all he said, interpolating an occasional word, to which he listened respectfully before beginning again.

24

The calls were made without Lucy and Mr. Treen. Lady Augusta gave her gracious consent to their driving to the outskirts of town to enable Mr. Treen, who had seldom visited London, to see for himself the great flocks of geese being driven in from the farms and sold for fattening.

As they left for this congenial expedition, her ladyship snorted, "He is such a gabble-grinder, that is to say, he is so—so *eloquent*. Undoubtedly a worthy gentleman who appears to be suited to Lucy, though how *my* granddaughter . . ."

She hurried to make ready and soon Emma, Sophia, and James found themselves driven as quickly as the crowded streets would allow from drawing room to drawing room, their entrance frequently rendering the company momentarily speechless. Lady Augusta dominated the conversation, contriving to sweep her companions away if awkwardness threatened. Sophia blushed sometimes at her aunt's mendacity, and James honored Sophia for her blushes and wished his future bride showed an equal sentience.

To Emma everything seemed unreal as she felt her spirit being drawn from her body after Lord Kinver.

That night they attended a musical evening, chosen deliberately by Lady Augusta since the performance would prevent much conversation. At last the long day came to an end and Emma retired to bed, but not to sleep as she lay hour after hour trying to imagine what could have happened had her first meeting with Viscount Kinver been different. If only he had not goaded her, if only Mama had been less convincing about the necessity for concealing her intelligence. But how was she to guess that her daughter would meet so unusual a man, one determined to hide his vulnerability beneath a cloak of cynicism and apparent addiction to pleasure? If only she had been true to her own nature. In the end Emma blamed herself. And the viscount had probably already forgotten her and might even now be sharing his bed with some easy woman. Yet still her whole being yearned for him and her senses betrayed her gnawing need.

She rose late the following day and shocked the maid by showing a complete lack of interest in what she wore. She had attempted to obtain Betty's reprieve from laundrywork, but Lady Augusta had been adamant that the girl should have known better than to accompany her mistress in nefarious activities and must learn her lesson.

The maid, seeing Miss Waring's pallor and the dark shadows beneath her eyes, chose a morning gown of palest-rose silk with a scattering of silken rosebuds on the hem and neckline. She dressed her hair in tumbled curls and pinned it with lavender ribbons, dusted her cheeks with pink Spanish wool, smoothed a little *pomade à baton* beneath her eyes, and touched the pulses at her wrists and throat with oil of damask rose. Emma descended the stairs to the morning room.

Sophia was quietly sorting out embroidery silks, her tambour frame on her lap. Mr. Waring was reading *The Daily Advertiser*. Lucy and her betrothed were studying a book, watched by Lady Augusta, who wore a flowing plum-colored velvet undress robe and a large lace cap. Her face expressed vexation.

"I comprehend that you find the diseases of cattle of absorbing interest, but it is not a subject I wish to hear discussed in my parlor."

Mr. Treen smiled deprecatingly. "I must prove myself a worthy steward of my dear future wife's estates, dear Grandmama-to-be."

Lady Augusta greeted Emma. "James is calling in half an hour to drive you in the park. You look well! The dark-blue cloth redingote and matching hat with the ostrich plumes with that gown, I think. Wheeler tells me the wind is somewhat keen today."

Emma tried to look as delighted as a young lady should about to be seen in public with an excellent catch so early in her first Season.

Mr. Waring said, "There is no reference here to your betrothal, Emma. Will you notify the newspapers, Lady Augusta, or shall I?"

"I think you, sir, as you are her father."

"Many people already know," pointed out Sophia. "I collect that you proclaimed it yourself, Aunt Augusta, at Lord Kinver's ball."

Her ladyship was testy. "A printed announcement in a newspaper ensures the fact."

The idea of seeing her betrothal set down in black and white deepened Emma's dejection and she had to make a tremendous effort to greet James. "I will get ready," she said. "A drive in the park sounds delightful."

She rose but had taken only one step when there was a loud knocking on the front door, followed by voices in the hall.

"Callers," exclaimed Lady Augusta. "What a lack of good manners! It is far too early. I am not dressed. Tell Bardsea I am not at home to anyone. Mr. Treen—Phineas—pray inform Bardsea that we are not at home to anyone."

Mr. Treen leapt to do her bidding, but before he reached the door, it was opened, and Gerard, followed by Anthony Downham and an embarrassed Lord Pembridge, entered.

"Must render apologies, your la'ship," murmured Lord Pembridge, bowing low. "Gerard *would* visit. Far too early, of course."

Gerard was too distracted to be apologetic. "Pembridge's valet said that Lord Kinver is in disgrace with the Prince and has fled the country. I cannot believe it! I am persuaded that we shall learn the truth here."

"Not like Kinver," explained Lord Pembridge. "Usually discreet."

"It is all true," began Lady Augusta. "That is to say, it is the truth so far as it goes."

"It does not go far enough," said Emma.

"What do you mean?" asked Gerard.

"His sacrifice will be in vain if you do not keep your own council," pointed out Mr. Treen, "though for my part I am shocked to discover the behavior of my dear Lucy's cousin."

"Are you talking about my sister?" demanded Gerard.

"I am a man of the cloth, sir. I have a duty to be outspoken however unpalatable it may seem to others, and shall continue to do so as long as there is breath in my body.''

Gerard scowled and moved menacingly toward Mr. Treen. There was a further commotion in the hall and yet more voices.

"Good God," exclaimed her ladyship. "This house is like Hyde Park in the afternoon. I will *not* receive anyone else. Mr. Treen, *if* you please."

Again Mr. Treen hurried to the door and again it was thrust open in his face. In walked Lady Kinver, followed by her grandson.

Emma stared unbelievingly at the tall figure in caped coat and dusty boots. He could not be real. He must be an apparition called into being by her longing.

Somewhere in the background Lady Augusta was protesting at this ever-increasing assemblage in her parlor at this hour, especially as it now included a gentleman who was still in his travel dirt, one, moreover, whom she had felt relieved to know was on his way to Greece.

Somewhere Lady Kinver's gentle voice could be heard asking pardon, but explaining that she and her grandson were so exhilarated by the discovery that all was well with the Prince that she had positively insisted that Kinver should bring her here instantly to share the rejoicing.

Emma heard it all dimly through a haze of wonderment. She took a step forward and stopped uncertainly, staring at Kinver's harsh-featured face. His eyes met hers and together they were wafted into a sphere that had no connection with the sounds and voices around them. He moved toward her. They were in each other's arms, their hearts beating in rhythm. The embrace lasted only seconds, but it was as if a bombshell had been detonated in the room.

There was a short silence.

Then Lord Pembridge, who was clear in diction if not in comprehension, said, "Thought you told me your sister was betrothed to Exford, Gerard. Odd thing for her to embrace Kinver that way. He ain't a close relative. Only distant cousin. Told me so yourself."

Gerard stared haughtily at his friend. "Don't care for criticism about my sister. A man always challenges in such a case. Name your seconds."

"Ain't goin' to fight you, Gerard. Ain't ever going to fight anyone."

Gerard kept up his glare a moment longer before capitulating. "Well, you're right. A lady betrothed to one gentleman should not be hugging another. As you say, he's only a distant cousin. Emma, Mama must have told you it's not done to—"

"Be silent," cried a goaded Lady Augusta. "Lord Pembridge is correct. Yes, in *this* instance he is correct. I am astonished, indeed, more than astonished."

Kinver took his arms from around Emma, but retained her hand in his. Emma was brought back to a semblance of reality. She was being fixed by such a variety of expressions she wanted to laugh. She would laugh—later—with Kinver. Her joy was welling from the center of the tight knot of pain inside her, melting her flesh and blood and bones with love.

Kinver recovered first. He bowed to James. "My dear fellow, I had not meant this to happen. I scarce know what to say. An apology is not sufficient, even should I really feel apologetic, which I fear I do not. I cannot fight you. Pray, forgive me. It is useless now to deny that I love Emma and she"—he glanced at the entranced girl, whose hand was holding his as if she would never let go—"is in love with me. We did not expect . . . we mistook our feelings."

James strode forward with outstretched hand. "Better far discovered before our marriage, Kinver. I relinquish Emma to your care. I know you will make her a good husband. Emma, I release you with my sincere blessing."

Emma could not help but notice that there was more than a tinge of relief in his voice and that he went at once to Sophia's side and stood with a hand on the back of her chair.

"Well! Mr. Waring, it is a good thing we did not insert the betrothal in the newspapers. I shall have to think very hard to explain away this roundaboutation to everyone. Young people these days!"

"The *ton* will love it," said Kinver. "They need a new talking point every day."

"My family has been the daily talking point for long enough," retorted her ladyship with asperity.

"You will have my support in any affliction you may endure," promised Lady Kinver gently. "Criticism will spring only from envy. Parents of hopeful young ladies will be cast down at how well your charge has done for herself."

Lady Augusta glared at Lady Kinver as she recalled for a regretful moment that her plan to unite Lucy with Kinver had come to nothing, then she sighed. "Well, our young people will do what they must, and you and I, dear Lady Kinver, can only watch and hope."

"A sound philosophy," approved Lady Kinver. "I daresay there may be much we shall agree upon."

"And much that we shall not," stated Lady Augusta.

"What an engaging notion," murmured Lady Kinver.

The ladies scrutinized each other measuringly as Mr. Waring walked to his daughter. "Is this what you truly desire, my child?"

"Oh, Papa!"

"I see that it is." He shook hands with the viscount.

Lucy watched with raised brows and Mr. Treen cleared his throat for speech.

Lord Kinver said hastily, "Pray, excuse us. We have matters to discuss." And Emma found herself in the hall with the viscount, who led her to the library. There he closed the door and took her in his arms, and this time he kissed her as he had longed to do since their first meeting, with open abandonment. The kiss sent delicious shivers along Emma's spine and made her blood race and her heart beat as if she had been running.

"I love you, Emma," he said at last. "I love you more than I ever believed possible."

"Oh, my lord, I've been desolate picturing you gone away. Poor James. But I would have made him a bad wife."

"Nonsense, my love. You could never be bad."

Emma gurgled with mirth. "You know how untrue that is. I have caused such tangles and brangles. You even supported my fib about where I had met Rowley."

"You made a brave try at helping me when Lowther was so obnoxious and landed yourself in a pretty scandal broth."

"Your false confession to the Prince was noble beyond anything."

"Your courage in absolving me was heroic past measure."

The couple gazed dotingly at each other.

Emma gave a sigh of immense satisfaction. "What made you return?"

"The other dear female in my life. Grandmama somehow got it into her head that we were in love and needed a push. She chased after me, then decided she was too frail to return to London without me. As soon as we entered the city, she demanded to be brought here. I imagine she hoped that sheer surprise would have exactly the effect it did. If this ruse had failed, she would have conjured something else. She wants you for her granddaughter-in-law, Emma. Almost as much, I believe, as I want you for myself."

"So you would truly have gone . . ."

"I could see no choice. You were betrothed to James. Was the Prince very angry?"

"Furious!"

"I gather he got over it. He is always moved by great beauty."

"I confess I used such charm as I can muster, but he was finally won over by a few tears and a great deal of toadying," declared Emma. "I am to dedicate my novel to him. You won't mind my writing a novel?"

"I shall insist upon it! In any event, Grandmama would be at outs with me if I attempted to interfere. She can scarce wait to become the patron of a famous literary lady."

"I was led to believe that any young lady who shows intelligence frightens away suitors."

"You certainly frightened me! I faced the horrible prospect of seeing you married to James."

Emma said slowly, "I am persuaded that James was not altogether sorry at my betrayal."

Kinver grinned. "He is an excellent friend, but not bookish."

Deciding that they had talked too long, Lord Kinver removed his coat, threw it onto a chair, and embraced his love again. "You smell of roses, as sweet as the first time I kissed you. What a fool I was to let you go."

Emma could not reply as he rendered her speechless with a kiss that she found rapturously devastating.

When he lifted his mouth from her quivering lips, she murmured, "Oh, Kinver . . ." She stared into his hazel eyes, which held such tenderness she almost lost her breath. "I cannot call you Kinver when we are betrothed."

"Will you marry me, dearest Emma?"

"I will. Oh, I will, my love."

"There! Now we are betrothed."

"So, what should I call you?"

The viscount pondered. "You may choose. I was christened Augustus Bardolph Robert."

Emma giggled and the viscount chided her. "You must show respect for your future husband and the names of his ancestors."

"I could follow Lucy's example. Do you care for Bardy? Or Gusty? I shall call you Robert," she promised swiftly as his brows drew together in spurious outrage. "Is that acceptable?"

"Certainly, my dear."

"You observe that I am prepared to defer to your wishes—upon occasion, sir."

The viscount looked appropriately gratified.

"My lord—"

"Robert . . ."

"Robert, I must tell you that my family has financial problems. I know you will be discussing money with Papa, but I think I should warn you. There is Gerard and his debts. And Sophia must make her come-out next year. I long to assist her. I have other brothers and sisters. And there is a little maid named Betty who must be rescued from a laundry."

The viscount looked impressed by the catalog. "She shall be my first concern and I will accept your family if you will take mine. There is Lady Augusta, who will insist on visiting us and instructing us on all matters concerning our lives. There is Lucy, whom I tried to convince myself I loved, but who, God bless her, knew different. And now, of course, there is Posty."

Emma and Robert contemplated their future.

A gentle scratching on the door preceded the entrance of Lady Kinver. "Have you settled matters, my children?"

The viscount smiled at her. "I have it in mind to marry soon and quietly and travel for a few months. I want to show Emma the beauty of Greece and any other country not pestered by Napoleon. And then we will visit my West Indies estates."

Lady Kinver was astonished. "You will do no such thing."

The door opened and Lady Augusta entered and heard of the plan. "Ridiculous! I agree with Lady Kinver. It will make your marriage look a havey-cavey affair. First Emma is betrothed to one and then another. And one moment you, Kinver, are in disgrace, and then you are not. There has been a surplus of tittle-tattle already and I see no reason why you should not face all the fresh speculation. You can take your bride trip later. As soon as Lucy is wed, I shall return to London. By then the talk will have subsided and I can enjoy Emma's triumph."

"What about mine?" demanded Lord Kinver.

Lady Augusta chose to disregard this frivolous query. "Meanwhile, Lady Kinver can chaperone you, Emma. The problems are solving themselves nicely."

The elderly ladies waited only to hear the happy couple's acceptance of their arrangements before leaving in rare charity with each other to discuss the essential matters of bridal gown, flowers, and suitable food for a marriage feast. "Mr. and Mrs. Waring cannot have the least objection to my assisting them in the affair," pronounced Lady Augusta just before the door closed. "We are related."

The viscount looked sternly at his betrothed, who was once again displaying a regrettable tendency to giggle. "Poor Mama!" She choked. "She will be quite overcome."

His lordship sighed, but his eyes were brimming with laughter. "Grandmama is awesome enough on her own, and Lady Augusta is a dragon. Together they are unnerving. Did you think James taken with Sophia, my love?"

"I would welcome him as a brother."

"After we are married . . ."

"In Papa's own church . . ."

"But naturally. As I was observing, after our marriage, and after a suitable time, we must take our bride trip. I long to show you the world."

"A wonderful prospect, dear Robert. And we shall always set aside time for writing."

"I will continue with my essays. I believe I lack your command of imaginative prose."

"I daresay I lack your extreme erudition, sir."

"Will you mind remaining in London after our marriage, my darling Emma?"

"I mean to enjoy everything I do so long as I am with you, my dearest Robert."

"It is exactly as I feel about you," exclaimed the viscount.

His arms went about her and he pulled her close. "And how I mean to enjoy this," he murmured. His lips touched her eyelids, her cheeks, the tip of her nose, her chin. He took possession of her mouth. His kiss, light at first, deepened as Emma's passion grew to match his. Her arms slid around his neck and she entwined her fingers in his hair, holding him as if she could never bear to release him.

At last Robert gently removed her hands and imprisoned them in his. He lifted his head to stare at her. Her skin was flushed, her lips moist, her eyes dark with desire. He said, in a voice filled with wonder, "To think that for so many years I've imagined I could get a fervid response only from women who—" He stopped.

Emma smiled mischievously. "Pray continue, sir."

"No, that I shall not!" He laughed softly. "Your glorious response betrays me into indiscretion. My adorable, clever, audacious, impassioned girl. Will you ever understand what it will mean to me to have a wife who will be one with me in love as well as in mind and heart? Your kisses promise all the delicious ardor I crave."

"My kisses tell you the truth, my darling. I love you so much." Emma freed her hands and drew his head to her once more. She molded her body to his and sensed his immediate response in the tautening of his muscles. "It is a marvelous joy to me that you want me for the woman I am, not a society butterfly without feelings. We can be honest with each other in love as in everything." She explored the contours of his face with feather-light kisses. She enjoyed the roughness of his skin where he shaved. She turned his head to fondle his ears with her mouth, obeying instincts she had not known she possessed. Her body was consumed with longing for the complete fulfillment of their love.

"Emma," he murmured. "My beautiful, tormenting Emma. You'll drive me mad. We must be married soon. Very soon."

"It can never be too soon for me," whispered Emma.

The world receded. They were wafted into their own sensual universe. They held one another close. Their fingers caressed. Their lips clung, parted to murmur messages of love, and met again. In consummate harmony they began their journey into the infinite realms of perfect love.

About the Author

Eileen Jackson is no foreigner to the world of which she writes. Born in Bristol, England, she has been resident near the beautiful west coast of Scotland for the past seven years. Her historical books reflect the fact that she has extensively studied British history, literature, and art.

She is married and has four grownup children and two grandsons. She has traveled throughout the British Isles and the Mediterranean countries. She plans to visit the United States when work permits.

Ø

Other Regency Romances from SIGNET